I0770859

WRITTEN BY
SHAWN PLUNKER
THE WORDLESS
BOOK

THE WORDLESS
BOOK

Copyright © 2025 by Shawn Spencer

First edition published 2024

All rights reserved. This book or any portion thereof may not be reproduced or used in any manner whatsoever without the express written permission of the publisher except for the use of brief quotations in a book review.

Publisher's note: This is a work of fiction. Names, characters, places, and incidents either are the product of the author's imagination or are used fictitiously. Any resemblance to actual events, locales, or persons, living or dead, is entirely coincidental.

Editing: Kristen Corrects, Inc.
Cover Art: Yosbe Design
Map Design: Marlon Felipe Ruiz
Interior Illustrations: B.A.W. aka Mata Tridatu | Connie Dragon | Setyna Art | Vanz | Lum Roger | Sereal
Book Design and Typesetting: Enchanted Ink Publishing

The text type was set in Minion Pro

ISBN: 979-8-9913689-0-2 (Paperback)

Thank you for your support of the author's rights.

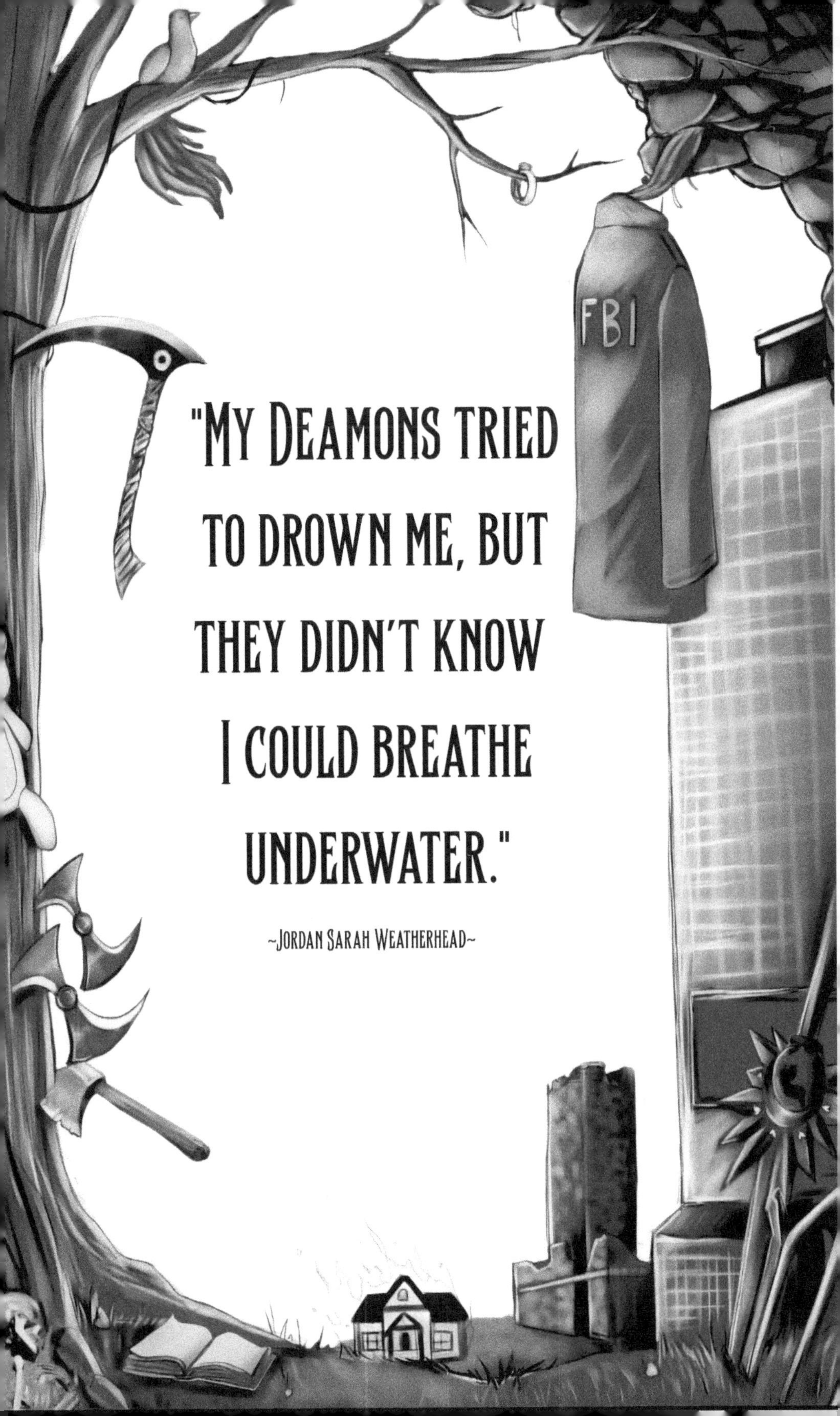

"MY DEAMONS TRIED TO DROWN ME, BUT THEY DIDN'T KNOW I COULD BREATHE UNDERWATER."

~JORDAN SARAH WEATHERHEAD~

CAMPS DIRECTORY
WELCOME TO CAMP WOLF CREEK 1
EVENTS 19
43 LEGEND HAS IT
FACING THE FLAMES 63
83 NATSU
97 WOLFS EYE DEN
FIRE DEADER'S 115
IMPOSSIBLE 137
163 RELEASE THE REAPERS

CAMPS DIRECTORY
CONTINUED
LIGHT THE WAY 183
SIXTH SENSE 195
215 BACK TO BACK
PICTURE PERFECT 233
257 ITSY BITSY SPIDER
271 Apiphobia
COAL MINE MASSACRE 297
CRACK IN' THE WALL 307
315 MOKUD

CAMPS DIRECTORY
CONTINUED
Hydrophobia 335

4
5
6
TARGET RANGE
WEST GRYM WOODLANDS
7
8
N
W
E
S
Grym Hollow's
Camp Wolf Creek

3
HOLLOW'S PEAK
2
1
WOLF CREEK
CANOEING

ONE
WELCOME TO CAMP WOLF CREEK

Robert's knees tremble while tapping his Brahma boots against the rubber flooring of a moving school bus. Random thumps from a bumpy ride along with chit-chatter from excited teens fill the space around him. The bus rocks back and forth, jostling him around, making the ride uncomfortable to say the least.

Both of his hands shake, one hand grips around a fist full of keys. They rattle, clinking together as he shuffles them within his fingers. His eyes squint to escape the impending reality of the upcoming hour.

Another hand as soft as an angel's heart and as supportive as foundation slides over his. Her ring finger is adorned with a glimmering princess-cut diamond ring shimmers like the sparkle in her eyes. His jittering ceases thanks to her care and compassion which radiates through him like electricity.

Robert immediately feels better, letting out most of his stress with a long exhale. He slips his hand from under her grip, sliding the keyring into his belts key clip.

"Robert, it's okay to be nervous."

"I know Jessica, we've my parents worked so hard to build this place. And-"

"And we finished it. Be proud of that. I sure am. And your parents would be, too."

"Ah, thanks Jess."

Robert's eyes embrace her endless sunrise-golden hair, shining bright as the sun. Those honey-sweet lips are rose-petal soft while her sparkling round eyes are an angelic amber. She's dressed in black shorts with red stripes and a gray long-sleeved shirt with the camp's logo on the front left of her chest and Happy Oaks Staff on the right side of her chest with the last name Hill on the back.

Jessica would describe Robert as a charming, thirty-year-old Korean American with coarse black hair, a chiseled chin, and calloused hands, dressing in a black and teal Camp Wolf Creek uniform with black Brahma boots.

They sit at the front of the middle school bus accompanied by fourteen other teachers and forty-eight seventh graders filling each seat perfectly.

Driving down a dark avenue overtaken by the shadows of the neighboring trees, the side of the bus reads: HAPPY OAKS MIDDLE SCHOOL. The sun's golden beams of light are hidden by the many interlocking branches high above the roads asphalt.

The bus brakes as they slow down around a corner, whooshing past a loose yellow-and-black street sign which reads: Camp Wolf Creek One Mile Ahead.

A bookbag rests open at Jessica's feet. She reaches in, revealing a red rose and black stem tattoo wrapped in a pink ribbon on her forearm as her sleeve shifts with the motion. She pulls out a bundle of retreat packets organized by paper clips.

Jessica's finger petting her nose is surefire proof of how nervous she is. A sudden exhale flutters her golden locks away from her eyes like door streamers waving in the wind. As she looks the packets over, Robert gently caresses Jessica's shoulder.

"Look, you have nothing to worry about. Everything's going to work out fine. We'll follow the event sheet, and everybody will have a great time. I promise. Geez, I thought I was the nervous one," Robert reassures her with a gentle kiss on her cheek.

"Yeah, you're right. Look at me. I need to relax."

"You're going to be amazing. Ah, hey, look Jess, we're here."

A wooden rectangular sign cut from the finest hickory tree stretches across the old dirt path reads Welcome to Camp Wolf Creek. Each hand-carved letter is painted a forest green over an orange background with the camp's symbol painted in a grey color.

"Wow, good job babe. It turned out great," Jessica gushes nudging him with her forearm.

An earsplitting screech forces them forward as the bus comes to a halt at Cabin 1 to let off the first group, consisting of two teachers and six students.

"Hold up," Jessica requests. Reaching out, her forearm mistakenly brushes against the leading teacher.

Jessica kindly hands over a walkie-talkie and a weekend retreat packet to the first two teachers. The packet is brimming with exciting content, such as an event schedule, a map, and a complete student roster with their parents' phone numbers.

The process continues as the remaining teachers and students exit the bus, one group at a time. As the bus arrives at its eighth and final stop, the brakes emit a piercing screech, and the door creaks open, revealing three boys and three girls eagerly waiting to embark on the adventure with Robert and Jessica. They sling their backpacks over their shoulders as they make their way to the bottom of the steps while Robert and Jessica are already there waiting for them.

"One, two, three, four, five, and… we have six kids, right? Hang on, Rob, I'll check."

Jessica enters the bus, making her way down the aisle. Her hands slide along the smooth warm brown leather seats as she looks left and right to find the missing child. Worry creeps in, gripping her heart with each row she passes. She holds her breath as she approaches the last row. A head full of brown hair peeks over the seat. The worry lifts like a ton of bricks as she is one more worry away from sweating.

"Ah-ha. There you are. Emma, you almost gave me a heart attack. Girl, you gotta stop playing like that."

"Yeah, I know." Emma sighs unable to make any eye contact with Jessica as she steps away from the bus seat.

Emma is an old soul, quite a humbling spirit for her age. Her dark brown chin-length hair sways like curtains in a gentle breeze while her chestnut-brown eyes are sweet and innocent like doves.

"Emma, what's the matter, sweetheart?"

"I've had a lot on my mind is all."

"How 'bout I help you to your room, and maybe later, you can tell me all about it?"

"Sure." Emma grins a timid smile. Her lack of confidence keeps her eyes locked at her feet as Jessica grabs her bookbag and they exit the bus.

"You guys have a good day now. I'll be back Sunday to pick everyone up."

"We'll see you Sunday, Debra." Jessica smiles.

"See you Sunday," Emma mutters with a wave of her hand.

The sliding door screeches to a close. The engine roars like a lion, warning others of its territory as it drives away, giving sight to the camps small mountain range.

The mountain's heaven touching apex stands proud and perkily against the baby-blue sky with specks of white cloud puffs as poofy as cotton candy.

"Shall we?" Jessica politely gestures with the wave of an open hand and requests Robert to take the lead of excited teens toward the door of cabin eight.

Full of excitement and hope for a memorable weekend, Robert gives a slight bounce to his walk and a shuffle before creaking cabin eight's door open.

"Here's the event schedule—hang it up on the refrigerator for me, please. I'll take the kids to their room so they can get settled in. We meet under the CAMP WOLF CREEK sign at 2:15 sharp. Just yell if you need me," Jessica says.

"Got it," Robert answers, pacing the shiny canyon brown kitchen, familiarizing himself with the event schedule.

His work keys shuffle in his hand, poking into his skin as he squeezes tight. Words fumble out from his mouth like a greased-up football, as if he is an actor fighting to remember his lines before the director calls out "ACTION."

"Looks like a really exciting day for the kids. I'm not sure 'bout canoeing, though. Not much of a swimmer. I was kinda hoping to get out of that one," he mutters, securing the schedule on the fridge with an apple magnet.

A subtle breeze creates a thumping noise, drawing his attention toward an open living room window. Plain white sheer curtains whip in the breeze, rocking a picture of an Asian man and an American woman holding hands on a cabin porch. SMASH. The picture falls, shattering its glass into several pieces.

"You serious?"

The warm fall air ceases against his skin as he shuts and locks the window into place. His eyes halt over the windowsill. Letters carved into its frame read: *I'LL NEVER QUIT LOOK-ING, PAPA.*

"How come I've never noticed this before? Huh."

Cleaning up the shards of glass Robert holds the broken picture frame out in front of him. His shoulders hunch while his forehead wrinkles. Robert carefully caresses the photo with the most care, almost afraid to touch it. Maybe his fingers would smear it, or maybe it would leave a mark.

"How I wish I could've gotten to know you," Robert sniffles, wiping away the single tear that escapes the corner of his wet eye.

BOOM. He jolts, cutting his finger along the only piece of glass that still remains intact within the frame. It was the upstairs door slamming shut. Several thumps down the stairs from six excited teens wearing their backpacks whip past Robert and charge toward the door.

"Thanks, Ms. Hill," the excited teens shout as they rush out of the cabin.

"What happened here?" Jessica asks, tip-toeing down the stairs, weary from the tension. A tension so strong she can taste its toxic fumes.

"The picture of my parents broke. I must've left the window open yesterday."

Robert sucks the blood out of his finger, checking its tiny slit as he tosses the glass into the trash. His approaching pinched fingers reflect off the remaining shard of glass still loosely fixed into the picture frame. Cautious of its serrated edges, he pulls it out with ease, placing the picture back on the wall with care.

"Ah, babe, did you cut yourself? Let me see."

Her gentle hand caresses his while checking on his finger. Her lips press against the back of his hand. The smell of strawberry shampoo enters his nostrils, coaxing him into a smile.

"See? I'm not bleeding. I'm fine."

Robert leans in for a kiss, swooping her luscious golden hair away from her face to caress her cheek. Their eyes close, the world is theirs. They're weightless, as if floating on a cloud of endless passion. Her lips, as soft as rose petals and as sweet as orange slices, press into his. Her right hand lays tenderly across his chest while the left rests against his lower back. His right hand caresses her cheek while his left wraps around her waist, pulling Jessica in close. Coming up for air they can taste each other's breath as their hearts beat against each other.

"Robert, we gotta go. Its two o'clock."

"Yeah, I'm sorry. I can never get enough of your kisses. And your hair. Smells so good."

"There's no reason to be sorry, babe."

Laughs and giggles from six happy teens direct their attention outside the kitchen window. Robert wraps his arms around her, holding her tight as they both enjoy the moment.

"You know what? I must reconsider my doubts. I'm beginning to think this is going to be amazing," Robert blushes, kissing her cheek.

"See? I told ya. You worried for nothing. You gotta stop doubting yourself."

"You know…"

"Know what?"

"When are we gonna have our own?"

"What? Children! Whoa, speedy. You gotta slow down there. We ain't even married yet."

"I can dream, now. Can't I?"

"Maybe one day, that dream will come true."

The picturesque cabin seven sits high on her throne of emerald-green amongst the warm rays of the suns golden embrace. At the bottom of that hill are many hills that roll like a fingerprint, rolling up and down, curving one way, then the next, all the way to cabin eight, where the teens embark on a game of tag. Emma is it, and she's having the time of her life.

"Looks like Emma's feeling better. How did you pull that one off?"

"I told her about the day we were having, and it cheered her right up. All including the canoe part. She loves the water." Jessica winks.

"I hate the water, but thanks for reminding me." Jessica's lips peck his cheek. "Come on, Robert. It's two o'clock, about time to start."

The cuddling ends as they separate so Robert can raise the walkie-talkie to his mouth. "Robert to all teachers: It's two o'clock—time to wrap up what you're doing and make your way to the Camp Wolf Creek entrance sign."

Jessica and Robert gather their six teenagers for a nice walk on the dirt path toward the entrance sign for the official meeting.

The mountaintops to the south are barely visible over the tall pine trees. The sun makes itself known from over the mountains with it's welcoming embrace. The honeyed light brings a frisson of joy to their skin through shafts of gold light that penetrate through the gaps of the trees.

Bugs swoop around Emma's face. Their wings hum and buzz, piercing her eardrums with a metaphorical knife that makes her cringe from the inside out.

"You okay, Emma?" Jessica asks.

"Yeah, just thought that was a bee. I'm fine."

"Emma, do you have your epi-pen with you?"

"Yes, Ms. Hill. It's in my bookbag."

"How 'bout you come up here with me, where I can keep an eye on you?"

"Coming." Emma breaks formation, double-timing to catch up with Ms. Hill.

Up ahead, the target range observable through the apertures of the tree line gives sight to six bales of hay. Tapered with the tree line is also a dirt pile or a safety barrier that towers over the targets.

Going east, they approach a shimmering blue lake that burbles under a long and very high suspension bridge approximately seventy feet. A dense forest full of assorted trees takes them past the canoeing area, and finally, under the Camp Wolf Creek's entrance sign.

It is so beautiful. The sun stands tall over the surrounding trees and proud over the clear baby blue sky. Browns, reds, yellows, and oranges decorate the lively elm trees on both sides of them. Leaves glide off their branches as gently as snow-flakes, blanketing the ground around them like confetti. The fallen leaves dance along the walking path in the gentle breeze from the fall air.

Robert, Jessica, and their group walk through the random chit-chat from crowds of scattered teachers and students loitering under and around the entrance sign.

"Is this everybody, Jess?" Robert asks.

"This is everyone." Jessica crosses her arms with her palms cradling her elbows, soaking in the sunlight from under the CAMP WOLF CREEK sign.

A small speaker and coiled microphone rest next to Jessica. Jessica flips on the microphone and speaker, unleashing a jarring squeal that can pop an eardrum.

The shrieking crowd of teachers and students plunge their fingers into their ears as if their eardrums are trying to escape out from their ears. They wince, clamping their jaws tight, releasing brain-bleeding groans that can barely escape between the gaps of their teeth.

"Hello, hello. Can you hear me? Okay, sorry about that. Is that better? Can everyone hear me? Okay, all right, we're finally here," Jessica cheers as the crowd applauds for a moment. "Like the sign says, welcome to Camp Wolf Creek, everybody, and welcome to 'Grym Hollow' or 'the Hollows' or 'Grym Town,' as some call it. We are in Max County. I am Jessica Hill; next year, some of you will have me as your eighth-grade science teacher, and to my right is Robert Lee. He actually owns this place. The two of us and the other teachers are like your camp counselors. Everyone, let's give Mr. Lee a round of applause—if it wasn't for him, all of this this moment and amazingly fun weekend we have planned for all of you wouldn't have happened."

The speaker releases a repetitive thump as her hand claps along the back of her hand. Jessica's eyes slide over at Robert, giving him a friendly wink as he gives her a respecting thumbs-up.

"Thank you," Robert mouths to her.

"All right, all right. I'm gonna pass the mic to the most infamous Robert Lee, Lee, Lee." Jessica's echoes fade as her lips curl from ear to ear as she slides the smooth metal handle of the microphone into his palm.

"Well, thank you, Ms. Hill, very much for that most thoughtful introduction. As Ms. Hill said, my name is Robert Lee; I am the owner of Camp Wolf Creek. I'm also responsible for the upkeep of this place, which has been in development for years. This wonderful place was founded by my amazing parents, who unfortunately passed when I was young. When I was old enough to take over this place, I knew I had my hands full. There was so much work to do. But, luckily, I met Ms. Hill, and three years later, Camp Wolf Creek is finished. I feel very fortunate to be here doing what I love, and that's putting smiles on your faces, and hopefully, along the way, I can teach you a little about the outdoors. After twenty-five years, this place is finally open, and you all are the first ones to stay here. During your two-day stay, we'll be canoeing, rock climbing, walking trails, target practicing, and much more. Jessica, the rest of your teachers, and I are really excited for you guys to spend a weekend you'll never forget. Now that you know who I am, I would like to know who you are. So, one at a time, come on up, take the microphone, introduce yourself, then pass it to the next person."

The mic passes from student to student, who range from shy to thrill seekers but all are equally excited to be there.

A very eager boy bouncing on his toes and waving his hands frantically catches Robert's attention. The boy begins to dance his way to the microphone, swiping it from Robert's hand.

"Travis Conley here. I'm five foot six inches, super athletic, and a short blond-hair Italian. I'm the dancing, singing, most amazing extravaganza on the planet, and probably the only one with these sweet self-tying shoes. Check them out." Travis presses his finger into the shoe app of his Android phone, swiping his finger in the main menu, passing the many choices of shoestring colors.

"Come on, come on, where is it? Ah-ha." Travis presses the tighten button, surprising the crowd of curious students.

Dale, a dark-skinned boy lanky as a recently planted tree with limbs like twigs, is tall, taking half the steps with strides as long as a race horse. He approaches the entrance sign rather quickly, taking the mic from Travis, whose eyes are busy gawking at his phone. "Hi, my name is Dale, Travis's more poor, quiet, respectful, and polite friend since the first grade, and most people know me because of my height and my long curly black and copper hair with a side part undercut."

Dale walks the microphone to Emma, who turns her head and pauses, appearing to be shy. Her eyes cement toward cabin eight. They appear opaque and white as foggy waters, but with her head facing away from them no one is able to notice. Her hand tightens around the microphone coming to a shiver but her trance like state comes to a halt when Jessica peels the microphone from Emma's shaking hands.

"It's okay. You don't have to if you don't want to." Jessica comforts Emma with a gentle pat on her shoulder. "Does anyone else want to introduce themselves?"

Emma's milky white eyes fade away to her natural brown color. Her trembling hands come to a stop as she eases her head back around; her eyes are stuck to the ground, struggling to uncover the truth of why she's an introvert in the first place. A hand barely visible in the crowd of teachers and students carries away in a frantic wave.

"Yes, you in the middle," Jessica blurts with a point of her finger.

She has short strawberry blonde hair with a perm, and her face is full of freckles, emphasizing her pale skin. A bright soul, born from the land of the thistles and kilts.

"Mrs. Hill, will there be a time we can use our cell phones? I'm Zoey, by the way."

"Good question, Zoey. There is no cell phone service here."

"Aww." The kids sigh with great disappointment.

"In fact, I left my own cell phone at my house. Cell phones are a distraction, and I want to give you guys my full attention.

We're here to have fun and learn. You can't do that if your face is glued to your phones. On the contrary, from ten a.m. to one fifteen p.m. is free time. For those of you who brought your board games and handheld electronics, or if you want to play on your cell phones, you can play at that time only. Now, each teacher was handed their own weekend retreat packet; with each packet is a map of the camp, a child roster sheet, and an event schedule. Each teacher has six kids they are responsible for. Everyone's event schedule times are different so there's no overcrowding at any event. This will allow you guys to have more fun and not feel left-out. Okay, how about enough talk and more fun?"

The crowd of excited teachers and students roars with applause, which soon diminishes to merely talking amongst themselves as the teachers group up with their assigned students. Jessica takes the microphone from Robert, sliding its button to the off position. "All right, Robert. What's our first event?"

"Looks like we go rock climbing first. All righty. Kids, Jess, follow me," Robert says, leading his group west toward the mountain range for rock climbing.

Everyone disperses with their groups, including Robert and Jessica, who march off, leaving Emma rooted to the spot. Under the entrance sign swallowed up by the shadows of dangling branches, she pants like a hot, exhausted dog. It's so terrifying, the trees begins to shiver. She forces out what little air she can, trembling like a leaf in a mighty hurricane.

The sun's light dims like dying batteries in a flashlight chilling the air around her. A hideous whisper transpires to a sinister voice – a voice that slithers around her making it impossible to pinpoint where it is coming from or even who or what is saying it.

- Thump, thump, thump. "Help us."

Directing her attention west, Emma pinpoints the voices location with little courage to face it. The brown in her iris transpires to a seamless white as her mind immediately departs her trembling body. Each and every brain cell is being called to work to bring her to the voice. But where?

She becomes light, so light her arms start to rise. The sensation spreads through her whole body, and then her feet lift off the ground.

Everything becomes a blur, as if she is moving at a supersonic speed blending her environment together like a smeared painting. The golden glare retreats under the horizon, making way for the harvest moon to shed its murky light over a dark camp so full of secrets. The breeze ruffles through the pine trees, the navy blue lake, the super cool treehouses, the fold mountains, and finally cabin eight which rests comfortably at the toe of the rolling hill.

The blur of blending colors fade back to their normal places as Emma's soul swoops under the front porch and into cabin eights crawlspace.

The thumping sound begins again becoming louder as she comes hovering over the bump in the dirt. It cracks, splitting wide open, releasing an array of colors that flare toward the velvet dark like fireworks.

Captivated by the lights mystery, she leans in to take a peek to see where the light is coming from. Crumbled dirt mingled with Saddle Brown leather brings a smile to Emma's face. It is like she found a buried treasure, but what is it?

She wipes flecks of dirt away flaring up plumes of dust, giving the hot air a musty smell. Her brain triangulates the surrounding area, calculating how long and how wide she needs to dig to extract the enigmatic item.

She squeezes her fingers into the gap between the dirt and the treasure's edges. She tugs, and tugs, breaking it loose from the grounds merciless clutches. Her mouth drops as she can't take her eyes off its front cover.

"It's a book."

ZOEY
TRAVIS
CANOEING
WOLF'S EYE DEN

Emma, you coming?" Travis shouts back at Emma who's glued to the spot from under the camp's entrance sign. She awakens from whatever awkward day-dream she was having and sprints back toward her groups line.

Travis gives a friendly pat on Emma's shoulder as she passes by to catch back up with Jessica. "You okay Emma? Looks like you seen a ghost."

"I'm fine, thanks for asking," Emma answers, glancing back, giving Travis a bogus grin. Her lips curl and drop instantly as she cuts back in the front of the line. She's unemotional, unsure of how to react or feel after the dark and evil experience she felt moments ago.

"Whoa, whoa. Let's stop here for a moment. We haven't gotten to meet the other three kids, in the group yet. Of course, we know you, Travis, we know Dale, and Emma. What are your names?" Jessica asks the other three kids who eagerly are ready to introduce themselves.

One camper full of courage steps out from the line. A real leader at heart and competitor in spirit, his short hair rolls like gentle waves into a fade, complementing his Kalahari-sand skin.

"I'm Caleb. I'm a pretty good rock climber. My dad and I go all the time. When I grow up, he wants to climb Mount Everest with me," Caleb says.

"Wow, Caleb. My father and I used to rock climb, too. That's really cool," Jessica says.

"Did you guys climb Mount Everest, Ms. Hill?" the unknown girl asks from the middle of the crowd.

"No, unfortunately, we never got the chance. We did allot of inside climbing. Now, what's your name?" Jessica asks.

"As I've already introduced myself, I don't mind doing it again. I'm Zoey. If you can't tell, I'm Irish and into fashion. I want to own my own clothing line when I grow up." Zoey smirks.

"Ah. Right. You had the cell phone question. I remember now." Robert giggles with a slight look of embarrassment crossing his face.

"Looks like Mr. Lee is a beamer." Zoey giggles.

A spoiled long blond-haired daddy's girl wearing diamond studs and expensive sunglasses lathers on her sun-screen. Chomping her gum like there's no tomorrow, she's excited to consume the attention from the group.

"Beamer? What does that mean, anyway? I swear, your Irish slang is starting to annoy me. Anyway, my name is Katelyn; we'll save the best for last. I'm incredibly smart with a very rich, and bright future. My parents are filthy rich, much richer than Travis's parents. I want to, no I'm going to be rich like my dad someday. He's a doctor, and my nails-they're to die for." Katelyn cheers showing off her shiny fingernails. "Matches my shirt. Cute, aren't they?"

"Are those Ray-Ban's?" Travis asks.

"Ray-Bans? So cheap. These are Anna-Karin's. I can buy several of those ridiculous and boring self-tying shoes for the price of these." Katelyn responds, flicking her layered hair behind her back.

"Okay. Those are good goals, guys. How about we continue? We have a ways yet to the mountain range," Jessica says with a gulp, a long exaggerated sigh, and a wipe of her forehead.

"Onward, melter, time for a dander." Zoey giggles, continuing to speak her Irish slang only to annoy Katelyn.

"What are you even saying? Ughhhh!" Katelyn complains.

Elm and ash trees line the trails on both sides and comes to an end before the mountain range. Next to the opening is a large handcrafted wood sign reading: Rock Climbing Ahead.

"That sign is amazingly beautiful. Fair play," Zoey elaborates cheerfully.

"Thank you. I made it myself," Robert replies with blushing cheeks as red as sweet apples. "You did, honey? Nice job!" Jessica compliments him with a proud smile so perky, she blushes herself.

They approach a round opening with two rather large cliffs at the trail's dead end. The round opening has surrounding pine trees as tall as the two cliffs.

Robert approaches the small shed on the right. Its tiny structure is the size of an outhouse, appearing as stable as a three-legged bar stool. His keys attached to his belt jingle as he slides them off the clip.

"What's in there? Looks filthy." Katelyn cringes.

"Rock climbing can be a dangerous activity, and inside here is what's going to protect you from falling."

Robert fumbles around the gear for the correct sizes. The metal hardware cling and clang as they collide with themselves as he finds the right sizes and exits the shed.

Caleb raises his hands in the air, running up to Robert with excitement. "Me first, me first."

"All right, you're first, Caleb. Show us how it's done."

"Move out of the way. Let me show you girls how a real man does it," Caleb says, bumping shoulders with Travis as he passes.

"Nobody bumps into me without a challenge," Travis growls. "Race, race, race," Zoey chants, shaking her fist in the air. She repeats the chant as all the other teens follow along except for Emma, who remains to herself.

"You are going down, son," taunts Caleb, who cracks his fingers and neck as Robert assists him with the harness.

Travis carefully takes off his new Jordans, holding them as if they are a precious treasure. "I'm not getting these babies dirty." He kisses his precious shoes before handing them over to Jessica.

Robert grabs the other harness, assisting Travis into it. His foot miscalculates and slides along the nylon strap, causing him to lose his balance and fall to the ground with great embarrassment.

The other teens laugh at Travis as the bully finally gets what he deserves. "That's enough, guys. Stop being so mean to each other," Jessica orders as she helps him to his feet.

"You're such a loser." Katelyn giggles.

"Yeah, shut up. Stop laughing at me." Travis rebukes her with clinched teeth and coiled fists.

"How does it feel? You laugh and bully people all the time," Zoey says.

"Here, let Mr. Lee and I help you."

"What do you know about harnesses?" Travis asks mockingly.

"Actually, Mr. Lee and I rock climbed here several times."

Robert secures the harness around Travis and latches the hook to the rope above. Looking up the looming mountain wall, they are mere ants to its massive presence. Blocking out the sun's light, they are blanketed in its shadow casting over them. Thank goodness the bell is in close range; otherwise, the climb would be insanely above their skill level.

"Is he good, Mr. Lee?" Jessica gives Robert a thumbs-up. "Both harnesses are secure, Ms. Hill," Robert responds, giving Jessica a thumbs-up in return.

Jessica and Robert back up to give Caleb and Travis enough space. "First one to ring the bell wins! Are you ready? Get set, go."

As everyone predicts, Caleb starts off strong with a grip like a spider gaining a massive lead as poor Travis neglects to find his footing.

With the crowd of teens cheering for both competitors, the pressure only makes it harder for Travis. Unable to get anywhere, time has run out for him as Caleb rings the bell and makes his descent to the ground, where he's met by the others to congratulate him.

Travis gives up making his slow descent, holding his head down and his self-esteem at his feet. His pride rejuvenates when the other teens greet him for some necessary encouragement.

Caleb detaches the hook from the rope, and the crowd surrounding Travis breaks away to make room for Caleb as he comes in holding his hand out for a high five. The encouragement lifts Travis's spirit enough to accept the loss and return Caleb's high five.

"I'm not a rock climber at all." Travis pouts, keeping his eyes to the ground, unable to make eye contact with Caleb.

"That's okay. You tried; that's all that matters," Caleb replies cheerfully.

"Yeah, I guess so," Travis says with an inspiration boost, giving him the confidence to look at Caleb.

Jessica hands Travis back his Jordans. Ding, ding, ding. The alarm on Robert's phone goes off, signaling it's time to change events.

"Aww," all the teens cry out in disappointment.

"So, what's next, Jess?"

"Looks like it reads: target practice."

All the kids cheer, while Travis and Caleb lead the way in a full sprint. The other teens follow, leaving Robert and Jessica behind, giggling.

"Hold up!" Robert rushes forward to catch up to the kids.

"Last one there's a rotten egg," Jessica says as she begins to run.

An open field stops dead at a steep hill. Spread out in front are six bales of hay with a bullseye attached to the front of each bale. The students are already donning the proper hearing and eye protection. They stand approximately twenty feet in front of their targets. Each shooter has their own table standing next to them.

"Everyone at the firing line. The BB gun next to you is a Barra 1911 airsoft pistol. They are already loaded. Do not, and I repeat, do not aim them at anything but the target in front of you. Okay, now go ahead and pick them up. Do you guys see the lever here on the side? Slide them up. See the red dot? Now, your weapon is ready to fire. Go ahead and aim your weapons at the target, but do not fire. Is that understood?"

"Yes, Mr. Lee," all the students shout simultaneously.

Robert stops behind Travis, giving him a confused stare before crossing his arms. Realizing Travis's goofiness Robert sighs while shaking his head. Travis is holding the airsoft pistol like he's too cool for school, pointing it out to the side with one hand.

"Check yourself, fool, before you wreck yourself," Travis blurts out to his target, like he's in some sort of action movie.

Robert, who happens to be nearby, notices Travis's reckless behavior and tells him to hold the gun properly. He reminds Travis that guns are not toys and he should never mess around with them.

Travis takes Robert's advice and holds the gun correctly, like he's suddenly realizing he's not invincible. Maybe if he takes it seriously, he can be better.

Robert walks off shaking his head in disapproval and before he can collect himself he catches Katelyn holding her airsoft pistol upside down. She's confident, acting like she's some sort of La Femme Nikita with her Anna-Karin's on.

"I got it," Jessica says as she assists Katelyn in turning her pistol around the right way.

"Ah, my gosh. This is so stupid." Katelyn complains when she notices a scratch on her pretty orange fingernails. She pants, waving her hands in a frantic way overly dramatizing the situation. "I'm done. I'm so done." Katelyn pouts, tossing the airsoft pistol back on the table.

"Katelyn, what's the matter?" Jessica asks.

"Look, your stupid gun scratched my nail. I'm going to have to get it repaired." Katelyn sighs. A single tear rolls down her cheek, and she wipes it away with the palm of her hand stomping off the firing line like a spoiled child.

Robert takes interest in Emma's progress. Stopping behind her he rests his thumb under his chin and his forefinger over his lips, taking in a sense of pride at her professionalism.

"When I give the command 'Fire,' I want you to fire ten rounds into the target, and once you're done, you are to wait for my next command. Does everyone understand?"

"Yes, Mr. Lee," all the teens with the exception of Katelyn respond joyfully.

"All right. Ready, fire!"

Katelyn continues to pout as she pounds her fist into the picnic table mumbling to herself random words of frustration. She scratches her nail when she lashes out in anger grabbing the air to strangle it. At her seat she digs into her bookbag for her fingernail polish to repair the damage she caused.

All the campers fire all ten BB rounds while Robert closely observes their performance, walking past all the kids like a stern firearm instructor.

The tall silhouettes of the tree line cast their dancing shadows over the towering dirt barrier sitting close behind six targets.

"Man, I suck!" Travis shouts, stomping his feet onto the many strands of green grass. Not a single hole is in his target.

Next to Travis are Caleb and Dale, who are in neighboring lanes, having their own competition, counting aloud every single round that hits the target.

"There's four. Five. And six. Ha ha, I have six." Dale celebrates, breaking out into a series of his finest dance moves.

Caleb tilts his head with a grin a grin that's growing as his trigger finger tightens. A thrust of air forces a BB to cut through the air and rip into the target's paper.

"Look at that. That makes seven. Looks like I win again." Caleb celebrates with a backflip.

The sun's brilliant golden rays hug the land, stretching its arms over the target range. The tree line's silhouette begins to fade to countless evergreen needles extending their arms toward the gold light to greet it.

Zoey cackles like a pack of crazed gorillas, hoping around in her imaginary cage not realizing she is only drawing attention to herself.

"That's right, that's right. I got eight. You guys got beaten by a girl. Ha-ha, boys suck." Zoey cheers with her hands in the air and her finger still on the trigger as about eighty percent of her shots land in the bullseye.

Zoey jolts as her finger accidentally squeezes the trigger. The BB whizzes past Dale and Caleb and right into Travis's butt.

"Ouch, ouch, dang it, you stupid girl." Travis runs around the firing range like his butt's on fire.

"Sorry, Mr. Lee! It was an accident, I swear." Her hands tremble, softening her grip and releasing the BB gun, which thuds to the ground. "Geez, I feel like such a plonker."

"Travis, are you okay?" Robert asks.

"Yeah, I'm fine, Mr. Lee. Feels like a bee sting."

"All right, everyone, enough horse play. Put your guns down on the table before someone else gets hurt," Robert commands.

"Travis, come here. Are you okay?" Jessica asks, showing great concern.

"The big baby's okay." Dale giggles while fist-bumping Caleb.

"Travis, I'm so sorry. I didn't mean to," cries Zoey.

"Phew, just a bruise. He's okay, everyone." Jessica hugs Travis. "Go ahead and put your guns and equipment away. Don't forget your targets."

"Yes, Ms. Hill," answers Caleb, Dale, Travis, and Zoey.

"Let's see your target, Emma." Robert walks with Emma down to her target, pulling it loose from the hay. With the paper target held in front of his face, his hazel eye looks through the center's near-perfect circle.

"You've done this before, haven't you, Emma?"

"Moon's my last name. Emma Moon. My grandpa's a hunter. He takes me hunting all the time."

"Do you want to keep it?"

"No, thanks. I never keep them."

Ding, ding, ding. The alarm goes off on Robert's phone. "Are you kiddos ready?"

"Ready for what?" Emma asks.

"To walk some trails," Robert replies.

"Trails are so boring." Zoey pouts. Her shoulders roll forward, her eyes on the dirt.

"It can't be that bad, right?" Dale asks.

"Got to be better than losing a race and getting shot." Travis winces, holding his bum to maybe catch some sympathy out of someone.

"You guys will love it. The beautiful fall leaves are so gorgeous. Not to mention the amazing pink-and-purple willow trees," Jessica chimes in with excitement.

"Pink-and-purple willow trees? Sounds boring." Travis sighs.

"Robert calls it 'Trail to Heaven's Willow.' That's where Mr. Lee proposed to me. Now, come on; form a line," Jessica winks at Robert with a smile, taking the lead of the short but adventurous walk along the narrow trails, which is quite pleasant.

The beautifully stunning scenery is a change of pace for all of them. Squirrels scatter and scurry up trees as the group approaches them. Leafless branches stretch across the sky, looking like veins of the earth. A hodgepodge of colorful leaves blankets the trails, rustling under their feet.

"Ouch!" Zoey pouts.

Jessica leading the line of students spins around to check on the commotion. "What's the matter?"

"Travis kicked a rock into Zoey. I saw it," Katelyn says.

"I'm sorry, Zoey, it was an accident," Travis pleads his sincerity.

"Are we getting close to the willow trees you were talking about? Shouldn't we be there by now? We've been walking forever," Dale complains, hunching his shoulders over.

"I think the wise guy took the scenic route." Travis pouts.

"Hey, guys. Check out the tree houses over there. Aren't they cool?"

Another directional signpost reads "Canoeing" and points east, while "Wolf's Eye Den" points south. At this point in the route, a massive suspension bridge spans the gurgling river below, which makes a gentle splash as it flows downstream.

On the other side of the bridge are many odd sequoia trees with large roots wrapping around them like bracelets and anchoring their welcoming hands into the ground. Each one holds three treehouses with a breathtaking view blossoming like flowers.

Rays of light pass through their windows, giving each of them a soul. The kind breeze sways the curtains with all its love.

Each treehouse is of hickory wood, with stairs spiraling around the trees to the ground. The kids marvel at the treehouses' brilliance.

"Can we go in one of them?" Katelyn asks, skipping to the front of the line to wrap her arms around Jessica.

Jessica attempts to persuade Katelyn with rational thinking. "We better not. We won't have any time to canoe," she responds.

"We can spare five minutes. Please. Come on, it will be fun," Katelyn begs.

Jessica shrugs. "Sure, why not? Get back in line."

Katlyn rushes back in line as they make their way over to the old suspension bridge, which appears to have been there for years. Jessica cautiously glances over her shoulder at Robert, who stands at the back of the line. While battling an episode of the jitters and with a shaky voice, she asks, "Is this safe, Robert? Ugh. I can't stop shaking."

"Of course it is. I cross it all the time, honey," Robert shouts from the back of the line.

The wood creaks from under Jessica's feet, making her wonder if it is going to hold. Her hands shake as she grabs the rope and her eyes peer through the gaps of the boards and into the waters below.

"You're gonna be fine, Ms. Hill," yells Caleb from the back of the line.

"If you can handle us, well, you can handle this," Travis encourages her.

Jessica finds it in her heart and soul to be strong, and with a deep breath, she leads the way across the bridge. The gem-blue river babbles and burbles over basalt and granite rocks. Leaves and twigs twirl along their journey across its glassy surface, telling stories from the trees they were once from.

"Earthquake!" Travis tries to be funny and rocks the bridge back and forth.

The excessive swaying puts Jessica in a fright. Her trembling hands lock onto the rope railing, developing rope burn in the creases of her fingers. But even then, it's too terrifying to let go. Her cold, clammy sweat seeps from her pores. Her skin crawls and her bones rattle. Every muscle screams of a horror unseen as her knees buckle and she collapses into the running boards.

"Travis, that's enough," Robert demands.

"You're gonna kill us!" Zoey screams.

Jessica opens her eyes as the swaying boards from under her stop, her spread open fingers reach a standstill. Her four hands become two as her vision converges back into place. The smell of fish and algae-covered rocks leap up into her nostrils. She shakes off the smell with a twitch and a sniffle, pushing herself to her feet.

"You okay, Jess?" Rob yells out.

"Yeah, Rob, I'm fine. How 'bout we keep going?" Jessica quivers.

"Sorry, Ms. Hill," Travis mumbles with a sigh.

Jessica cautiously leads the group with a tip-toe. Each stride forward is like a knife driven into her back. Her hold is strong around the rope but the fear outweighs the agony of rope burn.

Empathy abounds in the tiny campers hearts as they attempt to encourage her across the lengthy bridge. So lengthy the bridge between two cliffs bows in the center, beaming its smile at the camps gorgeous terrain.

Caleb marvels at the elegant treehouse. "Wow, this is so cool. Its huge." They stand in front of a sequoia tree. Robert's sore neck begins to ache as he strains to search for the top. His hand shades his eyes from the sun's beaming rays penetrating through the treehouse windows. Three separate treehouses are held in the grasp of three separate branches with stairs bringing them all together. The sun spills gently through the slivers between the wood-slat roof. Even if it was chilly outside, the tree house looks like the warmest, most comforting place to be.

"Now that's first-class. Did you build these treehouses?" Katelyn asks.

"No, I sure didn't. They were built by the same people who built the cabins, and you're gonna be the first group to see it. You ready? Okay, lets go." Robert leads the line of teens, one after another, up the steps with Jessica at the end. They disappear under the eerie shadows of creepy spider webs and branches high above them. Emma, the last teen in line hesitates. Her knees are slightly bent, and her nerves are full of fright. There is no way she is making any contact with any eight-legged creatures, and their icky webbing that may be hiding in the branches.

"Ms. Hill, I don't want to go up there. I'm scared of spiders."

"What do you mean?" Jessica asks.

"Look at all the spider webs up there. Let's not even talk about bees. I'm even more terrified of them."

"It's okay to be afraid, Emma. Even though I rock climb, the height still gets to me. Now, these treehouses are pretty up there."

"You're as scared as me, huh?"

Jessica leans in closer to Emma to not expose her secret. "Probably more scared."

Emma lets out a chuckle, and a serene breeze skims her hair away from her face. An ominous voice circles around her like a ghostly howl. Her eyes gaze around to pinpoint the grim and sinister whispers, but her wondering attention is cut off by Jessica's soft voice swiftly calling out to her.

"Emma, Emma. Earth to Emma."

Emma stands stiff as a board and in her own little world. Glaring over her shoulder, her thousand-yard stare ceases with the passing of the breeze as it sways the hair away from her face.

"Yea," Emma nods, grinning from ear to ear with relief as the spooky voice fades away. Now, she doesn't have to face her fear of those icky spiders.

"Robert, Emma and I are gonna hang out down here."

"All right, we won't be long," Robert answers, his voice carries down the stairs of the large sequoia tree like a distant wave.

Jessica takes a glance at the pink bracelet Emma is spinning around her wrist. "I love your bracelet."

"Thank you. Oh, I forgot I made you one." Emma reaches into her pocket of her black and white-stripe shorts to pull out a pink-and-white bracelet. It's the colors of home and memories of her mother, and is made of simple woven cloth and round plastic pieces. "See? Looks like the one I have on."

"I love it." Emma's heartwarming gift draws a tear to Jessica's eye as she slides the bracelet onto her wrist, holding it near and dear to her heart.

The giggling from the energetic young teens from above interrupts their heartfelt moment. The laughing grows louder, becoming aggressively obnoxious as the students lean their heads out the doorway with the sun's rays beaming past their heads.

Thump, thump, thump go the wooden stairs increasing in volume by the second. Jessica searches through the foliage when Robert emerges from the shadows, giggling.

"What's so funny, Robert? What did you do?" Jessica blurts out with her hands on her hips. Her eyes squint to search for the cause of Robert's giggling.

"Ask Travis." Robert laughs.

More thumping. This time, the pace is much quicker like the sound of a beating drum. Thump, thump, thump, thump.

The rest of the teenagers make their way down the steps, laughing all the way to the very bottom, all but Katelyn, who seems to be disappointed. "Ehh, it's okay. I was expecting much better."

Robert snorts, a small grin suppressed by the cup of his hand. Finally, Travis comes down last, holding his head low and away from Jessica in secret. She approaches his back. Before she eases her hand on Travis's shoulder, he turns suddenly.

"Boo!" Travis holds his arms up, waving them like a ghost.

A high-pitched yelp travels up and out of Jessica's chest and muffles against the back of her hand.

Robert and the teens release a chuckle at Jessica's reaction to Travis's clown-like face.

"What did you do to your face?" Jessica asks.

"Hey, Jess, don't look at me. I didn't see his face till it was too late." Robert chuckles.

Zoey nonchalantly slips her mom's petal bouche red lipstick in her shorts pocket. She makes eye contact with Ms. Hill, dropping her chin to her chest.

"Zoey, you know better than that. Why did you do it? Come on, Travis, let's go clean your face up," Jessica inquires as she waves for Travis to follow her.

"Who's ready to go canoeing? I'm not." Robert's hands fall to his sides, staring down at his feet as he leads the teens back over the bridge.

"No, no, I'm not crossing that bridge again. We're going around," Jessica urges with widen eyes and trembling hands.

"If we go around, that's like thirty extra minutes," Robert complains.

"You can cross it if you want. I'm going around. Come on, kids," Jessica dictates.

Several muddy footprints etch the ground from several excited teens mostly from the groups before them. Some life jackets scatter along the ground, while few hang over a towel rack where they belong. Wooden paddles lean over two large canoes, clanking against their upper edges by the rippling waters.

All the kids are helping each other with their life jackets, cracking jokes amongst themselves, all but Travis and Emma. Travis is standing in the river, washing the lipstick off his face, while Emma is the last person to don a life vest with the help of Mr. Lee.

"It's a little tight." Emma inhales sharply, as if the oxygen is taken from her while he loosens the straps.

"Now, how's that?"

"That's perfect."

Travis, covering his eyes, bumps into Robert, his face dripping wet. "Mr. Lee, is the lipstick off?"

"Looks like you got it. Here, dry yourself off." Robert snags a towel hanging off a handmade life vest rack made of PVC pipe and tosses it to Travis.

"Listen up. So, this is how it's going down; I'll take the girls, and Robert will take the boys. Be careful not to fall when you step into the canoe. It's easier if you grab the edge first. Go ahead and make your way in. I'll help hold it."

"Yoooouu re-remember my w-worst fear is d-d-drowning,

right?" Robert stutters, his body quivers as he shakes off a cold chill.

"Don't worry; the water's only waist deep. You'll be fine. Man up," Jessica jokes with a friendly wink and a kiss on Robert's cheek.

One foot steps into the water. Then the other. He gasps, anticipating a hike in his anxiety, stinging like a thousand angry hornets. He holds onto the canoe, battling his balance among chuckling teens. Robert dreads stepping into the canoe, questioning himself about why he agreed to do this in the first place.

The boys hold onto the canoe's edge, encouraging Robert as he takes a seat in the center of the canoe. His body shivers, and his heart feels like someone was wringing the blood out of it.

"You paddling, Mr. Lee?"

"Nah, Caleb. You and Travis can. I'm gonna hold on and hope this ends quickly."

"All right, boys, you see that rock out there? We go around and back here. Last one to make it back is a rotten egg."

Caleb and Travis grab paddles while Robert holds onto the sides of the canoe for dear life. Both eyes clamp shut, shutting out the calm waters around him.

"You're looking kind of woozy there, Mr. Lee. You're not about to get sick, are you?" Dale asks.

"All right, is everyone ready?" Jessica yells out.

Everyone is ready but poor old Robert, whose nerves remain uneasy. He is noticeably shaking as he holds onto the canoe, wishing he could jump out.

"Get set. Go!"

Zoey takes the lead, paddling from the front while Emma paddles from the back. Jessica and Katlyn sit in the middle, coaching and cheering them on. Their paddles dip into the cool waters simultaneously at opposite ends, taking the competition like pros.

"Caleb, come on, we can't let the girls beat us," Travis argues. In the front, he paddles harder than Caleb who sits in the back, causing the boys' canoe to drift to the side, putting the girls way ahead.

"Ha, ha, losers!" Katelyn yells at the boys. "Don't flip us. It'll ruin my Anna-Karins."

"You're not doing it right. Let me see the paddle, Travis." Dale, who sits in the middle with Robert, leans in to take the paddle from Travis.

"Boys. Stop this horse-playing before this stupid canoe flips." Robert trembles.

The canoe wobbles in the river's current. Water spills into the bow, sloshing against Travis's self-tying Jordans.

"Ah, no. My beautiful Jay kicks."

Splash! The canoe flips like a griller flips a burger. Robert panics, desperate to stay above the surface. It seems like some mysterious force is holding him down. The river grabs and drags him below the surface. His arms thrash violently to fight against the water's lung-crushing clinch until his aching arms are still. Only then is there complete quietness not a single sound, but a voice so soft it can't help but to be graceful, so peaceful it is calming to the soul and spirit, more soothing than a thousand kisses.

"Robby. Robby. Wake up, Robby. Come back to us."

A brown blob amongst the distorting surface casts a shadow over him like a solar eclipse. An unforeseen force hauls Robert out of the water of teal and into pure darkness. Robert, on his knees, gasps. His lungs inflate and deflate to normal rhythm. Laughing floods into his ears.

"Am I alive?"

"Stand up!" the girls yell simultaneously.

Robert opens his eyes, wiping the water off his face. The girls, including Jessica, are in the canoe close by him and the boys are standing around him.

Robert stands up, completely shaken in terror and humiliation. If looks could kill, Jessica would be dead right now. He growls under his breath as he stomps to shore, splashing the water with each staggering step.

"You boys aren't giving up already, are you?!" Jessica yells from within her team's canoe across the lake, hoping to give the boys some encouragement.

"Good job, Travis. You cost us the race." Caleb sulks, tossing his oar into the lake.

"I'm not worried about the race. My poor Jays," Travis whimpers, on the edge of shedding tears. He slips off his precious Jordans spilling water out the in-soles as he tips his shoes over.

"Ah, your shoes are stupid," Caleb blurts out, sloshing the water with each kicking step back toward the shoreline.

"Take that back, punk," Travis argues, splashing water at Caleb.

"Boys, boys, That's enough. Apologize, the both of you," Robert demands, wiping beads of water off his face.

"Sorry," Caleb says with a roll of his eyes.

"Yeah, I'm sorry, man. Friends," Travis pleads holding his fist out for a fist bump.

"Yeah, friends." Caleb pauses for a moment still holding onto his grudge, but gives in and returns the fist bump to Travis.

"Here, you boys take this rope and pull it back to shore," Robert says, drenched in water as he hands off the rope to Travis and Caleb and tramples ahead toward the shoreline.

"What's next on the list, Jess?" Robert asks.

"I figure after you boys change, the adults can hang out while the kids can play hide and go seek."

"You heard her. Put your life jackets away. We're going back to the cabin."

THREE
LEGEND HAS IT

Daydreaming outside and sitting comfortably on a patio chair, Jessica isn't immediately aware of the smile on her face as she gazes at the campsite, then back at the dying embers of the campfire by Cabin eight.

The darkness around her feels comforting and safe, and she can see the tall silhouettes of the elm trees against the grandeur of the night sky. A soft and gentle breeze brushes along her sun-kissed blond hair. Her legs cross as she rests one hand gently under her chin while the other holds a romance novel. The pureness of the moment is a story in itself.

Jessica takes in a breath, pondering on the intense intimate scene she's reading and taking one last glance at the blanket of stars before she continues to read her romance novel. She twirls her sparkly engagement ring around her finger, like she always does when she's reading. Deeply immersing herself into the story, her whole peripherals darken as if the entire world around her doesn't exist, as if she is the main character in the middle of the most intense dramatic scene of her life. Her wondering eyes arch as a shooting star graces her late evening with the warmest feeling in her soul. Her magical moment disenchants her heart when she's cut off by three teenage boys charging out the door.

"Where are they, Ms. Hill?" Dale asks.

"They're already hiding. Don't go too far. We're getting ready to go to Mrs. Crowe's cabin soon."

"We won't be far, Ms. Hill. We're getting tired. We're going to the tents soon," Travis says with a long drawn out yawn before running off with Dale and Caleb.

After a warm shower Robert exits the front door to join Jessica. He has a fresh shave with a couple nicks on his chin covered with a dry piece of toilet paper. The scent of Ocean Breeze lingers in his wet hair as he dries off with one of Jessica's purple plush bath towels. A giggle she can't suppress escapes Jessica's mouth.

"What's so funny?" Robert asks.

"I can't believe that boat flipped on you guys. You should have seen your face when you came up from the water."

"What do you expect? I can't swim. I was terrified." Robert tosses his wet towel at Jessica.

"I'm sorry, baby. I shouldn't laugh."

"So, what's next?" Robert grabs a bag of chips off the table and joins Jessica for a late-night snack.

"Amelia is supposed to be calling me on the radio when her students are done putting up their tents."

"It's kinda late to be putting up tents."

"They have to be about done. I figure our students can hang out with their students, then later, they can sleep in their tents tonight."

"We'll have the whole cabin to ourselves."

Jessica gives him a sidelong glance. "You're bad, but I like it."

"So, where's your phone? I know you can't live without it."

"Well, I thought of what you said earlier about cell phones being a distraction, so, I shut it off and left it in our room. No more distractions."

"No more distractions." Jessica gives him a seductive smile as he edges his hand toward hers ever so slightly, until she feels his fingertips brush her hand. She unfurls her fingers and lets his slip around hers until she can feel the heat from his palm pressing against her own. Robert leans in for a gentle kiss.

Radio traffic hisses from Jessica's radio. "Jessica are you there? This is Amelia."

Jessica releases Robert's hand. "I'm here. Are you ready for us to come down?"

"Yeah, actually, all the kids, including yours, are already in their tents except Emma. I figure you and your fiancé can come to our cabin, and we can all hang out. Don't forget the snacks," Amelia says.

"Where's Emma?" Jessica asks.

"Zoey said she wasn't feeling well, so she stayed at your cabin."

"We'll be there soon, Amelia. Clear." The radio hisses when Jessica releases its button before sitting on the patio table.

Jessica rips the bag of sour cream and onion chips from Robert's hands. "Don't eat any more of those. We have to share the chips with the other teachers."

"I'm sorry."

"You better be sorry. I'll make you sleep outside with the bears."

Jessica hands Robert his bookbag full of snacks. "Here, the snacks are in here. We should check on Emma."

"Yeah, I think you're right."

THUMP, THUMP. From the porch they gaze through the glass patio doors when they hear a banging sound from inside the cabin.

"What is that noise?"

"Must be Emma," Jessica says.

The hickory porch doors creak as Robert opens them. Robert checks the kitchen while Jessica veers off toward the laundry room.

"Emma, Emma, is that you?" Robert calls out.

Jessica checks the laundry room. "Emma, sweetie, you in here? Nope, she's not in there."

He checks the bathroom. "Emma. Nope, not in here."

Subtle groaning draws Jessica and Robert into the living room. The hardwood floor squeaks and groans from under their feet. THUMP, THUMP, THUMP.

Sitting on the bottom step and cradling her head is Emma. Robert kneels next to her, gently setting his hand on her shoulder. "What's the matter? Why aren't you with the others?"

Emma rocks back and forth, pressing her palms alongside her temples and clenches her teeth. "Voices in my head. Thumping won't go away, Ms. Hill."

"I think you're having a migraine. Come on, I have some meds I can give ya. Rob, can you help me get her to bed?"

"Of course. Anything further, princess? All right, girl, let's go." Robert gently lifts Emma and carries her up the hickory stairway to her room.

The moon's bluish light illuminates the bedroom, gleaming past the draping pink curtains and over the bed like a spotlight. The slightly open window invites the cool breeze in, scenting the room with the welcoming aroma of cedar embers, hotdogs, and marshmallows. A pink wool blanket lays neatly tucked over white polyester sheets, which are stretching so tight, you could bounce a quarter off them.

Jessica rolls the bedding back while Robert gently lays Emma on the bed. The springs squeak as she sinks into the spring mattress. Careful not to wake her, Jessica tucks her in for a good night's rest as she and Robert converse in a whisper.

"I'll stay here with her. You should hang with the others at Amelia's cabin. Cabin seven, I think. If we're going to be here all weekend, it wouldn't hurt for you to know them a bit. You can tell them how Emma's doing. I need to contact her grandparents. I'm sure they would want to know. A couple children's Tylenol will make her feel better."

"Migraines are horrible."

"I'm glad its not a bee sting. We would be in a completely different situation."

"I hope she gets better so she can enjoy tomorrow and Sunday. The landline's downstairs. I'll check back in later. Radio me if you need me. I love you."

"Love you too, hot stuff."

"Get better, Emma," Robert whispers, as she has already fallen asleep.

Robert scurries down the steps, taking the direct grassy route west and up to the tip pity top of the hill toward cabin 7, which is the highest point of the camp.

Robert's bookbag bears an open package of sour cream and onion chips. Each step Robert takes rustles the bag of chips, knocking a single chip out his bookbag and to the ground.

To the north-west are many hills that roll like scoops of mint ice cream. Standing tall behind them are gorgeous mountains that are pointy as arrow-heads, resting beneath the dark heavens while keeping their watchful eyes through the twinkling starlight.

To the south and running along the downside of the brink is a river. The luminescent river shimmers under the majestic moonlight, giving sight to silhouettes of ducks flapping their wings and splashing into the water for a good night's sleep.

Max County fairgrounds nestle next to the river, brought to life by the many colors of several fair rides and screaming guests.

Behind Robert and cabin eight going north east is a down slope. There, at the bottom, lies all the events they were apart of today, snuggling next to the camp's entrance.

From the brow of the hill, Robert peers at cabin seven which is made from logs of oak taken straight from the woods of Camp Wolf Creek. The view is priceless, gifting its guest with luxurious scenery, which can bring tears to their eyes.

Two lit windows on each end of the porch stare at him like a blood-thirsty killer. Its roof and yard are covered in the company of colorful leaves, and the creepy shadows from the branches above that looks like veins with a sinister and ghostly blood that keeps it breathing.

Burning embers of orange ascend amidst black smoke. The wood is charred and sticky with marshmallow chunks smeared along its bark.

Several tents occupied by sleeping campers scatter around the cabin's front yard. The fabric flutters in the gentle breeze. Robert tip toes past the tents, careful not to wake a single soul. Some snore and groan, and some toss and turn, while others the ones who are not quite asleep mumbles random chit-chatter.

Approaching the door Robert can hear a ruckus from within the cabin. He taps his knuckles against the wooden door. Tap, tap, tap. The ruckus becomes louder when the door opens before he can knock again.

A hardworking dark-haired girl whose hands are covered in tree dust with an armful of logs greets Robert. She pants like a deer fleeing from a hunter.

"Hi, I'm sorry." Amelia breaths heavily.

"You all right?" Robert asks.

"I will be. I was getting ready to stack these by the fireplace. Where are my manners? Here, can you take these? I'm so sorry; they're getting heavy," Amelia requests panting with deep breaths.

The logs' weight frees her hands, leaving behind crumbles of tree bark and saw-dust down her shirt and arms. She slips her hand into her shorts pocket in a bustle, pulling out her inhaler. A whoosh following a deep inhale and a generous repeat opens up her airway.

"It's the asthma. Kinda sucks, but I deal with it. Sorry, my name is Amelia Crowe, the students' art teacher. You're the owner of this place, right?"

"Yeah, I'm Jessica's fiancé, Robert Lee. Now my arms are getting tired. Where do you want the logs to go?" Robert asks, lowering his tiring arms.

"Just a sec, Mr. Lee." The door closes, creaking unexpectedly and bumping into the tip of his nose. His arms become sore and achy as the load feels heavier by the second. Before he can get a word out the door opens again.

"I'm sorry; come on in. You can put them on the hearth there by the fireplace."

"Well, it's nice to meet you, Amelia."

"You, too, Mr. Lee."

This cabin's living room is a little more spacious than cabin eight. The furniture is occupied by four other adults who are all smiles. They seem elevated by each other's presence with a hint of suspect sparkling in their eyes. A sigh escapes Robert's mouth. An instant relief in his arms as the blood flows back to his fingertips. The crackling and popping in the fireplace is relaxing, though something about the smell is off. It isn't the musky citrus from the cedar wood, but rather a musky skunky smell.

"Do you smell a skunk?"

"No. Don't know what you're talking about," Amelia asks.

The others appear clueless, unable to answer him, shrugging their shoulders with too little regard even to make any kind of eye contact with Robert.

"Smells like it's in here with us," Robert says.

"Dead skunks can be smelled from up to a mile away," Amelia says, gawking at her friends in an awkward silence. "Take a seat. Here have mine. You are the owner, after all. Let me introduce you to the others."

Robert takes a seat in the recliner. The tan fabric is teddy-bear soft, and he sinks into it like quicksand, while Amelia sits by the cedar wood on the fireplace's hearth.

"Hey, everyone. This is Jessica Hill's fiancé, and the owner of this beautiful camp, Robert Lee."

"We remember, she already introduced him earlier today by the front entrance. Speaking of Jessica, where is she?" a man asks.

He is practically bald. The stubble on his head is shorter than the five o'clock shadow on his face. He appears to have a bad temper and a heavy mind, twirling his thumbs and gazing deeply into the fireplace as if ignoring Robert.

"She's watching over Emma. I think she's sick."

"What's the matter with Emma, Mr. Lee?"

"Don't know. She spoke about voices in her head."

"Sounds like one of dos migraines to me. I sometimes get like a ringing noise like one of dos chime bells dangling in my ear. I'm Charlie Baskin, by the way. I'm clean dem turlets at the middle school. The bald angry feller over there on the couch is Blake. He's the middle school's math teacher. Sitting next to me here is my friend Linda. She messes with dem needles and fixes dos puckers."

"Hi, Robert. I'm the middle school nurse."

"Dem newbies over dur is Brittney and Sean. Dey in love with dem callin' devices."

"Hi, Robert. We're the new phys-ed teachers. We started about a month ago. I teach the girls, and Sean teaches the boys."

Charlie hocks a loogie into his empty beer can, straightens up his worn beer hat, and brushes wood dust off his hands before giving Robert a firm handshake.

"Sorry, Robert fer my dirty farm hands dar partner. Me and Blake's been helping Amelia carry in some firewood. I couldn't let da lil lady do it herself der. I'm afraid she has an oxygen condition."

"Okay, that's quite all right. I respect hard workers."

"So, what phone games are you two playing this time?" Amelia asks.

"Solitaire. Not many options when there's no internet service," Brittney says.

"Crap…phone's dead," Sean complains smacking his free hand across his leg. "Ah-ha," he blurts out with a smile Sean remembers his Android charger in his pocket. He wiggles his shoulder in a celebrative dance as he plugs his phone in the outlet next to him to charge it.

"Ah, poor youngin's calling device is sick. Linda, give dat boy's calling device one of dos band aids."

Sean ignores Charlie and stares over at Linda's phone for some secondhand action. Blake smirks, nodding at Charlie's funny comments.

"Hey, mama, can you get me another drink?" Blake asks.

'Mama?' Get your own drink. You got two feet," Amelia says.

"Bitch," Blake whispers under his breath on his way to grab a drink from the refrigerator.

"So, is this everybody?" Robert unzips his bookbag of sour cream and onion chips. The near-full bag crinkles under his grip as he sits the bag down on the coffee table amongst the other snacks.

"This is it. No one else wanted to come," Amelia says. Her

eyes are round as basketballs as she grabs the chips before any-one else can. "Ah, I love sour cream and onion. Umm, okay… how about a story?"

Blake rolls his eyes with a sigh as he cracks open a beer along the counter's edge with a sigh. "Oh, no, not that stupid story again," he sighs, leaning against the fridge for support.

"It's a great story; plus, no one here has heard it yet," Amelia says.

Linda sits up straighter, smiling from ear to ear and clap-ping like a spirited cheerleader. "Go ahead, I'd love to hear it."

The pop and hiss of Blake opening his beer reminds Charlie of his drink. He puckers, licking his lips while staring through his empty warm bottle of beer.

"I'm gettin' dry, and my hands are warm. I reckon I better refuel."

Charlie rushes to the fridge almost losing his britches and tripping over the strings of his hunting boots. Blake pushes himself off the fridge, with his shoulder to allow space for Charlie to quench his thirst. The glass bottles cling and clang together as he reaches into the crisper. Charlie pops open a shaken-up Budweiser. Foam overflows down his hand and onto the floor. GULP, GULP, GULP. He downs his beer and grabs another one before heading back to his seat. Everyone bursts out in laughter but Blake, who only smirks. Charlie catches his breath while cracking open a fresh beer. Wiggling into a more comfortable position, he releases a disgusting burp.

"Whoa, sheweee, I'm ready. On with your story." Charlie sighs wiping the excess beer from his chin.

"Okay, okay, this is a true story," Amelia starts.

"I'm going out to the log rack for more wood." Blake informs Amelia as she shoos him away. "Take your time." Amelia sighs with much relief.

"Huh, whatever." Blake pushes himself off the fridge once again and chugs his beer. The empty beer bottle clangs at the bottom of the trashcan as he tosses it in. Bang! The front door slams shut.

"Ugh. Ah, my, how do you stand him? I'm sorry, I know you two are married, but if Sean treated me like that, I would have been gone," Brittney says with a sigh.

"Ignore him Amelia," Sean says.

"On with ye storytelling." Charlie encourages.

"My mother's a paramedic here in the hollows. It was twenty-three years ago, on this very date. She was called here to Camp Wolf Creek for…unusual activity. This place was under construction still, far from finished. Supposedly, whoever was the witness of the 'unusual activity' called the police. What the witness described to the dispatcher was enough to send out the police, a fire truck, and an ambulance to the scene." Amelia pauses ominously.

"What did they see?" Sean asks.

"I'm getting to that. The caller was a local who was sitting on her front porch. This was before Androids, when most people didn't have cell phones. So, she ran to her landline and called the police. She said she saw a ray of light reaching to the sky, and colorful smoke which circled a bright light. She even heard screaming," Amelia says.

"Lights, colorful smoke, screaming…dat dur sounds like a country concert." Charlie chuckles.

Amelia groans. "Ha, ha…funny."

"I'm curious about what your mom saw when she arrived at the scene," Linda inquires, encouraging Amelia to continue when a whirling wind whistles around the cabin, rattling the windows. Lightning cracks the dark like an atomic bomb, shaking everyone out of their skin. Rain smashes against the roof, sounding like an army of raging bees.

"Is that rain?" Linda asks.

"Were we supposed to have rain? I didn't know we were getting any," Robert said.

"If we had Wi-Fi, we would have known. I can also tell ya how long about it will last," Sean says.

"Ah, shut up," Linda says.

"It's okay; it's just a little rain. I hope Blake and the kids are okay," Robert says.

"Yeah, you're right. We should check on the kids. Blake, he deserves to get wet for being a butthole," says Amelia.

"Look, Blakey boy and dem young people are fine. The winds not blowing much and it's only rain."

"It's raining hard, though. I'm going to look through the window to make sure they're okay." Amelia rushes to the living room window.

The rain hammers down on the tents. Lightning flashes a blinding light, sending a shiver through the camp's soul.

"See? Dur fine. If they weren't, they be screaming like a morning rooster. Let's get back to story tellin'. If dat wind hollers any louder, I'll go get dem myself. Amelia, please continue."

"Yeah. You're probably right. But they're coming in if it gets any worse," Amelia gasps as she returns to sit on the hearth.

"Okay, so where was I?"

"Ray of light, colorful smoke," Linda says.

"Okay, this is the weird part. While the ambulance was on its way to the camp, my mother saw the ray of light, which disappeared before she pulled into the entrance. My mother and the driver of the ambulance were the first ones on the scene. They saw nothing unusual but a little girl who was crying in one of these cabins. She kept repeating, I'll never stop looking, I'll never quit looking. Something like that," Amelia says.

Something perplexes Robert. His eyes face the ground in a thousand-yard stare reflecting on seeing those words carved on cabin eight's window framing from earlier today.

"The girl, her name was Christen Honeycutt. When she was loaded into the ambulance, the police and fire truck arrived. The police began to question Christen, asking her where her parents were. I guess her dad had been with her, but disappeared before the police arrived," Amelia says.

"Man, that's intense," Sean says.

"Poor little girl. I can't believe her dad would abandon her like that," Linda says.

"His daughter told the police that she heard voices coming from the book. Well, the police didn't believe the odd fairy tale she told them, and began the search around the camp for her missing father, but never found him. I believe she said his name was Marty or something like that. They say he still haunts this place. Supposedly, if you listen close, you can hear his voice calling out to his daughter."

Charlie chuckles. "Story-tellin' like dat is as windy as a sack full of farts."

"Well, you can put your stinky bag of farts down, cause the

super weird part was my mom was supposed to watch the girl. When the police officer made it back to the girl, she was gone. No one saw her leave, and they've both been missing ever since."

The wind snarls, slamming the front door into the wall. The creaking door wobbles back and forth, its knob pierces through the wall making a hole in it. Raindrops whirl in like bullets soaking the floor, and broken drywall flaps against the doorknob from the gust of wind welcoming itself in.

Lightning crawls through the inky void like a traveling snake. A muddy hand creeps in, slinking its fingers across the woven brown doormat. The earthly brown of fall leaves is so pristine, it is as if a single shoe has never been on it. Beads of rain and clumps of mud roll off its pale flesh, pressing and smearing the mud into the rug's fibers.

The girls cower behind Robert and Charlie while Sean does the same, but not until after he rips his cell phone charger from the wall. Charlie, who still has ahold of his beer, places the bottles neck out in front of him as if it is a blade. Leaning back with their arms waving in a frenzy, paralyzing fear sweeps over them all at what is crawling through the door toward them.

"OH MY! WHAT IS THAT?" Linda screams with a gut wrenching squeak.

Its head and face are covered in layers of mud that cousins the mighty swamp beast. The spark of its squinting cognac eyes and its tilting eyebrows resemble the look of pure evil.

Through the cabin's entryway, lightning colors the gloom a brilliant white, followed by a thunderous roar. Living room lights flicker, mocking the furious storm.

The electrical lines hum till the breaker pops, leaving the cabin as dark as the night. Thump, thump, thump. The thumping becomes quieter as if it's trying to sneak up on them.

"I can hear it coming toward us," Sean says.

"Power's out. I'm gonna check the breaker," Robert says.

"No, Robert, get back here," Amelia demands.

"Do we fight it?" Linda asks.

"Any of y'al teachers have some light?"

"Here, my phone still has some power," Linda says, aiming the beam of light where it was. The light shudders over the muddy rug smearing along the wood's grain, ending at handprints pressing into the red oak floor several feet in front of them.

"Where is it?" Linda says as they ease around the kitchen's island.

"Linda, shine dat light right dur." Amelia jerks open the silverware drawer. Metal forks and spoons cling and clang against the shimmering light. Her hand trembles as her fingers edge toward a kitchen knife buried under other loose utensils. She grips the kitchen knife firmly out in front of her, and it glimmers like bright snow from the phone's light.

"What are you gonna do with that?" Sean asks.

"I know wut she's 'bout to do with it. She 'bout to cream his corn."

Click. The cabin's lustrous golden rays light up the room. Beep, beep, beep sings the microwave as three green zeros appear on its digital clock screen.

The group hides behind Amelia, who guards them with the knife in her quivering hands. They peer around the island, gazing at the muddy handprints stopping before the kitchen's entrance.

"Where is it?" Linda asks.

"Wut ever it tis, it's a goner." Charlie breaks from the group, readjusting his John Deer hat, and moves in stride toward the front door. The group releases a long sigh, easing the tension and their shaky nerves. Rain surges into the cabin's entryway with a vicious howl. Charlie's feet splatter on the wet hardwood floor as he grabs the swaying door and closes it.

It's standing there, covered in mud from head to toe. Charlie jolts back, ready to attack with one clinching fist while the other wraps snugly around his beer, which spills over his fingers.

"It's me, it's me. It's Blake. Don't hit me, man." Blake pants.

"Fellers, cool yur britches. It's only Blake," Charlie says, wiping the sweat off his brow and chugging the rest of his beer.

Blake wipes the mud off his hands and face with a towel, holding his finger out like he is wanting to tell them something.

"You stupid ass, we thought you were trying to kill us. You're lucky I don't divorce you over this shit. You can clean up the mess you made. Dumbass."

"Are you okay, Blake?" Robert asks.

"Sorry 'bout the wall and floor there Robert. I'll make sure my idiot husband fixes it."

"Quiet, hush ye mouth. Looks like he's trying to tell us something."

Charlie places his hand on Blake's back. He can feel Blake's racing heart high fiving his hand like a pounding sledgehammer.

"Dang boy, your heart's beating faster den Chase Elliot's first lap on de track."

"Call call the police!" Blake mumbles, resting his hands on his knees, desperately trying to catch his breath.

"What's the matter with you? I'm so sorry for being so mean to you," Amelia says, kneeling down to his level, gently placing her warm hands along his gritty mud smeared face.

Blake points out the window toward cabin eight. After taking some deep breaths, he is able to catch enough oxygen. "Fire!"

BAW
2021

"Fire? Where at?"

"That cabin. Over there."

Robert gazes out the window past the raindrops drumming into the ground of sloshy goo, down the rolling hills of green pearl, and through the interwoven shadows of bony branches dancing under the breezy moonlight shading its bark like saw dust.

It's Cabin eight, resting beautifully down the rolling hills dropping off to the glistening navy-blue river dividing and blessing the camp and fairgrounds. The gentle sound of the waves rolling up the shoreline is calming enough to sleep to.

It reminds Robert of his father's accomplishments and makes him smile. Until he sees wisps of silvery gray curling their way toward the night sky.

Down the hill to the east, sparks dance up the inside of Cabin 8's window threatening everyone to keep away. Red-and-yellow ribbons of scorching heat flutter like the raging winds against thin fabric.

A pulse beats in Robert's ears, blocking out all the sounds, including the panicking teachers. He knows Jessica and Emma are in there. He wants to run to them but he is stuck there to the spot.

Robert can feel the cold air tickle his nose from off the window's glass. Several shimmering balls of glaring white light flicker like fireflies, disappearing like magic and appearing again larger with each passing second. A wicked flash splits the somber sky in half, and for a moment, it is brighter than daylight. It is the kids. They seem to pulse like strobe lights in the night before the darkness settles back in.

Robert can see the fire climbing up the window. Black smoke escapes through various places like a fire-breathing dragon is in the cabin.

The front door swings open. All seventeen kids flood in, hugging their teachers. All of Robert and Jessica's teens surround Robert yanking on his shirt. He might as well be a statue, not present in the moment, when the sound of his pounding heart pulls him out of his daze. Distant voices from worrying teachers and teens increase in volume, bringing him back to reality.

"Mr. Lee, Mr. Lee, listen to us," Zoey cries.

"Dude, snap out of it," Travis says, repeatedly snapping his fingers.

"Robert, Jessica's in there. What are we gonna do?" Amelia yells.

"I think he's in shock," Sean anxiously says.

"Wake up! We have to go, the cabin's on fire! Jessica and Emma are in there!" Linda yells.

"Linda, call the police," Robert blurts out as he awakens from his shock. He brushes the sweat off his forehead, struggling for the slightest bit of oxygen.

"How am I supposed to do that? There's no cell phone service!"

"Use your cabin's landline. Over there in the kitchen. Linda and Amelia, stay here and watch the kids. Guys, come on, lets go!"

Robert holds the cold plastic radio up to his mouth. "Jessica, Jessica, this is Robert! Are you there?"

There's no answer. Robert charges out the door leading the way with Blake, Charlie, and Sean behind him. They fight through the earth's breath, shoving rustling leaves out of its way as the wind whisks past their face gripping its windy paws onto Charlie's beer hat and tossing it into the nights void.

"Dag nabbit. I paid twenty dollars fer dat hat."

"Forget about your stupid hat," Robert says.

They stop at the door. Crash! The window to the right of the front door shatters to tiny pieces. The fiery oranges and yellows burn hotter with whites and blues climbing up the hickory walls.

"What are we gonna do? The fires getting out of control," Sean says.

Looking through the door's window, Robert can see Jessica's unconscious on the floor by the living room stairs. The smoke intensifies thickening till it consumes her from his sight.

"I can see her. She's inside by the steps." Robert cries out, grabbing the hot door handle, and instantly jerks his hand away, becoming red and blistered on impact with the scorching hot knob's metal surface.

"Jessica, Jessica, get up! Come on, get up!" He calls Jessica through the radio clipped to her shorts. "Jessica, Jessica, answer me." The radio chirps a strangling tune. Its red light flashes like a heartbeat, pounding as hard as his heart is. Its flash dwindles to black dying to nothing but a useless piece of plastic which is how he feels inside. "Shoot, it's dead." Robert drops the radio, cracking it like a coconut.

"Sean, we might get to steppin' to the back. Could be sum udder way in."

"You go this way, and I'll go the other," Sean shouts.

Robert's eyes harden, narrowing into slits drawling his eyebrows closer together. His knuckles whiten before he pounds the door.

"Jessica! Come on, get up." He rams his shoulder into the hard oak door, his bones make contact with each vicious strike, but the door stands firm. Rearing back, he kicks his Brahma boot into the door. The third time does the trick. Boom! The door's dead latch rips through the strike plate, splitting a chunk of hickory wood clean off the door jam and sending the door swinging open like a bat out of hell.

Black smoke rampages into Robert's face fogging up his vision and making him choke on his own breath as the smoke tears through his throat.

The intense heat threatens to scorch his face and collapse his lungs. He staggers backward out the doorway to evade any injuries, desperate for another taste of sweet oxygen. The woodsy smell of hickory and smoldering wires is so acrid and nauseating he scrapes the taste of ash off his tongue with his teeth. Although the smell was nasty it was better than choking.

Robert drops to his chest to spot any sign of Jessica's existence. His eyes flip around like a wild hose spraying out of control.

He spots an opening that is big enough to crawl through. Robert readies himself with a deep inhale, then re-enters the dragon's mouth this time crawling on his stomach.

Cough, cough. One forearm after another Robert scoots further into the cabin. The haze emits a dense layer obstructing his view from the hickory wood floor just under his nose. Cough, cough. Robert is screaming inside. Every last drop of oxygen is precious. Small rigid gasps escape his throat. Each second feels as if a blade is driving into his chest. He can feel his blood rush to his face and eyes. Cough, cough. Crackling and popping of blazing lumber surrounds him. Smoke rolls across the room like lazy waves, totally obscuring him from Jessica.

He wanders around aimlessly, spinning in circles, unsure of what direction to take. He becomes aware when a thin layer of smoke creeps before him revealing splotches of hickory.

Robert's eyes become bloodshot. Cough, cough. When both dry eyes spot the red stripes running along the seams of Jessica's shorts a rushing desire to save her bursts open his soul.

"Baby, stay with me, I'm gonna get you out of here."

Feeling around, he brushes his fingers along the back of her hand. He jolts with excitement, grasping her wrists and dragging her through the treacherous gauntlet filled with lung-collapsing smoke. The ceilings support unleashes a spine tingling groan bowing under its own weight. Boards split and crack till the living rooms ceiling comes crashing down over Robert and Jessica releasing a mist of bright orange embers across the room.

"Robert! You gotta get out of there!" Charlie's voice argues against the furious flames from outside the front door, unable to break through its force-field like barrier.

Robert stares into the broken ceiling. Drywall dust coats his face and the inside of his mouth. He gasps. Swiping off the drywall dust from his forehead. He slides from under the broken ceiling, crawling across the hot hickory floor pushing with his legs while fighting to drag his love to safety.

The dense smoke diminishes in a vacuum out the front door. He gasps, swallowing a surge of oxygen that whooshes into Robert's face, tasting like the finest meal. His dry eyes are wet now from the pouring rain. The vision of Charlie never looked so good right now.

"Here, newbie, grab dem feet."

They carry Jessica over to a tent, which shields her from the pelting raindrops. Her head rests gently over a red sleeping bag while the rain pitter patters against the fluttering tent.

Robert smears the soot across his wet face when his quivering knees go weak, dropping him into the soft sleeping bag. He places his fingers over her neck, and his ear over her lips.

"Does she have a pulse?" Blake asks.

"No, she's not breathing either." Robert weeps, a river of tears pouring out his eyes. He arches his back, and placing his hands on her chest to start compressions.

"Help me! Ms. Hill, where are you!"

"You heard that over yonder? I reckon dat must be Emma."

"Robert, Emma's still in there," Blake says.

"Dammit! I can't leave her," Robert cries, pressing his hands into Jessica's chest, this time more hurriedly.

"Robert, let me take over. You're getting tired. I can do this," Sean says.

"Please save her, don't give up." Robert leans in, pressing his lips against Jessica's soot-covered forehead.

"Saddle up, Robert, that youngin' needs us. I'll go with you," Charlie says, patting his shoulder.

They dead sprint through the weltering rain toward cabin 8. The flames are more intense now, consuming the first and the second floor. They roar, demanding more to eat, as the belly of the beast is empty.

The wind howls, yet the fire's not afraid. The rain growls, yet the fire burns brighter. The fire snarls back at the army of rain-drops, bullying them to retreating back into the void of the witching hour.

They stand there staring into the eyes of the fiery beast. Its blistering heat dries their wet faces. The whistling wind tires to a deadened sleep. The waving fire is massive now, standing tall in defiance.

"Dat fires madder den a wet hen. How you reckon we rescue dat youngin' Robert?"

"Emma! Emma! I wonder if she's in her room?" Charlie and Robert run to the side of the cabin where the girl's room is. Trying to gaze into the second story window with their feet planted on the ground, they can see nothing but flames. Flickering licks of hell light the room with ear ripping sounds of crackling and popping. Each pop is as painful as a blade piercing Robert's heart.

"Dat poor girl. I'm having awful feelings right now."

"Well, keep those damn feelings to yourself. EMMA! Where's that damn firetruck?" Robert ganders out toward the entrance of the camp praying to himself for the truck to show up or at least to hear the sound of those wailing sirens. But nothing, not a single sound, can be heard over the crackling flames.

Tap, tap, tap. "Mr. Lee. Mr. Lee." Emma springs up, opening the window.

"Ah, thank goodness. Emma, you have to jump."

"No, Mr. Lee, I'm scared. The fire's coming into my room."

"Look, I'm right here. I will catch you."

"What if you miss me?"

"Dat's why I'm here. To catch ye if Mr. Lee can't." Charlie side-eyes Robert, whose face is dressed with the most serious expression, and murmurs, "Don't miss."

"Okay." Emma's voice trembles. Sitting on the windowsill with her bookbag over her shoulders, she wipes the tears from her eyes and sniffles. "Here." She tosses her bookbag down to Charlie and, with a push off the windowsill, she safely lands in Robert's arms.

"You okay? Can you walk?"

"Yeah, I'm fine. My headache's finally gone. I'm worried about Ms. Hill, you gotta get her out of there. Come on, she's still in there. She'll die." Emma tugs on Robert's shirt. Her brave heart wants nothing more than to save her teacher and friend.

"About Jessica…I'm so sorry."

"Is she still in there?"

"No, dear, she's in the tent."

Crash! The roof caves in by the mouth of the blazing fire.

"It's not safe here. We need ta move like a fleeing horse from a burning barn."

They high tail it out of there, sloshing their feet in the mud. Robert leads the way toward the tent Jessica, Blake, and Sean are in. He hits his brakes, sliding in the sloppy mud, and catches his balance by the frantic waving of his hands. Emma comes in fast behind him, sliding like she's on ice, snatching the sleeve of his shirt to regain her balance.

Blake rests on his knees, blocking the opening and inside of the tent. Emma peeks around Robert like a turtle peeps its head out its shell. She rubs her neck, unable to make eye contact with anything but the ground she leans around him. She questions each careful step in the squishy mud as she inches closer to the tent. Robert turns his head as Blake slides out of her way. He squeezes his eyelids shut, hoping the tears will stop. Each breath is stressful and as choppy as a knife.

"Ms. Hill."

Robert releases a breathtaking gasp, bringing his hands to his knees. He feels like his heart's ripping out of is chest. The thought of Jessica's death is unbearable, but he has to look. He has to make sure of it. His head rotates as slow as the hand of a dying clock as both untrusting eyes raise and his hunching back straightens.

Robert isn't prepared to help mend Emma's broken heart. So, who is gonna mend his? Emma's arms wrap around somebody, and somebody's arms wrap around hers, but whose?

"Emma, your hands are filthy."

His face lights up bright as day at the sound of the familiar voice. His broken smile blossoms like Johnny Jump-Up flowers. Emma pulls back from her hug and sitting next to her is. It's Jessica, who sits there in a puddle of tears holding her aching chest. Her face is covered in soot, but still, she's so beautiful.

He feels stuck, unable to respond as if his imagination is toying with him. Is this real? Before he comes to any conclusions, Jessica charges, tackling him to the ground. He holds her close, afraid this is all a dream, and she will crumble under his grip.

"I thought you were gone."

"Sean checked on me after you left. I was breathing and I had a pulse."

"She didn't even need CPR. She was alive the whole time; she was just unconscious," Sean said.

"I don't understand. I checked your pulse."

"It was an intense moment for you. You must have not been doing it right."

"You okay?"

"Yeah, my ribs hurt. Besides that, I'm fine."

"Sorry, I was pressing really hard."

"It's okay, you were just trying to help. You did pull me out of a fire. I would have died if it wasn't for you."

"I love you so much, Jess."

"I love you, too." The outer darkness hiccups a mild flash of white off its lips following a mild cough of thunder fading from existence. Approaching footsteps clomp and squish against the earth's muddy flesh.

"It's Amelia," Sean says, realizing it through the golden hues of reflection that blankets her face.

Jessica releases Robert from their much-needed hug when Amelia recognizes the soot covering her face. Their eyes glisten with fresh tears. Amelia's nose twitches to ward off the itch.

"You okay, girl?" Amelia holds her arms out as Jessica comes in for a hug. She wraps her arms around Jessica like chains, and her tears are the lock that seals her hearts true feelings.

"Yeah, all I remember is after Emma went to sleep, I came downstairs to watch tv. I was tired, you know, so I fell asleep. I remember a loud bang. Well, I must have dozed back off. I woke up later to the fire alarm going off. I was coughing and I couldn't breathe. The cabin was full of smoke. I ran to the steps to get Emma, but before I got there, everything went black."

Amelia's hands wrap around Jessica's shoulders to open the gap. Her finger brushes the tears from her eyes. "Well, you're here. You made it. You're alive and, girl, you need to clean your face."

Both Amelia and Jessica burst out in laughter that is soulful and soft as a butterfly drifting over a garden of roses. Jessica wipes the tears away, smearing the soot across her face. The sparkle in her eyes dances like a disco ball.

"Ah, Amelia, I needed that."

"So, who's the hero?"

"My man, of course. He saved both of us." Jessica pulls Emma in close.

"Sorry, Robert, about the cabin," Amelia says.

"That's okay. The insurance should cover it."

"So, you guys know I've been getting a lot of radio traffic from the others about the smoke. I informed them what is going on, so they're aware of the situation."

"Yeah, Blake and I are well aware. As she was waking up in the tent, our radios were blowing up with traffic."

"Thanks, Amelia. Are the kids asleep yet?" Jessica asks.

"By now, they probably are. They were settling down when I left."

"I'm not trying to get yer knickers in a knot, but dat red truck ought to be here by now. I haven't even heard dose whirling sirens yet."

"Yeah, woman, what's the word on the firetruck? Everyone seems to be forgetting about the massive fire down there."

"Blake, you're an ass. Anyway, the firetruck, police, and ambulance will be here in about ten minutes."

"Yeah, and you're a witch."

"Whoa, guys. Stop fighting." Emma waves her hands around to gather their attention. "Guys. Guys. Let me see my bookbag, Mr. Baskin. I want to show you all something."

Every eye rolls toward Emma as she struts over to Charlie. She rips her pretty pink Jan sport bookbag from his chubby calloused hands.

"Emma, there's no time for any games," Robert says.

"Listen, buster, this is serious stuff."

"Well, hold on. Hold on to yer horses. Give the liddle lady a chance."

"So, while Ms. Hill was sleeping downstairs, I had a dream."

"Emma, we don't have time for this," Robert says.

"Let the liddle lady tell us her story," Charlie insists.

"That thumping I was telling Mr. Lee about. You remember?"

"Emma, that's just part of having a migraine." Robert sighs.

"The migraine came from the thumping, not the thumping from the migraine. Geez."

Everyone chuckles at Emma's cuteness like laughing hyenas at a comedy club. All but Robert and Jessica who are too stressed to release even a fraction of a chuckle.

"So, I followed the thumping noise downstairs. I knew it was close when the floor shook. What was shaking the floor was underneath me. That's when I started freaking out. See I've had these daydreams while I was here. They were so real. So I had to see it for myself."

"Wait a second. I didn't feel the floor shake."

"Cause you were sleeping. Duh."

"You got to get to the point, Emma. The firetruck should be here any moment," Jessica says.

I was standing overtop of a rug, so I pulled the rug back and found a trap door. I was under the cabin when I crawled over to the thumping sound. The same place from my daydream. I needed to know if they were real, so I began to dig. I dug and dug and dug."

"That explains why those hands are so filthy," Jessica says.

There's a clicking sound from the zipper of Emma's bookbag. Each tooth unravels from its slender brass body, unsealing like a treasure chest.

"Until I saw this. That's when I knew my daydreams were real. It talks, too. I heard it say 'Help us.'"

"Honey, daydreams are not real. It's just your imagination." Jessica says.

Emma draws out a mysterious book. Appearing ominous and grim, the book in no doubt creates a feeling of the heebie-jeebies from deep within the soul.

Its cover is a mud-brown faux leather that is rough as a seashell. Exposing its stitching gives the vintage look charisma. Rusty gears made of some kind of metal lay in the center of the book with engravings of five mysterious symbols and a key that is a mystery itself.

Charlie, Blake, and Sean gawk at the book with vacant expressions as blank as new paper.

What's even more sinister is the four skulls that attached onto the gear one on each corner but the top right which is vacant, and one in the center. Each skull bears a different orb-shaped color pendant in its forehead and a keyhole in each chin. A look of puzzlement crosses Jessica's face when she takes the book.

"That's them. The skulls there, she calls them reapers. The stones are pretty aren't they?"

"Reapers, red stone. You must have had one crazy dream," Blake says.

"More like a nightmare. It didn't last long. Don't know how or why it happened, but it sure felt real. I feel sorry for the girl. She's about my age. Another fake daydream I had. Anyway, the red stone is broken. I have half of it. Weird part is, when I pulled the loose part of the broken red stone from the skull this key went into its chin and red smoke flew out just like the one in my dream but I saw more than just red smoke. Teal was my favorite. Really pretty. The other half of the stone disappeared when I pulled out the broken piece. The skull on the book also disappeared. The bare spot there on the top right of the book is where his skull used to be. The skull in the center with the black piece of jewelry he's the scariest. I think he's the leader," Emma babbles.

"Sweetheart, it was only a dream," Amelia reassures her gently.

"I did see it. It was real. This actually happened, I swear."

"Maybe it was dat smoke inhalation. Smoke puts a hurtin' on the brain, you know. Cause dem hallucinations."

"Maybe she was daydreaming, Jess. I used to daydream all the time at that age. After my parents passed on, I would sneak over here and have visions of my dad walking around with me. He would tell me about his plans for this place. See, I knew they weren't real, but it sure felt like it. The mind can play tricks on you at times."

Robert delivers a side eye to Blake and Sean, seeking immediate guidance in aiding him with the matter. Their eyebrows raise, their lips press together, and they shrug without a peep.

"I wasn't daydreaming or hallucinating I promise. It was real," Emma says.

"All right, then. As I see it, we can't do anything till the firetruck gets here, so let her tell us her story," Sean says.

"I was over there, where the humongous treehouses are. A really nice girl was looking for her dad. She calls him papa. She asked me what I was doing there and told me I should leave. When I asked her why. That's when they came. The scary people in the smoke. There was red smoke, teal smoke, white smoke, purple smoke, and black smoke. They came whizzing by. We hid, though, in the bushes. When the smoke disappeared, I saw people dressed like trick-or-treaters," Emma is explaining when she's cut off by Charlie.

"Dey didn't take yer candy, did dey?" Charlie chimes in with a giggle that he conceals with the cup of his hand.

"Charlie, that's enough," Amelia says with a sigh. She crosses her arms with an expression of well-past annoyed with slanting eyebrows and squinting eyes. She would give him the finger if Emma weren't there.

Blake and Sean smirk, turning away not to upset poor Emma and not to be caught by the camp's owner. They try their best to refrain from bursting out in laughter. Blake even bites his finger, hoping the pain will make him forget how juvenile he's acting.

"I'm regretting smoking that joint," Blake giggles, unaware of the deep observation coming from Robert.

Robert's eyebrows scrunch together, his nostrils flare, and his eyes roll in annoyance. With both hands over his waist, he exhales in exasperation.

"Emma, please continue your story," Jessica asks.

"You shouldn't be laughing at me. You're my teachers. Whatever. They call themselves 'Reapers,' and they want this book for some reason. I don't know why. I never asked. They were after us, but I got away," Emma says.

"And how were you brave enough to do that?" Jessica replies, stooping down to her level.

"With this stone. Thanks to it, I zoomed out of there. I was so fast." Emma yawns silently, her eyes slightly pink, her limbs slouching, and the comfort of the bed calling for her.

"She looks pretty tired," Amelia comments.

"Amelia, you're right. Can you take Emma back with you? I think she's had enough excitement for today," Jessica says, running her hand over Emma's head.

"Come on, girl. Let's get you washed up and to bed. We

have another exciting day tomorrow." Amelia pulls Emma in close as they walk off together toward cabin seven.

Jessica can't help but glance at the book Emma gave her. "Spooky," she mutters.

Wailing sirens go silent, and the blur of the light welcomes a penetrating red gleam, coloring the entry way like Christmas lights. The night unveils itself to falling leaves and a gravel driveway crunches under the truck's rubber tires. The mother of the sky shines her beam of white gold light over the camp to make way for them.

"About time. I was about to put that fire out myself," Sean says, pulling out his cell phone to check his battery life. He smiles with a fist-pump. "Thirty percent."

"Heh-heh. Calm down dur, rookie. I don't understand what's be dat special 'bout a calling device."

"I'd say let the dang thang burn like my marriage."

"Do you hear that, Jess? The fire truck, ambulance, and police are here." Jessica veers toward Robert as if her soul is calling for him. Her luscious golden locks flutter in the gentle breeze and the glow of the moon.

Robert meets Jessica at the top of the hill facing east as they overlook the camp in its absolute brilliance. Thunder tickles the night sky as Jessica slides her sooty hands into his.

"Yeah, we should probably show them how to get here, and you should take the ambulance to the hospital. I'll go with you."

"I'm not going to no hospital. I'm supposed to be here with the kids."

"You can at least have them look at you."

"I'll do that, but I can't leave. I, we have a responsibility to those kids."

"You're right. Well, we better get going. Are you guys coming?"

Charlie is over the moon with glee in his heart, like a roller coaster enthusiast rushing to the front of the line when the rides open. "Ye don't have to ask twice, partner."

"Me as well. I'm not going back in there to argue with my crazy wife." Blake presses forward, leaving Sean behind to play on his phone.

"Hold up. I may be a rookie, but I'm still faster than you both."

"Lookie here, fellers." Charlie paces toward a tree at the familiar colors of brown and white.

Caught under the claws of a broken tree branch and tapping against the tree's base is the bill of his beer can hat. He puts it on his head with a smile and a twinkle in his eye before catching back up to the others as they continue downhill toward cabin eight.

A whiff of toxic fumes lifts Robert's nose. His throat dries like wet logs in lava as they avoid the blazing cabin eight. He coughs. The thought of being close to the flames again makes him shiver.

The book pulsates in Jessica's grasp. Her startled eyes cower in direct focus over its leather cover. Thumping arises from its sinister soul, sounding like the steady beat of Taiko drums. She becomes drawn to it. Its luring and uncanny dialect is possessing to the extent that she is paralyzed on the very spot. The top skull delivers a ghoulish smile, slipping away like a freakish nightmare.

"What the heck? Weird," Jessica mutters.

"Jess, you coming?" Robert turns toward her, curious about what is holding her up.

The roaring flames reaching toward the starlight seems to exchange secrets with each other. A palpable golden glow lights their skin like a lantern's light against a wall in the deepest depths of a cave. All eyes fix on Jessica, who is oblivious to the cluster of red smoke creeping past them like oxygen.

"You, uh, okay dur Jessica?"

"She's fine. We better get a move on. That fire truck's not gonna know where to turn at," Blake suggests.

DAVID LEE WOLF'S
CAMP WOLF CREEK
CABIN ONE

A h, come on, Jess. I'm ready to be done with this." Robert places his hand on Jessica's shoulder. His eyes follow hers to see what she's looking at.

"I say we leave her," Blake yells.

"Just give us a second, Blake," Robert pleads.

"Yeah, I'm good. My mind must be playing with me. I thought…" Jessica says.

"Thought what, Jess?" Robert asks.

The top skull cracks in various places. Lava seeps out from its wounds, dribbling down and off the cover of weathered grain. Jessica tosses the book like a literal game of hot potato, jolting backward before the scattering molten lava can melt into her flesh.

"How is it doing that?" Robert asks.

"Screw that crazy book," Jessica says, stepping back to stand clear of its impending danger.

The skull melts into ashes, and the wind whips each parti-cle around the burning embers of cabin eight, zipping past the treehouses of hickory wood, over the swaying canoes along the calming rivers, swooping under the camps entrance sign, and trickles down like falling stars by the shed next to cabin one. Each trickling particle lands in perfect harmony, forming an outline of something beastly.

The engines of the firetruck and ambulance growl as they pass cabin one and its solar light keeping its watchful eye over anything it sees. Their tires slosh through the muddy driveway pressing the sludge into their treads. The fire truck dips into a mud puddle splattering wet muddy browns over the clean shiny red.

"I can see the cabin from here, Scott." The firetruck driver points.

"Joe, why don't we just take the shortcut through the grass?"

"And what, get stuck? That's a bad idea."

"Well, we don't even know where we're going or what path takes us there. This place is huge. It'll probably be dust before we get there."

They drop into a mud hole, jolting Scott and Joe forward in their seats. The engine howls, but both tires keep spinning into the sloppy sludge.

"Damn."

"Ah, man, don't tell me."

"I'm stuck."

"Try going in reverse."

Both tires spin one way, then the other, but go nowhere like a runner on a treadmill. Distorting reflections in the wheel's aluminum leaves the question: From what?

A virtually invisible paw leaves a steaming print in the mud. It resembles the paw of a lion, but more massive.

It snorts and sniffles toward the doom-black clouds, booming like heaven's drum, and lights up like a shockwave of atomic bombs. Its snout hunts the air, locking its sniffer onto the very scent it is looking for. It snarls, scraping its claws into the mud as it prepares itself for battle. The beast launches forward, moving west, toward cabin eight, hidden by the dark woodlands of the walking trails without as much as a single spark.

Guys, check it out. I think the fire truck's stuck," Sean says.

A moment of silence brings every wary eye around cabin eight. Both emergency vehicles, no bigger than fireflies at their distance, flash their penetrating red lights of heroism. The two paramedics exit the ambulance to assist in pushing the firetruck up and over the mud hole.

"I reckon we ought to help dem out dur."

"Come on, guys." Robert pats Charlie on the back.

Before they can pass the cabin a monstrous growl bursts out behind the cabin like an explosion. Their souls suffocate in the crushing clinch of fear. Nerves wrap around their bones like vines, sealing them in place.

"What was that?" Blake's voice trembles like a leaf in a hurricane.

The smoke kisses the stars, and the flames roar up to meet it while sparks and embers rain down like winter's snow. One flame separates into three, shapeshifting into something horrendously terrifying.

"Robert, what the fuck is going on?"

Robert's sweaty hand glows in cabin eight's flame as he reaches for Jessica's. All their fingers interlock, cradling each other as if it is their last time. He holds her hand tight, and she answers back. The twinkling diamond of her engagement ring mirrors three vicious hell-hounds bulging out from the blazing flames.

Scanning the area swiftly to find its victims, a beastly howl from the three headed fire creature sprays scorching-hot slobber, arching at them like bombs. They jolt one way than the other, dodging the impact and splash of liquid lava and debris.

"Whoa, shit. Dodgeball was always my favorite class to teach," says Sean, who's almost struck by a burning piece of wood that slams into the mud.

The three-headed beast engages them in a bellow of rage. Its mighty roar shakes the earth and rips across the camp like a hurricane. Its putrid, boiling-hot breath singes Jessica's hair.

"Holy moly, what in tarnation is dat? Is this real, or am I high from dat marijuana you were firing up?" Charlie says, nearly tripping over his feet.

"I don't know, but I'm not staying here to find out. Fuck you guys. You're all on your own," Blake blurts out delivering both middle fingers as his welcoming farewell.

"Everybody…run!" Sean screams.

Everyone flees in different directions except Robert and Jessica.

"Jess, your hair's on fire." Robert panics.

"Put it out!" Jessica freaks out in a panic, hopping in place and waving her fists. While Robert taps the fire out, her once-golden ends char and sizzle like burnt chicken.

One head of the blazing hell-hound flares its grizzly snout. Liquid fire dribbles out of its mouth, sizzling into the wet sloppy ground below.

"Ah, impossible, I smell. It's so close I can taste its leather," the fire beasts growls. Its head contorts, pinpointing the book's exact location. "There's the book. Excellent. This ought to make Tate happy."

"Jess, it wants the book. Grab it," yells Robert, who is further from the book than she is.

Jessica slams on her brakes, sliding in the mud and slinging sloshy goo and chunks of mud behind her like she's amidst a deadly game of monkey in the middle.

The fire beast rears back with a ferocious, diabolical snarl. A sizzling, crackling, and popping sound alerts Robert to Jessica's imminent danger.

"Jump, Jess!"

The searing flames evolve into a blazing roar when explosion like dragons breath blasts its scorching rays at Jessica. With a dive, she slides along the slippery mud, splashing runny sludge into her face. She comes to a stop with her hands over the book.

"Get up, come on," Robert insists, dead sprinting back to assist Jessica to her feet when they take off toward Wolfs Eye Den.

"You can run, blondie, but you can't hide," the fire beast growls.

The horrific terror causes Blake to slip in the mud, giving Jessica and Robert the distraction they need to get away. Blake's arms lock, catching himself before smashing his face into the mud. He can feel the hair on the back of his neck singe as the center head of the beast towers over him releasing a menacing growl. It sizes him up, remaining furtive in the wake. His ears flutter in the rumble of its breath.

His perception keeps him rooted to the ground, trembling as he attempts to crawl backwards and away from the devilish hellhound. Saliva, scorching-hot like liquid lava, dribbles out of its volcanic mouth. He winces in pain as lava droplets burn his flesh. He bites his tongue, suppressing a scream with clinching fists, but the pain is too much.

A yelp escapes Blake's gnashing teeth when the fiery beast lashes out clamping its beastly jaws around him as it makes its ascent toward the sparkling moon dust.

"Let go. It burns. YOU'RE KILLING ME!"

Sheets of skin sloughs off his body as the fire rises. Black chunks of burnt flesh patters along the ground like a short hailstorm continuing to smolder and sizzle on the ground. Hot blood bubbles as it spills out from his wounds.

Suspending him high in the air above the trees, the fire monster looks into the melted eyes of a cooked Blake—then releases his charred body, which smacks along the ground.

"Blake!" Sean panics, putting his gym teacher skills to work. His athletic abilities come in handy. He reaches the wooded trails when the fire monster releases a ball of flickering flames at him.

Its intertwining orange and yellows light up the night with its molten-hot core. Sean manages to roll out of the way of the first fireball.

The explosive impact is like an erupting land mine. When he sees the second fireball coming, his heart skips a beat. A heat wave engulfs him as his neck hair rises and his mouth runs dry.

He hastily tucks and rolls landing on his back when the fireball slams into the tree next to him. Everything goes black.

Sean struggles to open his eyes when the smell of maple syrup and the choking taste of smoke enters his airway. He gags, fighting for oxygen. Opening his eyes, he looks both ways, which is like looking through stained glass. No movement, no texture, only a hodgepodge of colors.

Like the loading screen to a computer game, his brain begins to load, gaining focus each second. To his right, the texture of bark becomes clear; a tree is lying next to him.

To his left are scattered splotches of burning grass and trees painting the night orange, intertwining with the silhouette of the pine trees that wrap around the flames, making the backdrop look like a Jack-o'-lantern.

The crinkling and crackling from a large burning tree branch above cause Sean's eyebrows to rise. The crackling turns into snapping and the branch breaks off and plummets into his face, smashing it like a pumpkin.

Charlie sneaks over to take cover by the safer side of the cabin, unseen by the blazing eyes of the fire beast. It jerks its head, putting its snout to work.

It sniffs around, knowing Charlie's close, but can't quite pinpoint his location. He reaches for the coiled water hose. His rough hands tolerate the burning of its hot rubber coating. The feel of the bundle in his grip reminds him of calf roping. He slinks his hand over to the metal spigot valve, cringing with each squeaky turn.

He uncoils the hose, desperately trying not to make a sound, but the water spilling out is enough to catch its attention. With Charlie's eyes focusing on uncoiling the hose, he neglects to realize the beast is eyeing him from behind.

Its quivering upper lip lifts, exposing its gnarly molten hot magma coated teeth, fine tined as a shark's. Rivulets of liquid lava run and drip out its mouth like strings of melted cheese, sizzling onto the wet ground below. Steam rises as the lava cools.

With a huff and a puff from its gnarly snout, Charlie's beer hat rips off his head. "Please, be high, please, be high." With both eyes in a squint, one peels open. The beast shows mercy, allowing Charlie time to check his six in a staggering shiver.

"Where's the book?" Saliva shoots out its volcanic tongue, waiting for Charlie's answer.

Beads of liquid lava latch onto his face and burn into his flesh, abruptly congealing into warm rock as Charlie wails in a frenzy of torture.

Swatting the lava rock off his face, he digs in his flesh, picking out the ones that are still logged in his skin. The fire beast chuckles at his pain, purely the epitome of evil. Holding the hose over himself, cool water runs down his face, reducing the pain to tolerable.

"I'll be shit on a candlestick. You burnt my angelic momma getter, and you kilt my buddy dur, dur. Wat the hell are ya? You ain't some kind of devil, are ya?"

"Where's that girl with the book, or I'll make your death nice and slow."

"You's not communicating on dat eerie uh, um…"

"Book. Where is she taking it?" The fire beast growls with bared teeth. A boiling upsurge of temperature alters its angry reds and yellows into raging whites and blues. "Now!"

"Ah yeah, dat shit-covered bird cage liner dat Jessica has." Charlie wipes the sweat off his forehead. "Ouch, dag nabbit."

The fire beast creeps in, and Charlie leans back to avoid more burns to his face.

"Where is Jessica going?"

Charlie gulps with a regretful point of his finger in Jessica's direction.

"Good boy, and for that, I'm gonna let you live."

"Hey, hot dog. Hold yer horses, dur. I told you the wrong way."

"What? Last chance or I'll burn the flesh off your bones."

"You didn't think dat I was about to let you hurt me friends, do ye? It's time to cool you off!"

The fire beast bursts out in a diabolical giggle as Charlie finishes uncoiling the water hose. He looks up, aiming it in the monster's direction—but the fire monster is no longer there. There's no fire at all, actually, only a smoke-covered cabin.

"Wait a darn second, what?"

Lurking behind a tree, the three-headed beast camouflages itself under the shadows of the trees. It sneaks its way closer and closer to Charlie.

Smush, smush, crunch! The fire beast rolls its paw. Crumbs from a broken chip sticks to the pads of its foot, leaving the remaining pieces in the mud.

"Whoa, wat is dat?" Charlie spins around and sees nothing. "Who's dur?" Breathing heavily and teeth chattering, he is white as a ghost. Spine-tingling cold chills linger in his aching bones. Too anxious, he drops the hose to the ground, his cowboy boots sopping wet along the muddy ground.

Charlie digs around in his pockets for his keys and finds his keychain flashlight. Its three hundred-lumen light capacity doesn't fare well with used batteries.

Crickets chirp while the somber light passes over the grass and back up the trees. His hand tremors, clinging his keys together like jingle bells.

He turns around, scanning the flashlight past the cabin and over to the driveway, stopping on the charred remains of his friend and now ex-coworker Blake.

"I'm a sorry, partner. Dat varmint's gonna pay. I promise, buddy."

There's a crackling sound from an unexpected branch breaking, followed by a hoot from an owl, which frightens Charlie to a spastic panic.

"Who's dur? Come on. Show yourself. I swear, I'm gonna bull ride you right into yer grave, ye blazin' bastard. You lucky I don't have my rifle. I'd put a hole in ye."

His body convulses, dropping his flashlight to the ground. Wide-open eyes follow the beam of light to the sky, gasping for air. A gurgling sound forces blood to spew out his mouth.

He continues to gurgle, glancing down at his chest. His fists clinch tight while the convulsing escalates. His chest blazes orange, like forging steel melting a hole through him like burning paper, exposing the three-headed beast on the other side.

Charlie collapses to the ground. The putrid smell of exposed meat assembles a swarm of flies, burrowing under flaps and strings of flesh.

A dark red silk cloak draped over worn boots approaches Charlie's corpse. His boots sizzle on the wet ground with each step. He stops in front of Charlie's dead body and a his beer hat descends onto Charlie's face.

"Ew, disgusting. Well, they tried. I guess."

The three-headed beast snorts happily, bounding their heads forward in anticipation of its master's head rub.

"Natsu. You're so eager and quick to hurt people."

"Nobody must know of our existence, Master Tate. That's how this gets done."

"I'm aware of his rules, Natsu. Did you find the book?"

Their heads raise, aiming their snouts toward the gloomy clouds. With a sniff and a snuffle, the familiar whiff of leather and rust draws it further down the hill.

It stops, unleashing an uncanny and heinous growl. Lifting its massive paw, it points toward the entryway of Wolf's Eye Den.

"Good boy."

Natsu wags his back end, prancing around Tate with joy in his sinister soul, excited to start their venture for the book.

"Hold up, boy. I'm doing this on my own."

Natsu lays down with a whimper and a broken evil heart, placing his chin on the ground. His watery eyes veer away, ignoring Tate completely.

"Look, I know you're upset. But I promise after this is all over, we will have a lot of time together. Come on now."

"Fine." Natsu sighs with his ears down and eyes facing the mud.

With a twirl of Tate's finger, Natsu dissolves into ashes and embers, swirling like dust in a sandstorm. Each piece of ember and ash dances gracefully in perfect synchronization, as starling birds do.

They form together, creating the shape of a skull. A guttural growl rips through the skull's throat. Unnerving boisterous sounds become more distant as the forging embers and ashes condense into a steel buckle, latching onto Tate's belt.

A heavy wind bustles through the tree branches and howling leaves in a chanting tale of dark and grim lullabies. The view is magnificent. Higher than the trees, Tate peers down the hill and over the camp admiring its beauty.

Under the moonlight's gleam, the rock-climbing tower standing tall and proud lures a murder of crows to the open field, tapering off by pine trees adorning the target range with their shadows casting over it like umbrellas.

The winding twists and turns of the walking trails enveloped by many types of trees wielding a rainbow of leaves is shimmering under penetrating beams of silver light.

The canoeing river calmly sloshes against the shoreline, a jumble of navy and royal blue which glistens like the happiest star. Finally, the treehouses, the heart of the camp that's where Natsu claims the book is. Tate's cloak sways in the gentle breeze.

"Things have certainly changed since I was last here."

Tate converts into red smoke, only to convert back into himself immediately.

"Darn, out of power already." He lowers his head, peering at his broken stone. His severely grotesque and burnt hand embraces what's left of his stone.

"I really need the other half of my orb. It must be with the book. Oh, well, looks like I'm walking."

Welcome to
WOLF'S EYE DEN

Robert and Jessica's feet crunch over rustling leaves as they stop at the lakes edge leading into the woods of Wolf's Eye Den.

"Robert, hold up. I got to wash this crap off me."

Jessica nestles down along the riverbank, washing the soot off her face, while Robert frantically looks around for any sign of the fire beast.

"I'm good. Let's go."

Crossing into the entrance of Wolf's Eye Den, shadows of jagged tree branches take the shapes of claws, appearing ready to grab them at any moment until the trail's motion sensor lights are strong enough to devour the paths gloom.

"What the hell's going on?" Jessica pants as they scurry their way up the trail.

"Jess, hold up… Over here, I think we've lost it." Reaching the top of the hill Robert hunkers behind a group of shrubs where Jessica joins him.

"Who… What the heck was that?"

"Whatever it was, we have to figure out how to make it go away before people die. Did Blake, Sean, and Charlie get away?"

"I never looked back to check."

"Me either. I hope they're okay."

"What are we gonna do about the kids? You don't think it would hurt them, do you?"

"That thing looked pure evil. Definitely doesn't care. You know, if I still had my radio, I could alert everyone to get out of Dodge. Hopefully save everyone. Someone. But I dropped it back at the cabin."

"I still have mine. Here." Plastic rattles in Jessica's jittery hand, catching the radio's antenna in the bracelet Emma made for her.

"Ah, awesome, thank you, thank you. Hopefully, they're listening."

"This is Robert. Blake, Charlie, Sean, check in."

The pitter-patter of fine raindrops dripping off leaves and tree branches sings off key with the orchestra of unhappy crickets in Wolf's Eye Den.

His hand buries his mouth, staring blindly at the radio. It remains soundless. Not even a hint of static. He puffs, smacking his fist against his head at their failing response. He tries again.

"Blake, Charlie, Sean. If you're hearing me, please check in."

"This is Amelia. What's wrong? You're lucky you caught me. I was half-asleep."

"Amelia, you got to listen to me. This is no joke. Wake up

the other teachers. Everyone must lock their doors and wait for the police to arrive."

The radio crackles for a moment. "What are you talking about?" Amelia's the only one awake, half-asleep and on the couch in cabin seven, suffering from extreme bed-head.

"This is going to sound weird. But you have to believe us. There was this three-headed beast that came out of the flames of cabin 8. It may have killed Blake, Sean, and Charlie."

"Well, that just sounds absurd. You sound more drunk than Charlie. I'm going back to bed."

Jessica snatches the radio out from Robert's hand, eager to convince Amelia of the truth. "Amelia, this is Jessica."

"You okay, girl? You're not worried about the fire, are you? The firefighters will take care of it."

"Yes, I'm fine. It's not the fire. Well, it is about the fire. Kind of. What Robert's saying is the truth. There is a freakish three-headed beast, and it will kill all of us if we don't do something. Look, you haven't seen the guys yet, have you? None of them answered the radio."

"Yeah, I heard. Look, them guys love to goof off. They're probably playing a prank. At any moment, they're gonna jump out and scare ya. Especially my idiot husband. He's a bigger goofball than Charlie. At times."

"Amelia, we know what we saw," Robert pleads as he swipes the radio back before Jessica can speak.

"Okay, okay. All right. Let's say I believe you. Let's pretend this is real. What do you want me to do?"

"You may want to call the bus driver. Maybe she can pick you all up and get you guys out of here."

"It's nearly one in the morning. Debra's not answering her phone."

"Okay, call the kids' parents. I'll talk to the police about setting up some kind of rendezvous point for pick up."

"How am I supposed to call their parents? I don't know any of their numbers."

Jessica's finger presses against her lips, and her eyelids seal shut with a mind picking up speed like a racehorse. She springs her eyes open with a deep gasp. "The retreat packet. Tell her all their parents' numbers are in the retreat packet."

"Listen Amelia, all the parents' numbers are in the retreat packet."

Amelia sighs, fluttering her lips and removing her bangs from her eyes. "If I do this, do you promise to stop calling me?"

"I promise."

"This sucks. Looks like I'm not getting any sleep tonight." Amelia tosses the radio at the end of the couch back in cabin seven. Her hand comes across her face in disbelief, letting out a chuckle. "Ah, three-headed beast. Ah, man, I must still be high. I'm going back to bed." Amelia snuggles her head back onto her pillow and falls asleep.

That makes three of us," Robert says, looking at Jessica with an aching heart. Tears fill his eyes, but he refuses to let them spill. He has to be strong for her. "I'm sorry I dragged you out here. This is all on me."

Pride leaves his body like an exploding balloon. With his head down, he fights the tears while annoying shrub leaves flap against the back of his neck.

"No. Babe, look at me. This was my decision. This isn't your fault. I don't know what's going on. I'm sure it was lightning that started the fire, but whatever that thing was, I'm sure the police or the military will handle it."

Flashing red and blue lights look like an extension of a rave party, but without the loud thumping music. Robert's eyes hook like a fish on a line.

"The firetruck is finally unstuck, Jess, and look, here comes an ambulance. You're going to a hospital."

They begin to run on uneven ground, which is hard enough. Twigs snap under their feet. Squish, squish, in the mud. Splash, splash go the puddles, flinging mud up their legs.

The woods are vicious, as if made of tentacles and fangs. Branches hang low whipping into Jessica, biting her and leaving splinters cleaving into her flesh as Robert charges through them.

Some branches break off, while most don't. Sleeping starling birds awaken from their nightmares and flee north for their lives and over the bridge dangling high above the river.

"Why did you take us this way? I told you I wasn't crossing this bridge again."

"I'm sorry, dammit, but it's a shortcut. This is life or death. I figured it didn't matter. Otherwise, we would have to cross the river by the rock wall. You know how deep it is? Or we could have gone around the river, but then, we would be close to cabin eight, where that thing is."

"Fine. But this is definitely the last time."

Sizable roots from a cedar tree arch out of the ground like a venomous spider, ready to latch its fangs onto anyone who passes. Robert leaps over the roots, landing on slippery mud for the onset of a heart-pounding slip toward the seventy-foot drop off Wolfs Eye Bridge.

His feet zig zag through the mud, franticly trying to slam on his brakes, whipping around and seizing the rope with a locking grip. Momentum sends him leaning over the edge headfirst, and his pupils dilate as his wide eyes peer down and into the navy-blue abyss.

Jessica's foot catches the root of the cedar tree, launching the book out of her hands as she tumbles to the dirt and cracks her nose on the wet muddy ground unleashing a pool of blood oozing out of her nose like spilt glue. The book bounces and glides over the slippery mud, coming to a halt only feet away from the bridge's edge.

"Ow? Ah, shit, man. What the hell?" Blood trickles down her face and into her hand, but she can't tell which one.

There's two of everything. The world is shaking like a paint shaker as she stumbles to her feet. She can taste the metallic taste of blood as it dribbles down her nose and onto her lips. She wipes the blood away, smearing its goo along her shorts as she staggers past the book and over to Robert.

"Help me, Jess. Why you moving so damn slow?"

"Hold on? Geez. You can be an asshole sometimes."

She stumbles toward two Roberts hanging onto the side of

the bridge. Her double-vision corrects itself, converging everything back to one. The wooden plank creaks as Jessica steps onto the bridge. Her hands clasp one of Robert's, helping him climb back to safety.

"Thanks, hon. Jess, what happened to your face?"

"I fell onto the tree root, you asshole."

"Are you okay? I didn't know."

"I'm fine. I'm okay. Are you okay?"

"Yeah, I'm good. Here, pinch your nose and hold it up. Can you keep going? You need a doctor more than ever right now."

"Let's just go." Jessica winces with an agonized groan.

"Jess, look." Pointing north, the once-beautiful wooded trails are now feeble and under the control of the spreading flames of the beast's fiery wrath.

"Dammit, it's destroying the camp," Jessica blurts out with a fist full of her golden locks.

Both weathered ropes are timeworn from many trips across its wooden planks. Loosely anchoring to two wooden posts, the rope supporting Robert and Jessica's weight puts tension on each post.

There are two to the north, which is furthest from them, and two behind them to the south. The rope frays at the north end. Fibers split, leaving the rope half its size, but still holding.

"I'm so scared right now." Her voice quivers, struggling to get the words out.

"You got this, Jess. One step at a time."

She grasps the rope for dear life. Burns develop on her sweaty hands as they slide along the rope. The bridge sways back and forth, giving Jessica a sense of height vertigo. Creak, creak. Her eyes close, and her lips press together, releasing an exhale to help calm her nerves.

"That's it, take it easy; we're nearly halfway there."

"Robert, shut up. You're not helping."

Her quivering knees buckle, smacking them into the walkway. Her insides grow cold. A chill devours her like an illness. Goosebumps form all up and down her arm, raising her hair high and prickly as a porcupine.

Along the rope and around the post, tension increases. The rope continues to fray when… snap, snap. Both ropes break. Their blistering hands slip from the rope, and their stomachs fly up as they plummet toward the river below. The wind rushes through their hair. Mosquitos splat against their faces as their pounding hearts rip out of their chests.

Before the bridge can swing away from them, Robert and Jessica lunge for the rope. Jessica has the left side, while Robert has the right side. The bridge swings toward the cliff like a broken pendulum whooshing through the gale and whistling past their ears.

"Brace for impact," Robert yells. Both he and Jessica hold onto the rope with all their might.

Their eyes slam shut, and bodies become tense to prepare themselves for death when terrified screams erupt out their mouths. Boom! The broken end of the bridge smacks them hard against the side of the cliff. The wood groans, and the rope creaks as the hanging bridge sways back and forth. Their squinting eyes lift gently like feathers as if waking from a long peaceful nap.

Ping, pang, clang, splash. Their attention is drawn downward to broken boards tumbling into the water below. Inches away from the cliff, both Robert and Jessica let out a sigh of relief.

"You okay, Jess?"

"Yeah." Her voice quivers.

"Wow, were really high up. Are you able to climb?"

"I think so. Can we go, please?"

"Let's get moving before the rest of it breaks. I'm not going in the water. I'm not drowning. Not today."

Reaching the top, Robert helps Jessica onto the cliff. They fall to their backs in the sludge, hyperventilating, taking a moment to catch their breath.

"I can't believe it?"

"What's that?"

"After all these years, the bridge had to break now."

"Didn't your Dad build the bridge?"

"Yeah. It was one of the first things he did. If I remember correctly, he built it before the treehouses were built. They died a few months after. This bridge has been hanging there ever since. Two decades later I was finally able to finish what he started. Up until today my dad and I we're the only ones to have ever crossed it."

"What about your mom?"

"She was like you. Terrified of heights. At least that was what my uncle said."

Not so far from where they rest lies that creepy book, snug against the tree's root and open, baring its grungy pages. The left page remains blank, while the right has text reading:

Fire Deader. It's written in old-fashioned cursive under it is a drawing of a burning skeleton. Its ink crumbles to powder like some kind of dark magic. A sinister force flips the pages till the book's cover closes.

The flashing of reds and blues seize Roberts attention. He giggles, gawking into the gloomy night. His nose twitches as he bites down.

"What's so funny? Robert, what are you laughing at?"

"Ah man, this is a nightmare. Look, the emergency vehicles made it to cabin eight. All this trouble when we could have stayed there."

"And what? Be burnt alive by that thing.?"

"Yeah, you're right. Phew, can tonight get any worse?"

Distant yelling of hardworking firefighters putting in some honest work echoes across the camp. The dense smoke places its gloomy veil over the emergency vehicles, camouflaging their lights like a total eclipse. "The cabins good and clear, sir." "Good. Everyone, back in the truck. Let's get a move on it before that wildfire gets more out of control." The fire truck moves northeast and downhill toward the blazing trails.

"Ahem. Look, ah, thank you, thank you. They're coming our way."

"Good. I can't wait to get you seen by a paramedic. I'm so worried about you."

Thump, thump, thump, thump.

"What's that noise, Jess?"

"Not sure, I thought for a second it was coming from this pounding headache."

A toneless guttural voice tears into their ears. "Anulus Ignis." The sinister sound surrounds them as they spin around to find the source of the noise.

Flames erupt from the ground, creating a perfect circle around Robert and Jessica—too high to jump over, but low enough to be unnoticeable by the fire truck, police car, and ambulance parking by the rivers bank.

A small portion of the fire itself takes the shape of a human. The fire hovers into the circle, transfiguring into an individual in a frayed and dirty dark-red cloak.

"Who are you?" asks Robert with anxious eyes. His pupils shrink to tiny weary pencil points, as if the rest of them cowers in the backside of his eyeballs.

"My name is Tate. I'm the Fire Reaper, manipulator of fire, second in command to the Death Reaper."

"What is that three-headed thing?"

"You talking about Natsu? He's harmless. Usually."

"Did this Natsu kill Charlie, Blake, or Sean?" Jessica gulps. She is made quite timid by his threating essence; she stutters her words.

"The book and the other half of my orb. Where are they?" Tate is angry, but is restraining it by patience and wisdom. His desire for the return of his master's property is not slipping past him.

"What book? What orb?" Robert shakes his head in confusion as his body leans back to avoid the uncomfortable heat venting off his smoldering cloak.

Jessica is discreet, remembering where she dropped the eerie book. Both amber irises hang at the corner of her eyeball with the slight gaze over her shoulder as stealthy as a shadow in the dead of night.

"Come on, I don't have all day—tell me now or she dies," Tate demands unsheathing his axe, lowering it down by his side.

"Please leave her alone. Don't hurt her! We don't have what you're looking for. Please. She needs a doctor."

"I'm not talking about your little girlfriend, Jessica."

"How do you even know my name?"

"That dead overweight redneck ratted you out. He says you ins dur have dat shit-covered bird cage liner. Ha, stupid redneck." Tate mocks Charlie with a sadistic laugh.

"He's as dead as the other two. More will die unless you give me the book." Tate waves his hand, parting the ring of fire and revealing a shaken Emma under layers of fright.

"And we'll start with the girl."

Rage flares from within Jessica's spirit. With clinching fists and squinting eyes, she stomps her foot. "How dare you?"

A delicate breeze waggles the flames to pardon itself to a very familiar scent.

Tate lifts his head as if the smell possesses him. With a sniffle, the aroma of leather and brass mixes with the musky smell of the woods and the steam off his cloak.

"Ah, yes, yes. We're very close. I can smell it." Tate rests the wood handle of his axe over his shoulder.

"You okay, Emma?" Robert asks.

Each cautious step Emma takes toward Tate is like fire walking on burning hot coal. She quivers like a leaf, placing her hand over her wet eyes to stop the pool of oncoming tears.

"That's far enough."

Emma halts at Tate's side with a whimper. The shaking spreads to her legs like a raging disease. Her knees buckle unable to carry her weight as Tate presses the cold steel blade against her neck.

"Now, the book or Chris dies."

"Who's Chris? That's not Chris. No one here is Chris. I think you've mistaken us for someone else," Robert trembles, easing toward Emma to rescue her from the blade of Tate's axe.

"Don't even think about it. You guys are liars. Don't play me for a fool."

"We're not," Jessica blurts out with a quiver in her voice.

"So be it. The Death Reaper wants Chris alive, and that girl looks like her."

"So, see? You can't kill her, then. This Death Reaper guy will be mad."

"Stop talking, I'm done playing around. So hand me the book and orb before things get heated," Tate demands.

"Master Tate, I can feel the orbs' presence. We're very close. My sense of smells is never wrong," Natsu says from within Tate's skull belt buckle.

Emma moves her hand in secret. Slow as a sloth and careful as walking on thin ice, she pulls out the broken red orb, gripping it from behind her back. "Come on, come on. Do it again," She mumbles.

Robert stares at Jessica with a hint of caution sparkling in his eyes, speaking softly. "Where's the book?"

"I sense fear in you guys. You may want to—" Tate says, but he's abruptly cut off by Emma.

"I'm sorry. It's not a stone. It's an orb." Whoosh! Emma's gone, vanishing from existence, leaving nothing behind but a trail of red smoke and wonder in Robert and Jessica's eyes.

"So, you've had my orb all this time, huh?" Whoosh! Tate also vanishes, leaving behind a red trail as he follows Emma.

"Did you see that? How? Where did they go Jess?"

"Your guess is as good as mine. You think she got away?" Jessica's eyes are wider than her mouth. The magic was stunning, making it hard to push her words out.

"I hope so. Why did he call her Chris?"

"Emma mentioned a girl from her story. Is it the same person?"

"Listen, this story of Emma's I'm starting to believe it," Jessica says.

"Yeah, I think you're right. We need to talk to her. See what else she knows," Robert says, but he's cut off by a gust of air.

The whoosh of air rips through their ears like an atomic bomb, reverberating in their bodies like plucking a guitar string.

The red smoke creeps closer and closer to them with each beat of their pounding hearts. Breathing becomes more of a battle with the sinister growls and eerie screeching lurking inside the red fog.

The impenetrable smoke swallows them, clouding their vision with a red fiery haze with floating embers burning like a lamp. Augmenting weeps from Emma are bound within its belly.

"Emma, it's Mr. Lee. Can you hear us?"

"Come back. Let us help you," Jessica pleads.

"Emma, where are you?"

"It's too foggy. I can't see anything, No, stay away from me."

"Give me back my orb, Chrissie. It doesn't belong to you."

"You can't have it. You evil red freak."

"You will, or you'll never make it out of here alive, little girl."

"Hey, you bastard, leave her alone," Robert says.

Emma struggles to crawl through the red enigma, her legs under the control of Tate, who camouflages in the smoke's density. Tears flood her face as she pants herself to exhaustion. She reaches her hand out, fighting to escape his evilness. With one final reach, she loses control of the red orb. Its rigid edges bounce through the sloppy mud and knock into the steel toe of Robert's Brahma boots.

"How much do your friends really care about you? We're about to find out. If they want you back, they better have his book with them."

"Let me gooooo!"

"Emma, it's Ms. Hill. Where are you? We can't help you unless we know where you are."

WOOSH! The cluster of smoke moves east, taking off like an F-18 jet breaking the sound barrier. The red fog clears when Robert feels something hard under his boot. He kneels, peeling the red orb out of the mud and peering into its glowing translucence.

"What the hell are we gonna do now, Jess?"

"We get Emma back. The ambulance is out of the question. The police aren't gonna believe a single thing about some fire manipulator."

"Yeah, but your friends are dead. The police need to know."

"And what are we gonna tell them? Some three-headed fire monster killed them? They'll think we're hiding something. We'll go to jail."

"Calm the heck down. No one's going to jail. We've done nothing wrong. We have to get Emma back. We can't depend on the police to find her. We know he wants that book and this orb. So, I say we use that."

Jessica makes her way back to the book. Stooping over to pick it up; she wipes the mud off its leather cover giving her a clear sight of its sinister appearance. "Good, I say we just give it to him."

"After this is done, I'm getting you to a hospital. The ambulance may be gone by the time we get Emma back."

"Looks like finding her won't be too hard. This Tate guy left us a trail."

"All right, let's go get her."

Robert and Jessica gander east at the top of Wolf's Eye Den, gloating over the patches of fire left behind by Tate.

"What a mess." Robert wipes the surprised look off his face.

"You're right, Rob. Emma needs us. We can't let her down, and we can't give up on her."

"This fire's going to destroy our camp. What my father worked so hard to build. I hope the fire department is able to save it."

"I just want this day to be over with," Jessica says, swatting away annoying mosquitos, though their bite is more tolerable than the pain in her heart. She holds her head down, gazing into the shadows of Wolf's Eye Den.

"Yeah, so do I. This all doesn't seem real. How can we get so unlucky? Everything was so good. Before I had the chance to make my dad proud before it was swiped away from me."

"Your dad is proud of you. Look how far you've come. This is just a minor hiccup. Everything will be okay. We'll get through this. So, not to change the subject, but how's your uncle and aunt?" Jessica asks, wiping the tears from her face.

"They're fine. Missing my parents, of course. I can't believe it's been twenty-three years since they died. You still coming to the cemetery with me to visit them?"

"Well, yeah, you goofball. You know I support you."

Jessica gently rubs his back affectionately. Her soothing touch is calming enough to hypnotize the trees' swaying branches into hibernation as they cower from the threatening flames to the west.

"Thanks, Jess. You always know how to touch me. So, have you heard anymore from your dad? I'd like to meet him. I figure it's only right if I get his blessing."

"You know I haven't seen him in years. I don't get it you know. Everything was so good with us. He would take me to the climbing wall at Vertical Sanctuary gym every Saturday. We always joked 'bout climbing Mount Everest. My dad knew the thought of it terrified me. Then one day, he just disappeared without explanation. Not even a letter to me or my mom. He's probably dead. He had a dangerous job. Mom thought people were after him. Who knows?"

"Sorry, honey. I figure, I mean, I was hoping he contacted you. That's all. We're not around each other all the time. Wishful thinking. Maybe things will turn around for you and he'll call," Robert says gently and with a bit of regret for making her sad.

"Yeah, I kind of gave up on that idea. I have better things to look forward to," Jessica says, puckering her lips, waiting for Robert to kiss her.

As their lips meet, a tingling sensation runs through their

body. In that moment, nothing else seems to matter. From behind them, a south wind carries a continuous trail of dark grey smoke, whisking past them from the blazing trails.

Dirt and leaves kick up from under Robert's boots as he smothers any small patch of fire that he can. The radio hisses like a snake guarding its territory a noise so annoying Robert is ready to throw it. He's not in the mood for any more bad news.

"Robert, Jessica, this is Amelia. Emma's missing, and the police are here. They want to talk to you. They're asking me all these questions about Blake, Charlie, and Sean. You haven't seen them, have you? Did they prank you yet?"

The radio eases to Robert's mouth while locking his teary eyes with Jessica's. Her head lowers, shaking in dismay. She rubs his shoulders to comfort him, and with a deep sigh, the radio clicks under Robert's reddened fingers.

"How long ago did you realize Emma went missing?"

"A few minutes ago. The officer had me do a count on everyone. I'm so sorry I didn't believe you earlier."

"How's everyone else?"

"Half of us are gone. I actually got ahold of Debra. She's on her way here to pick the rest of us up. She's supposed to drop them off at the church so the parents can pick them up there. Have you seen Emma? With everything going on, I'm scared for her. You know my asthma flares up when I'm stressed."

Robert presses the radio up against the wrinkles of his sweaty forehead. A moment of silence to purge out the stress is cut short by the rustling leaves and the orchestra of singing crickets.

"Amelia, we saw her."

Jessica's bulging amber eyes latch onto Robert like an intercepting missile, so intense and terrifying, no amount of defense can combat it. Robert instantly realizes his mess-up, but the hole he's dug is too far down to crawl out of. "Why did you tell her that? Now what are you gonna say? This fire manipulator took her. What police officer's gonna believe that? Things are looking bad for us right now."

More hissing escapes the speaker of the radio. "Well, good, Robert. Tell her to get back here so Debra can take her and the rest of us home, and maybe we can forget about what a crappy night this has been."

Amelia sneaks out of the living room and away from the police. The back door latches into place as she slides it shut.

"Robert, you got to listen to me. I overheard the police—if you guys refuse to come back soon, you'll both be considered suspects and once they find you, they will arrest the both of you."

"How can we be arrested for something we didn't do? Amelia, I have to find her. She's got to be scared out of her mind!"

"Look, I believe you and I understand. Be safe and stay in touch. Please tell my idiot husband once he and his boys make it back, I'm gonna beat his ass."

"Okay, I will. Take care Amelia."

Amelia sneaks her way back inside the cabin, easing the sliding door closed. She makes her way around the kitchen corner and into the living room, where a cop is questioning Linda.

"Are they coming?" the officer asks Amelia.

"I don't know; he didn't say," Amelia carefully answers as she slides the radio into the back side of her waistband.

The front door bursts open revealing a very anxious rookie officer so anxious she can hear his gun rattle in his holster. His hat lays slanting along his pale forehead.

"There were three dead bodies out there," the anxious officer says.

"What do you mean there were? Dead bodies don't simply vanish," The Officer questioning Linda says.

"Dead bodies? Is one of them my husband? Blake Crowe is his name." Amelia sobs with panic. Her breathing escalates past her control, causing her to pull out her inhaler. She inhales deeply as she presses the button.

"You okay, ma'am?" the questioning officer asks.

"I'll. Be okay. Just. Need to. Rest. For a sec," Amelia pants, taking a seat on the couch, hunching over, trying to regain her composure.

"Hush it. How 'bout you tell me over by the door?" the questioning officer whispers to the rookie officer.

"Sorry, anyway. The ground took them. Like quicksand," says the anxious officer.

"That doesn't make any sense."

"I know what I saw, I'm calling it in," the anxious officer whispers clicking his radio. "220 to dispatch."

"Go for dispatch."

"We have three dead male adults that are missing, two additional missing adults, presumed alive, one male and one female, and one missing minor female, who is also presumed alive."

"Copy, sending out an additional ambulance and detectives. Do you need additional backup?"

"Affirmative, dispatch, on additional backup. I need assistance finding the three missing witnesses. We also may be dealing with a 134 on that minor female. The FBI may need to be involved."

"Copy, 220."

I can't believe you, Robert. Now we have the cops after us! Maybe we should go back and let the police find her. It's their job, anyway."

"You heard what he said. If we don't get him that book, more people will die, including Emma."

"I get it. It's the only thing keeping me from turning around."

What happens next is completely unexpected even more unordinary than the nightmarish hell they've already endured. The red orb piece seated in Robert's fist begins to flutter. He uncurls his fingers to gaze at its uncanny actions. It glows bright red and begins to spin faster and faster until it begins to hover over his hand.

An ominous smoke leaves the orb and creeps to the book. First, there's a spine-tingling twitch following a heart jolting shiver. Then, it begins to spin and spin and spin finally descending back into the palm of his hand.

"What the hell?" Robert says, tucking the red orb in the safety of his nylon pants.

"What was that about?" Jessica asks with a forehead full of wrinkles, as if her mind is unable to accept what she saw.

"Now, I've seen everything," Robert jokes with disbelief.

"Wait a sec. The books moving," Jessica says as her hand leaves the fore-edge of the pulsating book, switching her grip to the spine when the book flips open.

Crumbles of ink dust break away from the old pages of the book. Flecks of ink dust mutate to embers, greeting the grass with scorching hot kisses shriveling each strand to a crisp.

The flurry of blazing embers leads them on a journey through the woods and into a clearing, where patches of fire are scattered throughout. They continue their search for Emma, stomping out the fiery patches along the way They part the tall grass and bushes, only to find the dirt from underneath them.

"I know this may not make sense, but it's almost like the smoke from this orb just…woke it up."

"Yeah, you're right. That doesn't make sense. Ahh, shit," Jessica blurts out with a screech in her voice. Her trembling hand covers her mouth, her eyebrows narrow to meet it.

"What? What's wrong?"

Their eyes wander the glade, set forth on an expedition like migrating butterflies. Some rustling in the distance gathers their attention, but they can't decipher where exactly the noise originates from. Is it coming from the grass, the trees, or is it their imagination?

"It's probably a squirrel or a raccoon."

"What's wrong? You look a little scared. What, no balls? Well, I say keep calm and spook on." Jessica snaps her fingers while spinning in circles acting a tad arrogant as she approaches the vicinity of the noise.

Two blazing bushes ahead give the glades life, looking like raging eyes. The grass around them is like the beard of a were-wolf. The tree line in the background is like a cat's arching back with its hair standing on end.

Jessica's back is covered in the fiery hot shadows dancing like starving frogs fighting over a single fly. The heat is as comfortable and cozy as a campfire, giving her a dazzling glow as she gets rather close to the flames.

"Come on now, stop acting foolish. You're getting too close to the flames."

Emerging out from the burning bush and creeping toward Jessica's back is what seems to be a twig, but indeed, it is something much more frightening. A practically fleshless ant-infested skeletal hand skims across Jessica's shirt, and with a curl of its disgusting fingers, it fails to take her in its grasp.

"Relax, Robert. Lighten up a little. Geez." Jessica bursts out in a nervous laugh.

"It's just hard to right now with everything going on. When this is all over with I'll lighten up then."

"Whatever, let's keep-" Jessica neglects to finish her sentence, as the book's rough leather spine rips from her grip and thuds along the ground. But how or what caused this to happen?

A tingling dread creeps through her body as she eases around. Her voice freezes in her throat as she battles to breathe with a shuddering pant. She locks eyes with Robert, waiting for him to tell her everything's okay. Her awareness is so keen, she can feel his lips against her ear.

"Jess, get over here. Jess, get out of there," Robert whispers.

She gathers the courage to face it with clinching fists and chattering teeth. Her knees buckle at the horrific sight of two hideous skeletal creatures emerging out from the burning bush. They're mostly skeletal, with some layers of decaying flesh, muscles, and tendons still hanging off their rotten bones.

Their black claws slightly curve coming to fine points, so sharp and fierce they can cut through steel.

The smell hits their noses immediately, a smell so putrid they can feel it in the back of their throat, as thick as syrup. Lava drips from their mouths when an unsettling gurgle sound mixes with a hasty series of nerve-pinching clicks.

Jessica's amber eyes rise to the void of their eyeless sockets. Her mind, adrift from the present amidst the shocking terror of the dead, is instantly swept away when she is launched into the air by the foot of one of those bony creatures. She smacks her back hard against the emerald beard of the glades. Robert rushes to Jessica and aids her to her feet.

"You okay, Jess?"

"Mmmm. Yeah, I'm okay." Jessica groans. "What the hell is that thing? How's that possible?"

"Considering what we've seen so far, I'm not shocked by anything at this point."

"Orb," a creature growls with a point of its finger.

"What?" Robert glances at the glowing red orb in his hand.

"Looks like that Tate guy's not the only one after the orb."

"What is so special about this orb?"

Whoosh! Both creatures combust into flames, wearing the

yellow and orange like knight's armor. The bony freaks begin to approach them like wild hungry beasts.

"Over there, Robert, the tree house!"

"Perfect, let's go."

Robert trails close behind her, dodging the closest bony creature as it lunges for them when they pass. They manage to move out of the way, forcing the creature off-balance and smacking its skull hard in the mud.

The bony creatures light up the night like torches as they charge up the spiral stairs after them. A broken tree branch held together by splinters sways in the gentle breeze, only inches above them.

"Watch out, Jess; I got an idea."

Robert moves ahead of Jessica, wiggling his hands through the mesh of twigs, taking scrapes and scratches by their pointy claws. With a strong grip around the branch, he yanks as hard as he can. CRACK! He snaps off a piece of the broken branch, grinding his palms around its scaly bark.

The sizable branch drops onto the steps with an unrelenting thud, separating them from each other, knocking Jessica and the creatures off-balance and tumbling down the steps and back to the wet muddy ground.

"Jessica, get up. Come on." Before either creature can curl their fingers around Jessica's singed golden hair, she crawls to her feet and dashes toward the stairs.

"What do I do? I can't get to you. The stupid branch is in my way." Jessica shrugs. Tremors erupt through her that could convulse the entire camp.

"Can you crawl through the branches?"

"I don't know. I'll try."

"You gotta do more than try. They're coming!"

Jessica slides in between the branches, taking on scrapes and scratches as she wiggles in-between the branches tight gap, using them as a barrier from the skeletal creatures.

"ROBERT!" She screams as a raging, stumbling skeleton bounces off the branches as she struggles to spin through the thicket to face its horrific actions.

It releases a jarring clicking sound as its teeth smack together while attempting to reach its bony hand in to grab Jessica.

"I can't reach you. The branches are in my way."

"What do I do?"

"Kick 'em Jess."

She leans back using the twigs as support, and with a thrust, she kicks one of the fiery creatures down the hickory stairs. Thump, thump, thump. Robert aims the broken branch at the other flaming bag of bones, driving its narrow end over and over again through the layers of twigs, but with each thrust, he misses. With one final drive forward, he loses control of the branch when the skeleton's grisly claws snatch it right out of his hands sending it plummeting to the ground.

"Ah, dang it."

The fluttering flames consuming the skeletal creatures tickle the preceding branches, altering their smoldering dry roughness into a spreading flame.

"Robert, it's burning! Get this branch off me before I burn with it."

Stuck inside its flaming cocoon, Jessica bursts into a rage-filled scream, jerking, shaking, and shoving on the branch fighting to free herself. Shriveling leaves smolder to orange embers that trickle downward from the branch.

Robert grabs the meatiest branch worth grabbing. He can feel a muscle-ripping stress in his aching back with each lifting attempt but it's too heavy.

Shadows from the twigs and the flames' light dance across her face as Jessica peers into the pool of yellow and orange. Her ears shriek at the grueling snarls and growls of the fiery creature lurking on the other side of the flames. She sways and ducks, coughing and trying to avoid the surge of black smoke passing through her. "Robert, do something."

"I'm trying. This stupid thing's too heavy."

A low groaning sound emits from the branch, which is quite unsettling. If it breaks apart, it could fall on her or worse than that. It can fall off the stairs, it could take her with it.

"Jess, over here. Can you make it?"

Robert creates an opening from the backside of the burning branch just enough for her to crawl through. The exit looks promising but the scorching hot flames make her second guess her chances.

"Come on, stop being a wuss, and get your ass over here." Robert waves his hand, reaching for her with all his might.

The branch continues to crack and pop as the splinters gradually tear away from it. The blazing branch slides off the edge of the stairway, dragging Jessica along with it. She fights, leaning back with all her weight to push the branch back. Her calf muscles tighten, but her muscles aren't strong enough to stand against the branch. The branch ultimately catches on the stairs' edge, barely holding on by only a few splinters.

Jessica maneuvers through the thicket, staying away from

the branches that are burning. Before she can exit, though, a hot sensation wraps around her calf. "OUCH!" Its hot bony fingers sizzles into her flesh like a skillet full of grease.

"Here, take my hand," Robert pleads, reaching through the mesh of twigs.

Jessica stretches with all her might, reaching for his hand, but what seems like miles apart is merely inches. He leans in a little more, stumbling off balance about to fall over himself.

Their fingers brush up against each other like a gentle lover's first kiss. Both fingers curl, locking tight, while their eyes lock together like puzzle pieces saying a thousand words to each other without speaking. Pulsating hope pounds in their beating hearts, lingering for what feels like an eternity.

Snap! The heavy branch breaks from the tree, pulling Jessica closer and closer to the stairs' edge and free from the burning skeleton's grip.

She presses her purple air runners into the hickory wood, but their grip is no match for the branches pushing force. The twigs curl up off the edge of the steps, swinging downward like a sledgehammer, lifting the branch vertically. Its flames regurgitate a cloud of embers like a hellish sneeze. The branch stands vertical for a moment, stuck there like a picture.

"Hang on, Jess."

"I see an opening. I think I can get through." Jessica slides between the twigs. Its prickly ends are quite nettlesome. They snap, crack, and break off as she pushes through.

A raging human carcass bursts through the flames, breaking and ripping through the burning twigs after Jessica.

"You're doing great. You gotta hurry, Jess. That things right behind you."

The twigs bow under the weight. Cracking, snapping, and a tearing bouquet of splinters brings the branch toppling over.

"Here, grab my hand."

Her hand collapses into his as the tree branch plummets to the ground, taking one of the bony creatures with it. Robert and Jessica peek over the stairway's edge, looking at a burning tree and the rubble of bones disintegrating to burning ashes.

"You okay?"

"Yeah, son of a bitch burnt my leg."

"Can you walk?"

"Oh, yeah. It feels no worse than a sunburn."

Robert takes heed to the remaining threat lying senseless at the bottom of the steps. His forehead wrinkles, honing his eyebrows like a fine blade. Pulsating veins erupt from his head like a volcano as he comes to his feet.

"Robert, what are you doing?"

"What I should have done earlier."

"No, no, no. Leave it alone, babe. It's too dangerous."

The book is nestled serenely next to the skull of the still fire creature. Robert re-locates the broken branch, wielding its sequoia wood in the fury of his grasp. A kick to the skull will suffice to see if this thing's still alive or not.

"What are you, anyway?" Robert mumbles standing over the skeletal creature with the sharp end of the branch aiming over its head, ready to attack it at will.

"Is it dead, Rob?"

"I think so."

The book eases with a sinister turn toward Robert, perhaps to angle itself for a better look. Gaining his attention, the four skulls leave a ghostly aurora penetrating his soul. Their sunken orbitals are the hypnotizing gateway into its never-ending darkness. Its warm leather cover flings open, catapulting many withering pages toward the books middle.

"Jess, come look at this crazy book."

"What is it?" Jessica strides down the stairs, remaining vigilant and keeping her distance from the dead human skeleton. She brushes her singed hair around her ear, waiting, hacking and coughing as she hunkers down for a closer look. "What am I looking at?"

"Just watch the book."

"That's weird. The pages are blank," Jessica cries.

Hieroglyphics summoned by some sort of bewitchment etch onto the page. It's a drawing of a burning skeleton dissolving to dust. From the depths of the page looms a warm, sultry voice as soft as melted butter and as smooth as red wine. "They're called Fire Deader's," says the faint voice.

"Fire what?" Robert widens his eyes in puzzlement.

She tilts her head to the side pursing her lips into a fine line as she fiddles with the bracelet Emma made her.

"How's it doing that? I'm this close to freaking out." Jessica sobs, wiping the tears from her eyes. She holds her arms above her head to help herself breathe.

"I wish this was just all a really bad dream."

Ink dust hurls out of the book and swirls past them, spiraling into the blazing sequoia branch that lays broken next to the base of the treehouse's staircase.

While their wary eyes gaze at the blazing branch, the fire deader lying dead close tenses its metacarpals in the mud. Crumbles of dirt and sludge roll off its facial bones as it wobbles to its feet with a heinous growl.

They both jolt, closing their eyes to filter the overwhelming anxiety that rattles their nerves. The fire deader creeps toward Jessica, reaching its pointy claws at her, ready to rip into her flesh.

"Hey, bonehead. What, no guts?" Robert intervenes, taunting the fire deader before it can touch Jessica.

"Robert, be careful." Jessica trembles. The deader's neck bones crack with a jerking motion as the insults provokes its murderous revenge now on Robert.

"All right, skinny, let's go. The score's tied; I'm 'bout to crack a four banger right on your skull." Robert gives it his all with a line drive swing, knocking its skull clean off its neck. Its useless head rolls, bumping into Jessica's shoe. A slimy and sticky brown worm slithers its way out from the skulls dark and lonely orbitals.

"Eww, yuck." Jessica quivers from the inside out, kicking the skull from of her sight, where it crumbles to a burning ash.

The skeleton falls to its knees, disintegrating into a fiery ash before its bones can crash to the ground. Gentle air grabs Jessica's hair, but the burning heat defeats it. Flames gnaw at the large branch, consuming it like a disease. Twigs crackle, snap, and pop, unleashing a pepper of sparks greeting the stars with a welcoming handshake.

Flames wrench upward, wreathing around two more Fire Deader's emerging from the slamming branch. The Deader's's scorching heat is hot enough to melt through their eye sockets. They edge closer toward the treehouse as both Deader's commence in a chase after them amidst the luminous moonlight.

"We gotta go, Robert." "To the treehouse. Go now."

Robert snags the book from the clumpy layer of mud it lays in. He digs deep to find his balance, mushing it's brown slop into his boots tread while he's skating in place. He finds what little dry spot there is, and his Brahma boots grip against it, driving his momentum forward tearing through the wet grass toward the treehouse stairs.

"We should go to the highest treehouse. We'll be farther away from them there," Jessica urges.

They race up the spiral stairs leaving the pattern of their muddy soles behind on each step. Bursting through the door and slamming it shut behind them, they scurry around the room, searching for something to barricade the door with.

"Jess, the couch. No, no, the other damn side," Robert pleads with the point of his finger.

"Okay, okay. Sorry, geez," Jessica complains.

Its wooden legs scrape across the hickory floor as they drag and slide its heavy weight against the door. With a few minor adjustments the couch is snug against the door.

"What the hell are those things?" Jessica panics. "What are we going to do?"

"This book said they're Fire Deader's." Robert rests the book on the kitchen table. His eyes clamp shut with both hands anchored along the table's edges. He scoffs with a shaking head, knowing how ridiculous he sounds.

"Robert, do you know how that sounds? Books don't talk."

Robert ganders out the window at the two Fire Deader's climbing the steps, second-guessing his stupid decision. The blazing flames consuming the Fire Deader's lick the hickory steps. Scorching hot bony feet burn into them. Charring footprints wreathed with flames are spreading like an infection.

"We need a plan. We don't have much time."

"There's not much we can do now, is there?" Jessica shakes her head, glancing out the window with her arms crossed.

"Look, it's only a matter of time before we burn in here."

THUD, THUD, THUD. The Fire Deader's drive their fists into the door, sending a shudder through the portico with each blow.

"They're gonna kill us."

Robert approaches the table, his eyes glued to the book as if it's the Holy Grail. Its spine is partially tattered to the back cover. The smell is a perfect mixture of mildew and musk.

Caked in dirt and grass, he blows the layer of earth's remnants off the four skulls on the front cover. The hard leather creaks open growling its final warning to keep away. The rustling pages stop at a graveyard drawing with Charlie, Blake, and Sean's names written on the caskets.

"What are you doing? You're wasting our time with that stupid book."

"Jess, I'm telling you, this book spoke to me. Maybe it's worth a shot. We don't have many options."

"Okay, whatever, hurry up. We don't have much time for these games."

"Weird." Robert flips through the pages of the book carefully viewing each page as they slip from his fingers.

"What is it?"

"This book."

"What about it?"

"You said it earlier about the pages being blank. All of them are. Not a single word in it. Huh, it's also missing a couple pages," Robert says, opening the book to show Jessica its blank interior as well as the torn remnants of pages hastily removed.

"I'm surprised it's not missing more than that. It looks really old."

All is quiet except for the sound of the Fire Deader's growling and clawing at the door.

"Great, it's only a matter of time before they break the door down and they eat us alive."

Before Robert can snap the book close that same familiar voice emerges from its blank pages. The sound is breathy and light. Its long drawn out pitch is as spine-chilling as a ghost haunting.

"Wait," whispers the book, etching each letter onto the page.

Jessica continues staring out the window, completely oblivious to what he's witnessing. "I wonder if we can make it to that tree over there."

"Jessica," Robert mutters, awestruck and in wonder.

"I think we can if we have a running start." Jessica measures the gap, taking steps to help calculate the distance.

"Jessica." Robert speaks loud enough this time to get her attention.

She looks at him with utter annoyance. She rubs her hand through her hair, flinging it out of her way with a scoff.

Robert motions for her to come over with a sense of urgency, his eyes locked onto the book's intricate leather edges.

His fingers circle over the bare outline toward the top, which appears to have once held a skull.

"What's so fascinating?" she asks, curiously.

"Shh, watch," Robert responds, his voice full of wonder and amazement as he continues to gaze at the book with a look of pure admiration.

EIGHT
IMPOSSIBLE

They marvel at the blank pages as the word Abeamus appears from nowhere. The red orb begins to throb from within his pocket like an aching muscle that won't stop twitching.

"What? Abeamus."

Red smoke slips out the opening of Robert's pocket, crawling down his leg like London's deadly fog.

"What's up with your pants?"

A breeze rips through the shutters, greeting the red smoke whipping around them like a banner waving in harsh winds. Translucent orange and yellow beams through the window, lighting up the room like a glorious sunset. The floor begins to tremor. The shutters smack against the windows' framing. Loose boards rattle free from their nails as the breeze escalates into an unforgiving whirlwind.

"Robert, what's happening?"

"I think we're in the middle of a tornado."

"In the fall?"

The rotation of the wind becomes more powerful with every second, making it difficult for Robert and Jessica to keep their balance. They latch their hands on the table. The tree house rocks back and forth but under all the chaos, the book remains still.

Bolts once fastened tightly and holding up the treehouse begin to wiggle loose against their brackets. The nuts steadily spin from their bolts but the treehouse still holds strong.

The kitchenware rolls out the cabinets, smashing onto the wood floor. Picture frames embracing memories of the camp's development, including a portrait of a young Robert and his father, jump off the wall, shattering the camp's history into tiny pieces.

Gravity becomes nonexistent. Everything, including what fell to the floor, is now floating. Their eyes bug out at the tugging sensation, dragging them toward the book like a mighty vacuum.

Robert's shirt slips from the clutches of Jessica's grip, like when a chain breaks from the collar of a mad dog who has the scent of a cat under his snout.

His feet slide along the hickory planks gaping as far apart as the teeth of those deadly boneheads. He jerks back gazing into her loving eyes. Her burning soul urges for his hand. Before he has a chance to reach for her, both of his hands are consumed into the red vapors. He's under great dismay, a gut-wrenching mess, powerless to stop the inevitable. Where is it taking him? Before he has a chance to think of it, his body entirely becomes smoke, pulling toward the book like a losing game of tug of war. Jessica takes a risk, lunging to save him, and she too is taken by red smoke spiraling downward into the book.

A surge of air barrels across their face; they become immediately aware they're flying through some sort of organic dark cave infested with a nest of sleeping crows.

An impressive darkness cracks open the tunnel, casting shadows as black as the core of a the black hole. It's relentless void swallows them up into non-existence.

The consumption of emptiness lasts for a moment, yet the gloomy grays and black clouds are frozen behind their retinas. Coos and caws unleash an echoing chant in the distance perhaps a mob call to alert the others Robert and Jessica are entering their territory.

An inky ball of black explodes through the fog, startling Robert. With a jerk of his head, he evades the attack, taking a nick to the ear as it projectiles past him.

The dense haze clears to the vast expanse of a navy-blue sky and somber clouds frowning over the ashy ground and polluted river below. Departing out the mouth of a frightening and uncanny skull cloud, they immediately are aware of the overwhelming rush of falling as they shoot toward the ground, leaving behind a trail of red smoke.

Everything is black, and nothing exists, like swimming in space without light from the stars. Sounds of the ocean bring forth polluted waves rolling over Robert's fingers. His body presses firmly into a pile of wet ash. The putrid swampy smell of rotten eggs and carcasses is enough to make him vomit.

Distant footsteps crunch over crumbles of bones and ash, which rapidly draw nearer.

"Chris, Chris, is that you?" A man's husky voice strikes Robert like a whip, conveying masterful authority, slicing, dicing, and cutting through the air like a samurai's sword, but also as calm and patient as still waters.

Filthy ocean water splashes onto his face. Robert's eyes spring open, first to his broken radio. Surrounding it are its remnants. Secondly, he sees someone in a Friar Tuck-style brown cloak holding an empty bucket. "Well, looks like using this radio is out of the question." A yelp escapes Robert's lips while his point of view adds to a blurry layer of superimposing worlds.

"You're not who I thought you were," the man mutters with a sigh.

"What?" Robert winces.

"I'm just a little disappointed. That's all. I see you're still alive. Come on, get up, kid. How did you get here? What orb do you have?" The old man lashes out with a throaty growl.

Robert wipes the wet contaminants of ash off his face as the blur escapes his eyes. His memory recovers, and the thought of his dear Jessica embraces his heart. "Jessica where's Jessica? What's going on?"

"I don't know who you're talking about, but if she's here, she can't be far. Here, dry yourself off." The cloaked man throws Robert a dry towel. "Hurry boy we don't have much time. Now, what orb do you have?"

"You talking about this?" Robert replies, pulling out half of the broken red orb.

"Ohh, yes. That's the fire orb. It's broken. Did you break it?"

"No, it was like this when I got it," Robert says.

Pushing himself to his feet, he wipes the remaining sticky ash off his face. His eyes gaze over the odd environment, which is unlike anything he's ever seen.

The filthy black swamp water goes as far as the eye can see, wrapping around a very small island with a sizable rock taking the shape of a skull resting at the island's center.

The shoreline and beachfront are not the beautiful white sands one would dream of, but about a foot of ash and bone. Facing away from the water is a hill tall enough to block the rest of the horrific territory.

Awaiting at the top of the hill is the cloaked man, standing tall like an unbeaten titan, waiting for Robert to join him. His hands lace over a golden staff that grinds into the ash under his weight. His cloak blows in the wind like the cape of a superhero.

"What is this place?"

"It's Impossible."

"Yes this is impossible."

"No, it's called Impossible."

"Yeah, I know what Impossible means."

The cloaked man buries his face in his hands, unable to fully convey his exasperation. He sighs with a mutter. "Ah, out of all the people in the world, I get this guy. It's going to be a long day."

"What did you say?"

"Never mind. Welcome to the Impossible, the middle world between your earth and, well, the other place."

"Ah, I see. This place is called impossible."

"Yes," the cloaked man says with great frustration.

"So, there's also another place?"

"It's where I'm from. Well, enough about me." The cloaked man doesn't seem too eager to talk about it.

His shoulders droop slightly. Looking down, his soft voice

is as sensitive as the wing of a butterfly. He is brief and slow to answer.

"So, how did we get here?"

"You can only enter and leave here with an elemental orb."

"A what?"

"The elemental orbs. There's five of them. Each one manipulates a different element."

"And this one manipulates fire, huh?"

"That's right."

The threatening fumes around them are bound to be toxic. The lingering and vile aroma settles deep within Robert's nostrils. "What's that smell?"

"Death."

"Yeah, that's about right. Where are we?"

"The Impossible. Didn't I tell you that?"

"I know what you said, but where exactly is—"

"Well we're inside the book, of course."

"The book?"

"You know what book I'm talking about."

"I heard the voices. It came from that wordless book. Was that you that spoke to me?"

The man chuckles. "No, how could I possibly do that? If that was me, I definitely wouldn't have told you to come here."

"Those Fire Deader's. What are they and how?"

"They are the remains of all the people he's killed. The reanimated corpses are…powered by the source of energy of their kind. What influences them to your world? I'm sorry but I don't have an answer for that. Come on; I have much to tell you."

The walk feels more like a tour, which gives enough time

for his experience to settle in. "I can see why they call this place the Impossible. None of it seems real."

The cloaked man's heartfelt chuckle tickles Robert's ears. "You don't like it here, do you?"

"No, of course not. It's quite terrifying, really."

Beautiful red roses edging the walking trail wilt and die as they pass them. The malodor reeks of a putrid carcass and sulfur. Piles upon piles of human bones congest the open field in all its disgusting glory.

"Woooo, it's getting a little bit nippy out here." Robert rubs his hands together before coming to a shiver.

"It's the woods. Its creepiness is literally chilling. Do yourself a favor and stay away from there. The gasses are poisonous."

They're approaching the tree line of an eerie woodlands and out of the ground rise red gasses as they pass a wooden sign reading Forest of Shadows.

The trees are rather different in appearance than our earthly trees. Each tree is smoking and as black as a silhouette with a trunk resembling a skeletal spine. Each meager branch is lanky, down to the twigs, which are bent, resembling human fingers. Each branch is home to many crows, which emit a black vapor from their mouths as they exhale. From a distance, the crows look like leaves, but scatter as you approach them, leaving the tree bare and lifeless as a skeleton.

Passing the forest of shadows, they stop at a decrepit and venerable bell tower. The bourdon bell dongs a blood-curdling tune that is anything but welcoming.

Its walls are gray, wearing layers of moss that scale the wall like an army of hedge-hogs blossoming in every possible nook. Most arched windows are broken for reasons unknown. The

FOREST
OF
SHADOWS

breeze cares not if the edges of the glass are sharp or smooth, dirty or clean, and there or not.

"Is this your home?"

"It was much greater before. Before all this. It used to mean something. Well, it's their home now. I live here… for now." The cloaked man speaks softly with a gentle heart while eyeing his wrist.

Above them hangs a rustic wrought-iron sign that reads "The ones who tried." It creaks an eerie warning not to enter under its leaning archway. Its protective coating must have worn off years ago.

Past the archway is a well-kept graveyard with tapering gravestones arranged into several rows. Several rows of caskets stand up-right, glaring under the moon's light, clean as a whistle of all but the sprinkle of dirt that lies on top.

"What is this place?"

"You sure ask a lot of questions." The cloaked man chuckles, answering Robert before he can speak. "These are the ones who tried to take down the Reapers and failed. I filled up the castle first. The space promptly depleted. Left me no choice but to build this graveyard for any other poor soul who doesn't make it. The caskets, they're standing above ground. After the Reapers kill someone, their casket appears, rising out of the ground like one of his trophies. Those three popped up just recently."

Robert proceeds toward the three caskets with a cautious mind and a humble spirit. The moon's gleam drifts over the caskets as if it wants him to read them. A certain kind of creepiness brings his warm veins to a chill as his hand slides over the etching on each casket.

Sean Thatcher is first, Blake Crowe is next, and last is Charlie Baskin. Robert lowers his hand leisurely down the woods grain, curling his fingertips around the lid's flange of Charlie's casket.

Robert flares his nostrils with a deep inhale. He is more of a rip-the-Band-Aid-off type person. He rolls his eyes shut, tightens his grip, and jerks the door open with a long exhale that lights his face like a cherry. He can't help but gaze briefly into the hole of Charlie's chest. The unbearable site is nauseating. Sheets of dry flesh hang from his orifice. Its pungent smell hosts a swarm of flies that dwell within the hole in his chest. The site repulses Robert into shoving the casket door closed.

"They were friends of Jessica's. Wait a sec, you said Reapers. Do you mean Reaper, the pyromaniac in the red cloak?"

The bell comes to a halt. A low hum flutters the cloaked man's grizzly silver beard. He lifts his eyes over the roof and into the dark-blue and granite-gray clouds. He grinds his teeth and balls his hand into a fist.

The crows turn silent, resting their aching wings on the roof and window edges of the castle, gazing in the same direction as the cloaked man, as if they're to welcome someone.

"Magmus Pias, Magmus Pias, Magmus Pias." The spectral sound reverberates off the inner walls of the old castle.

The cloaked man and Robert look toward the door at the enhancing sound of their chants and echoing footsteps.

"You must go. Come back later, and I'll explain everything."

"But how?"

"The fire orb you possess can do more than get you here and take you back. I'll explain more later. Do you remember the word that got you here?"

"Uh, uh, yes, I remember."

"Okay. Now go back to earth."

"And what?"

"Survive. Protect the book and the orb with your life. Now go. They're coming. You'll have to come back later."

"I can't leave without Jessica."

"Go!"

Tip-toeing backward and around the caskets, trying desperately to avoid detection from the Reapers, Robert takes cover behind them. The hard wood presses against his back. He jolts with a sigh at the slight movement of the casket. Careful not to knock it over, he eases his weight off it.

Robert peeps his head around the casket when the door to the castle bursts open. Death, who's first to come out, stands front and center, waiting for his loyal cohorts, who are late as usual.

Robert's knees begin to shiver when, unknowingly, the casket door behind him creaks open. His eyes bulge out of his sockets.

Something has ahold of him. Someone's hand clinches at the wrinkle of the back of his work shirt. His heart leaps out of his chest at the tugging sensation, which pulls him inside the casket, causing the door to slam shut.

The cloaked man verifies Robert's safe location as the Reapers launch out of the bell tower and plummet down like missiles in front of him. With a huff and puff, he murmurs in disappointment, "You idiot. You were supposed to leave."

In the darkness of the casket, Robert can feel hot air on the back of his neck, making his hair stand at attention. Chills shoot up his spine, swelling his lungs to near-suffocation. He hunches his shoulders to hide his head from the lingering threat from behind. Is it Charlie? Is it Sean or Blake? But their dead. Maybe its someone or something that's almost dead. One of those deader's perhaps.

His hands tremble as he inches his head around first. Then his body which tremors more than his hands. Peering towards the back of the casket, it's too dark to tell what or who is breathing on him. The sudden teeth-chatter induces a panic in Robert that makes him ball up like he's about to be someone's dinner. Leaning his head back against the casket, his hands rise to defend himself from getting his face bit off.

The moon's light beams through the cracks of the casket exposing the shine of her frizzy sunrise gold hair and her beautiful amber eyes. To his surprise it's Jessica.

"Jessica, you've been in here the whole time?" He gasps with quick repetitive breaths, lowering his hands to his sides until the shaking dwindles to stop. She can always calm him.

"Shh, they'll hear us." Jessica eases open the casket door to eavesdrop on the Reapers' conversation with the cloaked man.

"Where are they?" the Death Reaper demands with a deep raspy voice.

"I don't know who you are referring to." The cloaked man shrugs.

"Don't play me for a fool, you feeble simpleton. It's been a long time since that bell rang, and you and I know it. Actually, you were our last visitor. That bell hasn't rang since."

"It only rings when we have visitors," the cloaked man says under his breath.

"Yes, yes. The bell only rings when we have visitors. So, tell me where they are, or I will end your pathetic life where you stand," Death demands with a vicious growl.

"They're gone. They took off. They could be anywhere!"

"Did he send them here? Was it Magmus?" Viviane says as a giggling Seth fist-bumps Ira.

"Enough with his hideous name. Magmus Pias." The Death Reaper sneers with a stomp of his foot.

"Sorry, master. We knew it bothered you," Seth says, wiping the smirk off his face. "We was only playing. No worries." He smacks his fists against his chest, followed by a peace sign.

"Stop the games," the Death Reaper demands. "I'm your leader. What has Magmus done for you? Remember, he's the one that made me who I am. I'm the one who protects you. Anyway, someone pulled the fire orb from the book. Since Tate has escaped, it's a matter of time before it's our turn. If we're lucky, Tate will already have Chris when we escape."

"Sorry, Master," says Viviane. She backs up and bows her head.

"The only way into the Impossible is by the orb. Split up, find who ever is here. They may have Tate's orb." The Death Reaper turns to the cloaked man. "After we destroy them, you can bury their remains with the rest of them." Death jerks his head toward Viviane and Seth with a hideous growl. "Why are you still here?"

"On it, Master," Seth says as he heads off toward the lake.

Viviane strides down the first row of standing caskets slipping out her snake-like whip from her inner cloak. Lightning snaps through the sky, flashing its white light over her when she begins to snap her whip, smashing through each casket door as if it were a sledge hammer.

Ash and tiny bone fragments kick up like dancing ice-skaters, twirling and spinning in a gentle glissade back to the ground.

"What are we going to do?" Jessica whispers peeping at Viviane through the crack of the casket's door as she advances closer and closer to them.

"Shh, I'm thinking," Robert says.

Ira shoves the castle doors open. Their rusty steel handles crack the concrete walls as they slam into them. A whistling gust of wind hurls through Ira, welcoming her back into the castle with an impatient whirling bundle of dead leaves. She stands firm at the entranceway like a mother lion protecting her cubs.

Long, dark, and dirty velvet black curtains line the corridor to the right. They wave along the ground, displaying the moon's light and unveiling a layer of dust that fills the room.

"One Reaper, two Reaper." Ira points at the first curtain, but nothing happens. She drops her head to her chest, forgetting for a moment that her orb is vacant and still in the book. No power. "I miss my orb. Things would be much easier if I had my beautiful precious orb. If I had a heart, I would cry." She grips the velvety fabric, slinging each curtain open on her stroll down the corridor. "One Reaper, two Reaper, three Reaper, four! One of us will find you, then you'll be no more!"

Robert and Jessica gaze at Viviane through the crack of the casket door as she continues to sling her whip into each casket. "One Reaper, two Reaper, three Reaper, four! We'll escape the book, and that is for sure!"

Seth walks along the shoreline, pulling out his trident from his inner cloak. With a snap of his hand, the sword-size trident extends to its full length. He twirls his trident around like he's some kind of martial artist. "One Reaper, two Reaper, three Reaper, four! Your life will cease to exist, as we rip it from the core!"

Ira exits the castle. Weak in the knees, she drops to them, wailing, slamming her fists into the ash and bone like a frantic psycho. "No, no. It can't be. I can't stay here any longer. I must leave this dreadful place."

"Ira, Ira, calm down. Patience is not your strong suit," Seth says as he collapses his trident to sword-size and holsters it back into his cloak.

"They're not in the castle, master."

"Yea, I figured." Death sighs.

Seth takes his place beside Ira. His back arches and his shoulders hunch, too afraid to make eye contact with Death. He gives him his answer with a disappointed shrug of his shoulders.

"Figures. Where are they?" With a sinister murmur, the Death Reaper whispers, "One Reaper, two Reaper, three Reaper, four! Those pathetic humans better"—the Death Reaper turns around and waits for Viviane to open one of the last caskets—"be behind that door!"

The cloaked man, the Death Reaper, Ira, and Seth gawk at the casket, impatiently awaiting for the door to open. Viviane slips her whip back into her cloak as she inches her hand toward the casket door. Suspense lingers in the air like a foul odor; anxiety and tension course through the veins of the curious.

Viviane curls her long grotesque fingers around the casket door, its screws and hinges corroded and layered in rust. The door sounds off with a spine-shivering creak as Viviane eases it open.

Hope lingers for the Reapers, but their patience runs thin. Her shockingly hideous lavender eyes, full of the ooziest gooiest parasites and as crispy as burnt chicken, peer around the doors edge and into the casket. Viviane gives the Death Reaper a look of discouragement. "It's empty, master."

The Death Reaper steps forward, balling his rotten dead fingers into a fist and shaking them with rage. "What?"

The cloaked man unleashes a grand smile. He hasn't given a smile for over twenty-three years. He sees a slight build in confidence, perhaps a glimmer of hope for the old man. The man shoves a fit of laughter deep down in his gut. He fights to suppress the possible explosive celebration, swallowing the evidence with a gulp. The risk of punishment is a guarantee if Death saw him happy.

The Death Reaper approaches the casket, sliding Viviane to the side. "Out of the way, Viviane! Let me take a look." The Death Reaper pulls poor Sean's dead body out of the casket, carefully observing every crevice of the casket for any clues of his new visitors.

BAM! He slams it shut, breaking the top hinge off the door, smacking its edge along the crumbles of ash and bone along the ground. Death's boiling point puts him in a fit of rage. "Where are they? Somebody didn't search well enough—or maybe someone here is lying. WHO'S LYING?! Ira, did you check every room in the castle?"

"Yes, Master, I did. The castle is empty. I, I swear. As soon as I find whoever it was, I'm gonna cut off their eensy-weensy tiny fingers with my girls here and feed them to your Dead-

The One Who Tried

er's…Master," Ira says, holding her cloak open, exposing her two boomerangs with a hint of sarcasm. She bows her head in fear, careful not to anger Death any more than he already is.

"No. You'll bring them to me alive. If you bring them to me dead, you'll spend the night in the basement with my crows. Again."

Full-body tremors blow through her like a hurricane. She can feel the crows pecking at her, chained to the wall and helpless, their beaks penetrating her frostbitten eyes and flesh, their claws scratching, ripping at her, digging into her bones. She screams in terror, waking her from the hellish memory. She snaps out of the traumatic incident, focusing on her breathing.

"You okay, Ira?" Viviane comforts her, rubbing her back with her charred and reddened hand. So reddened parts of it are split open like a burnt hotdog. Ira nods with one last inhale and exhale to bring her nerves to ease.

The Death Reaper glowers at Seth's immature actions as he continues to do the robot dance. "Seth."

"What?"

"Were you listening to me at all?" The Death Reaper scoffs. "You know what? Never mind. You guys are all idiots. At least one of you has half a brain, and that's Tate."

Up in the treehouse of Wolf's Eye Den, Tate stands in disbelief over the wordless book. It's been years since his freedom and now he's in full control. The book, still lying there open on the table amongst the mess of debris that surrounds him, and the two fire deader's, who stand there next to him, flameless, and awaiting orders.

Tate's forefinger and thumb prowl around the remaining four orbs of the book. He becomes hesitant while his fingers dangle over the black orb. Tensions rise, making a prompt decision skipping the Death orb and grabbing the snow orb instead. He grips the white orb firmly with his fingers. Gears turn, unlocking the key, causing it to spin clockwise on its dial.

The gears crank as the key spins, halting on the wind orb's skull, which sits in the top left corner of the book. The key reaches into the skull's chin, and with a clink and clank, unlocks the snow orb, bringing it to a wobble. With ease, Tate lifts the white orb out of the wordless book.

"We will be together soon, my love," Tate says, admiring the snow orb. Its lustrous white light is full and radiant as LED headlights. The flashing light burns dim when, most abruptly, the orb begins to dissolve into tiny snowflake particles.

Out of Tate's peripherals, he catches Emma trying to escape out the door. She whimpers, more on the inside than out as she tip toes toward the exit. She eases her hand toward freedom. The doorknob rattles. Click, click, click.

"You're wasting your time, Chris."

"It's Emma, okay? And I'm leaving."

"It's locked."

Emma kicks the door, angry at her failing escape. "OUCH! Ohh, dangit. Stupid door."

"Where do you think you're going, anyway?"

"Away from here, and away from you. You got what you wanted, now let me go," Emma yells, tugging on the doorknob, but the doorknob itself becomes red-hot. "Ouch! Why did you do that?"

Tate's fiery hand still points at the doorknob. With a roll of his wrist, the flames recede from whence they came. The smell of hot metal fades away as the red doorknob changes to its original color.

"Come on, Chrissie. The Death Reaper wants to see you."

"Again, for the third time, I'm not Chrissie."

"Yeah, well, tell him that."

Tate's trembling hand hovers over the other three skulls with a heavy heart and a conflicting mind. His hand lowers close to Deaths orb as it lights up to expose the lingering dead souls floating around like a witches crystal ball.

The skulls sizzle from the intense heat emitting off his scarred flesh creates an expanding ball of burnt residue over the ornaments surface.

One and only one single thought clutters his mind. Is he actual reconsidering not releasing his master from his imprisonment? Although Tate wasn't keen to backstabbing anyone, Death would be the exception.

His hand retreats from what can be his most inevitable mistake. The tremble in his hand transpires to fear in his heart and it's that fear that awakens the other orbs.

Each orb still bound to the books cover begins to shake unleashing the next chain of events. Three remaining keys enter into the three chins still holding an orb in its skull.

His smoldering eyes are like partially burning wood with glowing red and orange particles with embers covering its surface. His pupils dilate extinguishing the embers to grey ashes.

The Electric orb, Water orb, and the Death orb rises out of the skulls forehead and hovers there. The Water orb dissolves into a puddle, their Electric orb breaks down into electrically charged particles, and the Death orb dissolves to ashes. Each particle from the three orbs make their spiraling descent into their own separate skulls adorned on the books cover.

"Now that the orbs are removed from the book. It's only a matter of time before they show up. Looks like we're moving to Plan B." Tate mutters.

From out of his palm is a tickle. The snow orb fragments rise from his hand. Those snow flake particles belong to his love and that thought, that longing for her arrival reignites the flame in his heart and combusts his expanding pupils back to smoldering embers.

"Wow." Emma's attention is immediately drawn to the floating orb fragments swirling in Tate's hand.

A slight and gentle breeze carries the snowflake particles away and into the mouth of the skull that once held Ira's orb.

"I don't have a need for the book anymore. Looks like I have some collateral for my missing orb," Tate says with a low, guttural growl while scowling at Emma.

Ira scuffs her palm as she slides her hand up to grip the headstone. The unforgiving gale shows no mercy, lifting Viviane and Ira off the ground as if gravity doesn't exist.

Lightning strikes in the horizon of the Impossible, following a gust of wind, which whips around the Reapers like a boomerang. The Death Reaper looks at Ira and Viviane. "It's not us. How could we without our orbs?" Ira says, shrugging high enough both shoulders touch the hood of her cloak.

A wicked roar unleashes in the somber sky like a mighty wind with enough power and force to stop the earth from spinning. The skull cloud, a face of horror in every feature, emerges ominously out of the gloom. The mouth lies open, its eyes slant, and its body swells with rage. Its brooding presence emits a horrific threat like an oncoming storm.

"Ah, coooool, look!" Seth says, pointing at the sky.

Thunder roars through the murky skies like an exploding volcano. The trees flex and bend down to the roots. Leaves shred from their twigs and rain down on them like a violent hailstorm.

A chuckle escapes Death's mouth. "Good boy Tate. It's about time."

Four separate clusters of glowing orb fragments spiral out the mouth of the skull cloud and directly into the Reapers' ribcages. Each Reaper gazes at their sternums as their orbs appear. The symbols around their orbs glow brighter than bright while the orbs' power surges through their bones.

With a deep suction from the mouth of the skull-like cloud, the pulling force picks up power. A surging inhale from the colossal skull cloud kicks up ash and bone fragments that color the Impossible like wintry confetti.

The wind sweeps Viviane off her feet and slams her body onto the ground. Dirt packs into her sordid nails as she drives her long, grotesque fingers into the dirt.

"What's going on?" She yells, her voice barely able to penetrate through the massive whistling blizzard.

A casket hurls past her and slams into a light-post, snapping it in half. The hanging electrical wires begin to spark like the grand finale at a firework show that blazes through the ash like campfire embers.

"Who's going first? I'm betting it's you, Viviane. Tick, tock, tick, tock. Up the gale and through the ash, into the skull's mouth, out the book, I won't look back, tick, tock, tick, tock," Ira sings. "Ha ha ha ha, I just love the wind," She yells with a joyous glee through the relentless gale.

Ira reaches out to grab Viviane's hand. Their fingertips graze each other's, and Ira slips off the headstone, smacking hard against the ground. "Ha, ha! This is kind of fun." Ira laughs.

The Death Reaper feels weight on his leg. He gazes down, and to no surprise, it is Seth who is holding on to him. "Let go! What's the matter with you?" Death sneers.

"I'm scared," Seth cries.

The Death Reaper shakes his leg free of Seth, who manages to catch the Death Reaper's cloak, hovering off the ground like an indoor sky diver. "Get off me! Stop being so clingy."

"Are we finally getting out?" Seth asks. The Death Reaper's cloak slips through his weary grasp as he is carried away into the mouth of the skull cloud.

"How long have we been here for, anyway? I'm soooo ready to leave. The views starting to bore me," Ira says before she's carried away into the cloud. "Remember, whatever happens, together, we can't be defeated," Viviane says as she's taken away into the skull cloud.

The Death Reaper gawks at the cloaked man with a chuckle. He's standing there at ease as if the high winds are of no threat to him.

"Laugh all you want, you backstabbing bastard. You bound me here, and that's temporary. I will find a way out of here, then you and your other goons will fall. Karma's gonna get ya," the cloaked man says.

"You're never getting out of here. You're pathetic. I'll make sure to bring your daughter's dead corpse back here so you can bury what's left of her with the rest of them." The Death Reaper laughs standing tall in defiance.

"You better not touch her."

"Don't worry. After I kill you, you'll still be serving me as one of my favorite Deader's."

Looking high in the sky at the skull cloud, the Death Reaper chants. "Silence, locate the book, the time has come. We are the keepers of the elemental orbs; bound and motivated to the cause, the dead will rise, and the living will fall because we are…the Reapers."

The high winds inhale the Death Reaper through the mouth of the skull cloud bringing the wailing gale to an immediate halt.

The cloaked individual stands confidently by the castle peering up at the skull cloud as the whirling ashes and debris trickle to the ground. With vengeance in his eyes, a clinch of his fists, and hope in his heart, the man mutters-

"We'll see, we'll see."

NINE
RELEASE THE REAPERS

Red smoke seeps out from the wordless book like a leaky exhaust pipe. Jessica and Robert land hard on the treehouse floor, as if the floorboards are stretching out toward them, greedy to have them in their clutch. The levitating and trembling wordless book collapses back to the table like a heavy load of snow.

"Are you okay, Jess?"

"I think so. This place is a mess." Jess jerks her hand from the floor. "Ouch! Why is the floor so hot?"

"I was going to say the same thing."

With aching bodies, they gradually rise to their feet as smoke surges through the gaps of the floorboards. A crackling noise from outside tears into their ears, and their desperate attention is drawn to the window.

The rubber soles on their shoes have become soft and sticky like a gooey marshmallow. The floor is hot, as if they are walking barefoot on blacktop on a scorching summer day, making the walk toward the window a literal hop and skip.

Robert rubs his eyes in a state of confusion at the layer of haze that veils the once beautiful view. Their eyes swell up at the horrific site at the entire floor and balcony underneath them is burning. Rising flames begin licking the mezzanine, and smoke rolls in, swiftly filling the treehouse.

"Oh, great. After we die of smoke inhalation, we'll burn to death. Like we don't have enough in our lungs already." Cough, cough. "Then, when the floor caves in, our burnt bodies will fall fifty feet to the ground, shattering every bone we have." Cough, cough.

Frustrated and struggling to breathe through the smoke, Jessica shakes Robert by the shoulders. "Stop being so negative. We're not dying here. Help me think. Hurry, or we'll die. We got this."

Robert tries to shake off the musky smell of burning hickory from his nose as he hops over to the window and leans out, holding his feet off the hot floor while scoping out the best escape scenario.

"Well, broken legs sound better than burning to death!"

"Are you suggesting we jump?"

"Not yet." Robert veers toward the emergency cabinet, covering his mouth with his hands, hacking and coughing as he drives his elbow through its glass door and rips the fireman's ax from its clamps.

"What are you going to do with that?"

"I'm not going down there without some sort of protection. Now, grab the book, and let's get outta here."

Before she can grasp her fingers around the book's rough faux leather, the skulls' eyes light up in their separate colors. "Wait! What?" Jessica jolts, evading a burst of teal, white, purple, and black smoke that explodes out the center skull of the book, sails through the smoky haze, and swoops out the window. The three corner skulls on the book vanish, leaving the one in the center still present.

"Was that them, Robert?"

"It has to be. Let's hope that ambulance is still here."

"There's no time to go to the hospital. We have to warn everyone. We don't know what they're capable of. Come on."

Jessica snatches the book, and with a shove the shutters fling open as Robert aids her out the window and onto the balcony, coming in close behind her.

"Ouch, ouch. Robert, you need to hurry; my feet are on fire. How are we supposed to jump off with the railing burning?"

"Watch out, I'm chopping it down."

Robert slams the axe into the railing over and over again. Visions of his camp's destruction flicker in his mind as each swing becomes more violent than the next. He pushes the broken pieces over the edge. Their long journey to the bottom ends as they shatter into pieces.

"Jessica, can you make it to that tree over there?"

"It's too far. We'll never make it. No, no, I'm not doing it." Jessica panics.

"We do it or we die. If we miss, maybe the pile of leaves will break our fall."

"Ha, don't count on it. Hmmmm, shit. I hate heights. Robert, I-I-I can't do this." Jessica breaks down in a panicked full-body shiver.

"Yes, you can. Look at me. We will die if we stay here. It's now or never."

Robert tosses the fireman's axe over the balcony. Its delayed impact makes the distance a reality and brings doubt to his confidence. With a dreadful gasp, they fist bump each other, both reciting a special quote with passion in their eyes that bleeds a gentle melody.

"Never above, never below, always beside you is where I belong," they both quote simultaneously.

Robert gauges the hazy distance with a squint of his eyes for his landing mark. The come and go of rising smoke offers a moment of a clear view one second and a cloudy veil the next. He calculates for a clear opening. With a couple deep breaths, he charges across the balcony, lunging off its edge. The rush of clean air is refreshing for him as he inhales deeply. His arms and feet swim through the air, reaching out to grab the earth and drag the tree closer to him, but he isn't strong enough.

Robert lands on his mark on the adjacent sequoia tree branch. The impact to his stomach takes the wind out of him. He clamps down with a mind-boggling wince and a moan as soaring as a high-speed locomotive approaching its crossing.

"You did it, baby," Jessica cheers, hopping for joy.

He grunts and groans till the pain subsides unexpectedly, sliding off and catching the branch with his hands. His arms drain their energy with his slipping fingers rolling toward him first his pinky, then his ring finger. He begins to reposition his grip when his fingers are a landing zone for a meddling crow pecking its long pointy beak into his fingers. A puncture to his flesh seeps blood that dribbles off his hand and cascades to the ground. Biting his tongue to ease the pain his hand twitches to shake off the crow, and he feels his weight drop to his feet. With a few agonizing pecks his fingers slip off the tree branch making his long descent to the ground. His body is no match for gravities grip as it pulls him down. He contorts his head for one possible last glance at Jessica, who becomes smaller and smaller by the second as be descends down each branch.

He lands onto a wet pile of twigs and leaves, which is a huge relief, even with the mixture of worms and ants crawling over him.

"Ah, my gosh!" Jessica covers her mouth in a bloodcurdling shriek. "Are you okay?"

"Ahhh, yeah, I'm fine. My back is a little sore, that's all. Come on down; it's completely safe. You can do it. I won't let you get hurt. I promise." Robert rises to a sitting position, wiping off the wet leaves and icky pests.

"I'm terrified. I'm just going to stay here and fucking die. Ow, dammit! My feet."

Jessica looks down warily. "What if I miss miss my mark? If I don't land in the right spot, I'm dead. I don't want to die."

"Then jump! I promise, I'll catch you if you fall."

"You know what? Fuck it," Jessica mutters.

The blaze lights the treehouse like a torch, glazing an orange hue over Robert like stained glass. Two narrow shadows breach the orange tint over his face, leaving him on high alert, but what are the shadows from? Branches, maybe. Lucky for him the axe is a hop away.

Moving shadows make this a now-or-never situation. The squishing muddy sounds grow louder and quicker by the second. Coming to his feet, Robert comes face-to-face with two Fire Deader's.

There's something slightly different with one of them. A red glow pulsates and hovers within its ribcage. Their teeth chatter and jaw joints pop. A sinister growl mixes with a repetitive clucking sound that is as threatening as a snake hiss.

The axe lays halfway in between the Deaders and Robert. Is the temptation worth the risk, or should he run? Or maybe he can stay where he's at? Robert's mind is like a drying machine full of thoughts whirling, bouncing around in his head.

A ticking movement forward prompts Robert to be hesitant when the Deaders gnash their teeth, swinging their claws at him, ready to tear him to pieces at will.

It's black rock like beating heart amplifies to a pounding thump that thrashes against its ribs. A bright orange ooze seeps out the cracks of its heart. The intense heat gives off a thermal current that spreads toward him like a contagious disease.

"Jessica! Get your ass down here! I could really use your help right now."

Robert reaches his finger toward the oncoming haze, and its blazing heat lets off a sizzle like a hot dog on a grill. He jerks his reddened hand back, placing its burnt tip upon his wet lips. "Jess, Jess!"

The heat is overwhelming, drowning her in sweat. In tears, her trembling hand covers her mouth as she creeps toward the burning edge. "Ouch!" She lifts her feet off the hot balcony, leaving globs of melting rubber behind on the floor.

The burning steps creak and crack, charring around their bolts. Her head jerks at the terrifying sound. The stairway crumbles without warning, crashing hard against the ground. Jessica anchors down, readying herself for the jump.

"It's now or never." She tosses the book over the balcony. In full sprint, she leaps off the ledge of the patio, soaring high in the air like an eagle, totally awestruck by her courage. She comes in fast, landing hard on her mark.

"AHHHH!" Both arms wrap around the branch in a heart-wrenching landing. The popping noise in her shoulder leaves her in excruciating pain.

"You okay, Jess?" Robert shouts.

"I think I popped my damn shoulder out of socket!" Jessica yelps, but the adrenaline boost gives her the courage to motivate her descent. She fights the pain and continues dropping down one branch at a time, snapping the last one in two and thumping into the pile of leaves.

Safely on the ground, she crawls out from the pile of leaves, holding her arm. She comes to her feet running while supporting her dislocated shoulder.

Robert stumbles backward, crawling away to evade the air's smoldering heat, but the bottom hem of his smoking pants erupts into a flame.

"Robert! I'm coming."

Her achy shoulder joint grinds together as Jessica scurries her way to Robert, first grabbing the axe that lays close by. She drags the fireman's axe along the ground, scraping clumps of mud onto its steel blade.

"Jess, don't come any closer. It's the air. It's scalding hot." Robert panics, trying to pat out the growing flame off his pants.

She stops behind the Fire Deader's, who seem to be taking a sick pleasure in Robert's torture as the ring of boiling current traps him to the very spot. Her eyebrows lower, and her lips curl inward. Jessica is in full adrenaline mode, ready to crush these Deader's.

"Get away from him, you motherfuckers."

A single water droplet lands on her forehead. Jessica gazes at the stellar gloomy skies. Thunder rumbles in the darkness, and the moist drips of rain dribble down her cheek. The scalding-hot air sizzles as each droplet battles through its blistering barrier. The moment of peace regenerates within her as Jessica continues her stare off with the two Fire Deader's.

Eye liner smears, running down her face. A sense of relief flows through her when she realizes the rain has extinguished Robert's burning pants.

"I can't get through. The air it's too hot," Robert elaborates, jerking his sizzling finger back.

Her courage sprouts like a budding flower that is equally as sinister as the Deader's themselves. She can feel a sense of energy coursing through her own bones.

The Fire Deaders' bones smoke, sizzling with each drop of rain that splashes on them. Looking up at the rain and back down at themselves, they suffer great disappointment when their own flames are gone too. Jessica, realizing they are now a lesser threat, gains a boost of confidence with a vengeful smirk. The one's bright red glowing heart is as eye-catching as rave lights in the void of the desert.

Jessica marches toward the heartless fireless deader, slicing its head clean off the neck bone, turning it into burning ashes before its head can smack the ground.

The rain ceases when an unsolicited breeze scatters away the remnants. The remaining smoke evaporates into the night air bringing a moment of calm as if the battle is already over

with. She eases the axe by her side, her grip loosens letting the wood handles grain slide down her palm slightly. Her chest rises and lowers to a normal rhythm when the snap of a twig startles her easing mind.

The remaining Deader with the pounding heart balls its metacarpals into a tight fist, raging like a rabid dog. Jessica rears back sharply as the Deader leaps in the air at her. With the axe out in front of her, she prepares for impact. Both grotesque hands collide, wrapping around the axes handle and forcing her to the ground, fighting to free the axe from the Deaders fusing grip.

Molten-hot lava seeps out from the Fire Deaders grip and drips onto the sizzling, wet ground next to her. She dodges left, then right to evade each life-threatening drip.

"Keep fighting, Jess."

"I'm trying! What do I do?"

The hissing ring of fire ceases its unrelenting heat, leaving behind lingering steam and Robert's dire urgency to aid Jessica. He slips his hand once more toward the rising steam. Each cool pelting raindrop against his hand is like a barrier from the heat that makes it bearable to the touch.

"Ah, yes," Robert blurts as he rushes through the warm air toward Jessica.

Robert plunges his boot into the Deader's ribs over and over again but its hands remain fused to the axe's handle. The Deader muscles its way closer to Jessica, its pounding heart beating rage-fully, as if it has a mind of its own and wants to attack her itself.

Inches away from its gnashing teeth, Jessica can smell its sulfuric breath, the repulsing stench of rotten eggs. She manages to overpower the furious Deader by pivoting the angle of the axe, aiming its pick end up.

Robert follows up, slamming his foot into its spine, and with a downward thrust, he gives the bag of bones one final message. "Ashes to ashes, dust to dust."

Driving downward the pick side of the axe impales the Fire Deaders heart, disintegrating it to burning ashes.

Jessica wipes off the individual pieces of ash that linger around her like fireflies. She delivers a pained groan, holding her arm close to her body. Robert aids her to her feet, giving her the warmest hug as his hands slip around her, pressing her in close and tight.

"Are you okay?" he asks gently as a whisper.

"Other than my dislocated shoulder, I'm fine. And you? Are you okay?"

"I'm fine. Thank goodness you are. I was so scared you were—"

Tears flood their eyes as they close like curtains. They lean in, feeling the warm air from each other's breath. The rain and gloomy skies part, making way for the sprinkle of stars that gather to witness the pure moment of bliss.

Their souls embrace each other like Heaven's welcoming arms amid the glow of the lustrous moon. Her heart-shaped lips press into his while he's running his fingers through strands of her burnt crispy hair.

Their picturesque moment is cut off by four careless brushstrokes of different colors smearing along the blackened canvas. They arch like enemy arrows, curving back toward the earth and propelling toward Robert and Jessica like raging cannon balls.

First to make their crash landing is Ira. "All right, hot stuff, where are you?"

Viviane lands next, wiping ash and bone fragments off her cloak. "Finally, something other than the smell of death."

Seth lands next. "I don't remember much about this place, but I can't wait to see more."

Lastly, Death lands in all his menacing wickedness. He follows the patches of fire to the dilapidated spiraling stairway. He stops on the blazing flames of the treehouse with the point of his fleshless forefinger. "There. That's where we came from. That's where my book is, and my right-hand man. Ira, get him down here."

"Tate, baby, come on down to momma. We need to find your orb. You know what happens when you lose it," Ira says.

"Ha, ha, ha, ha. Looks like your loser boyfriend went off and left ya." Viviane giggles.

"How are you so sure Tate doesn't have his orb in the first place?" Seth asks.

"If he came back to the Impossible, why would he hide from us? Am I the only one here who still has their brains? Well, it's a pleasure to be brilliant," Ira boasts.

"You are by far the smartest one here," Viviane is saying when she's rudely cut off by Death.

"Enough, Viviane. Iras's right. Someone else has Tate's orb," Death says.

"Master, maybe Tate's orb is in the treehouse. Do you want me to put the fire out? I can make it rain. Cooler than that, I can create a tidal wave from the lake over there. It'll be so fun. Woo-hoo, I'm so glad we have our power back. I can't wait to use it." Seth chimes in with his best celebratory dance moves.

"No, the rain is not my thing. The thought of it makes me itch," Viviane says.

"Nah, nothing's up there anyway. Let it burn. Destruction is so beautiful," Death mutters.

"How are you so sure Master, neither of them are up there?" Seth asks.

"Death's instincts are never wrong, Seth," Viviane says.

"They're actually underneath our noses," Death growls ominously.

Twigs crack amongst rustling leaves from somewhere close by. The abrupt crunching piques more than Death's immediate curiosity.

"There they are." Death giggles as he raises his head to the crunching sound behind him.

A devilish outcry escapes the remaining skull on the book. Its roar is sharp enough to cut through Robert and Jessica's chilled bones.

"What the fuuuuuccckk?" Jessica mouths to Robert, who takes cover behind a tree. She bounces to release an uncontrollable horde of the heebie-jeebies.

"We gotta move, Jess. Don't forget the book."

"Did you hear the noise it made? I'm not touching it. You're outta your damn mind if you think I'm grabbing that creepy thing. I'll get the axe," Jessica whispers.

"Fuck it, let's go," Robert says as he snags the book.

"There it is. What are you doing? Get my book!" Death demands.

Viviane rushes in fast with Seth trailing behind. Robert's foot splashes in a puddle as Viviane swoops past him, sending a bolt of voltage into the puddle, which shocks him to his knees in a jolting collapse before he falls to his face.

"Leave him alone!" Jessica shrieks. She runs to help him when she notices a teal smoke darting past.

Before she can reach Robert, Jessica's brand-new Puma Speedcats are immersed in a sloppy mud puddle. Robert comes to, shaking off the blow, waiting for the dizziness to subside.

An aquatic hand lashes out from the puddle Jessica is in and latches onto her ankle. The starving mud puddle gulps her leg like quicksand as the aqua hand drags her under more and more. A wail of terror unleashes from her mouth as the aquatic hand drags her and the axe completely into the puddle of water.

Semiconsciously observing his beloved's descent into the puddle, Robert's brain fights to send a signal to his limbs to get up and save her, but he can't move.

One final scream from her is the boost he needs. Robert feels the warm blood drain to his fingertips and toes when his fingers curl into a raging fist. "Come on!"

Crawling as fast as he can, her reaching hand is the last thing he sees as she fully submerges in the puddle. Face wet and full of gnats, he drives his hand in after her, losing balance and slipping in himself. He manages to grasp onto something hard and rigid. The Reapers speak sinister whispers of discouraging gurgling from all around him. With all his might, he manages to pull and pull and pull until the axe's blade and handle reaches out of the puddle. Robert grunts and huffs, pulling with all he's got. Jessica's hands grip tightly around the wood handle as he pulls her out of the puddle and onto the surface.

"Thank goodness." He gasps, panting like a dog out of breath.

She gags, and coughs, gasping for the tiniest bit of air while Robert comforts her with a gentle rub on her back. The gagging and coughing culminates in normal breathing as he helps Jessica to a sitting position. He gives her the tightest hug he's ever given her.

"Where did they go?" Jessica grabs onto her injured shoulder, rotating it with ease.

"I don't know; they disappeared. What's wrong with your shoulder?"

"My shoulder?"

"Did I hurt you?"

"No, it feels better, actually. I think you popped it back into place when you pulled me out from the puddle. How the literal hell is the puddle that deep"

"We need to get you to a hospital more than ever right now. We'll let the police take care of those psychos."

"We should have gone to the police in the first place. Emma would probably be home with her grandparents by now."

"What about the Reapers?"

"What about them?"

Robert's face twists into a scowl, and his brain crashes in befuddlement.

"Robert, what's wrong?" Gazing into the refection of his eyes Jessica can see swaying branches. The rustling of leaves brings her head to a U-turn. They watch as they sway back and forth from one tree to the next, awaking sleeping birds fleeing for their lives. They stand holding each other's hands as they starlings ease their way backward. Branches begin to twist, turn, and curl, taking the shape of a lion's head, while other branches stretch out on both sides to look like wings.

"What the hell? Are you seeing this, Jess?"

"Maybe we shouldn't be standing here. Come on."

"I agree."

The mouth of the lion opens up, letting out a monstrous roar, and a heavy wind rushes at them like a hurricane. White smoke dashes out from the mouth too. It's Ira, and she's coming in fast.

"Baby, we got to move!"

Ira hovers over them, pushing her hands outward, throwing Robert and Jessica in opposite directions. Robert's back smacks against a tree, while Jessica slides along the mud.

"Now, I end you," Ira roars.

Twigs and leaves blow past Robert as he tucks his head into his arms to hide from the whirlwind of dust. The nearby tree splits its trunk and tilts in his direction, sounding off its final crack. He rolls out from the line of impact. BOOM! The Death Reaper, Viviane, and Seth drop in next to Ira, taking formation behind the settling dirt and leaves.

"Did you get 'em, Ira?" asks Seth.

"Of course she didn't. Ira's losing her touch."

"In order for you to insult me, I have to first value your opinion. Good try, though. Anyway, my hubby's missing. If they're the ones that showed up at the Impossible, they must have his orb. Or they know where he is."

"Tate was a waste of time. I say we kill those intruders, take Tate's orb, and finish what you started, master."

"I ought to take a lightning rod and shove it up."

"Girls! That's enough shit talk. Look, there they are."

Jessica runs to Robert's aid. "Get up, they're coming! Come on, we got to move!"

"Blow it down," Death commands, making eye contact with Ira whose threatening presence weighs heavy like a mountain on her nerves.

Leaves and twigs scoot across the ground. The trees' branches flap their wooden wings faster and faster. Leaves and debris, including empty bags of hotdog buns and marshmallows, dart past the Reapers. The wind grows heavier, bending the trees to their limits, but the Reapers stand there like it has no effect on them at all. The Death Reaper signals Ira to stop with a wave of his hand.

"They're here. I can smell them. Bring me their corpses. One of them has the book. The one who brings it to me will be on my good side."

"Yes, Master," all the Reapers say simultaneously.

The other Reapers fly off in a game of hide-and-seek while the Death Reaper hangs back to supervise.

Jessica and Robert take cover behind their own separate trees. Death scans the woods for movement, pulling out his chained kusarigama to ready himself for the hunt.

Its metal chain clings and clangs together before the spiked ball strikes the ground like a clap of thunder.

"I'm starting to get tired of these games," Death growls.

Jessica waves her hands urgently, staring a hole into Robert, trying to gather his attention, but he remains attentive to the Reapers' whereabouts. As he's mumbling a plan to himself for their safe escape Jessica begins tapping the axe against the tree. Maybe a little noise will do the trick.

"Hey, pssssst. Robert."

"Shh, be quiet! They're coming."

"Robert."

"What?" Robert blurts.

"Look, your pocket."

Robert looks down at his shirt pocket and observes a red glow as bright as a glow stick. He pulls out the beautiful red orb and shows it to Jessica with a look of befuddlement.

"Why's it glowing?"

"Put it away. They'll see us."

Robert stares deeply into the bright-glowing red orb, completely mesmerizing him with its beauty. He scans up at each glowing orb in the Reapers' chest.

"They all have their own orbs too. Just like this one," he says.

As the fire orb's glow dissipates, Robert ceases his lingering stare, placing the orb back in his shirt pocket.

Easing his head around the tree, Robert takes note of the Reapers' location. The Death Reaper, through the thicket of a thousand branches, is at a standstill, scanning the woods as a hunter seeks his meal. Viviane and Seth advance on the left side of him, while Ira advances on the right side.

Jessica places her focus and trust on Robert. Her trembling hands wrap around his in a unbreakable clinch as solid as concrete. "What do we do?"

He can't hear her through his pounding heart, but can read her lips. Also curious of their location, Jessica peeks her head around the tree, careful not to unveil her location with nerves that rolls her head like dice. Death edges his malicious focus in their direction. She snaps her head back scuffing her forehead along its bark realizing Death may have seen her. Sweat rolls down her forehead, and her head presses firmly against the tree. Her axe lays ready in the tight clench of both her hands.

She is panicking. She clamps her teeth down before becoming self-critical. "Stupid, stupid, stupid," she whispers. The overwhelming anxiety feels like her flesh is melting off. Closing her eyes eases the tension. She inhales holding her breath before she exhales.

Robert waves at her to gather her attention. "Relax and be still." He gestures his hands downward in a pushing motion. With a gentle nod, she builds the confidence to take another look, and immediately, Ira's boomerang explodes into the tree. The penetrating blade misses her face by a splinter. Several wood fragments and pieces of bark ricochet off her cheek, while others stick into her hair.

"Found you," Ira mutters with a taste of revenge on the edge of her tongue.

Jessica leaps up to her feet in a dead sprint for her life. Ira charges after her, ripping her boomerang out the tree as she passes by.

Saving the love of his life is a must. Robert can't take the thought of losing her. So, he does the only sensible thing. Gripping his hand tightly around the book's spine, he pulls it into his chest protecting it with all his might as he darts after her.

Before he can reach out to grab Jessica's hand, the Death Reaper darts past, knocking the book out of his hand. Black smoke devours her. Consumed into the black gloom, Death and Jessica spiral into the center skull of the book before the book can smack the ground.

"Come on, dammit. How do I get to the Impossible? What word was written on the book?" Robert lashes out in a panic.

Robert grabs the book in full sprint with Ira trailing close behind him. She comes in fast too fast for him to see it. "Need a lift?" With a wave of her hand, Ira sends a gust of wind throwing him and the book across the woods of Wolf's Eye Den like a rag doll. Viviane and Seth meet up with Ira, flying together in perfect formation after him.

Robert's back wraps around the steps of a treehouse with a moan and groan of aching hell. The excruciating impact is paralyzing. Time to man up and quench the pain. The grass crunches under his palms and knees as he crawls around to search for the book.

"Come on, where did you go?"

Viviane swoops in with a series of kicks to his ribs, knocking him back to the ground before he can stagger to his feet. Her laughs cut deep and are annoying like a hyena.

"If you wanna do something right, you got to do it yourself. It's time I end you." Vivian pulls out her electric whip and lashes it at Robert. SNAP! Dirt flies, barely missing him as he rolls out of the whip's way.

Jumping to his feet, Robert takes cover behind a tree, again dodging another crack of Viviane's whip by using the tree as a shield—bad idea.

The whip wraps around the tree, lighting it up like a raging thunderstorm, burning through it like a plasma gun. With great force, the tree swings up, and the breathtaking blow hits Robert in the chest and knocks him on his ass.

"Seth, are you gonna do anything, or just stand there?" Viviane shouts.

"Fine." Seth summons his mighty trident, raising it high in the air for the final blow. Robert hides his face with his forearms. The pure darkness is far less horrifying than observing his approachable death. It's quiet. For a moment, it's all like a dream. His eyes roll open to the cluster of red smoke that surrounds him.

"What's happening?"

Thick red smoke wraps around Robert like a blanket leaving him marveling at the sight. Although his eyes wonder around like a kid in a candy store he still remains alert at the lingering threat on the other side of the smoke.

"He has Tate's orb. Give it to me at once. Where is he? How did you?" Ira lashes out clinching her fists around her boomerangs. Her voice is deep, rumbling like an earthquake and shivering with rage. She lunges forward, launching both boomerangs through the red smoke, holstering them once they return back to her hands.

Ira, Seth, and Viviane impatiently wait for the smoke to clear. Between Seth's fidgety hands, Ira's tapping feet, and Viviane's bouncing leg, they halt only to suffer disappointment at Robert's absence.

"Looks like he's getting away," Seth says.

"Well, let's not let that happen," Ira suggests.

From inside of the smoke, it appears as if Robert is running at normal speed—but from outside the smoke, he's moving at a remarkable speed.

"HE'S MINE!" Ira growls as she takes off with a sonic boom that tears through the branches in her path.

Clumsy and clueless as a newbie at his first job, Robert loses control, zigzagging all over the woods and ricocheting off random trees like a pinball game, yelling out random obscenities on impact with each tree.

"Ah, I think I got it."

His confidence lasts a moment before plummeting into another tree, stopping him dead in his tracks. The red smoke clears as he shakes off the near-concussion.

A boomerang whooshes at him from behind, cutting through the air with each spinning rotation, and the sound reminds him of the whistling whirlwind back at the treehouse. He can remember the word that appeared as his eyes gazed at the book's worn blank pages.

"Abeamus." Robert vanishes like scattering embers before Ira's boomerang can take off his head. Red smoke whirls around him like an anxious tornado.

Robert dwindles down to near-rodent size making the trees skyrocket upward to the size of mighty mountains. A deep inhale snatches him and swallows him into the bowels of the book, and he barrels out the mouth of the Impossible's hellish skull cloud.

He forces his eyes open through the windy torrent. It roars and groans, stabbing his ears and cutting into his anxious bones. The bell dongs announcing his arrival, dinging like an annoying alarm clock that won't shut up.

The dense somber clouds become sparse, making the bell tower visible through the transparent vapor. Robert arches like a Hail Mary, staring into the darkness of Death's hood as he lands superman style next to Jessica. She's on her knees with the axe in arm's reach. The tip of the cold steel blade of Death's kusarigama pokes the back of her neck.

"You hear that bell? That's the sound of perfection. See, I knew you were coming. How 'bout you give me my orb, and I won't end your girlfriend here. Can you believe she tried to use an axe on me? Stupid bitch," Death growls.

"Fuck you. Got ya, Jess. Abeamus," Robert shouts with his hand on Jessica's shoulder. They take off like a rocket, bursting out the wordless book and back into Wolf's Eye Den before the Death Reaper can finish Jessica off with the blade of his kusarigama.

"Nooooo!" Death yells, rearing his head back toward the dense gray clouds that blankets the black sky with their weightlessness.

Seth, Viviane, and Ira are playing scavenger hunt for the book. Seth rummages through the tall grass, stopping at the blueberry bushes for a snack. Ira and Viviane walk the trails in opposite directions.

"Ah, boy, how I wish I was still alive. Well, what the heck?" Seth places a blueberry in his mouth. His lack of flesh leads to an oozy leakage of blueberry mush out of his neck hole.

"Leave the berries alone, Seth. You know our taste buds don't work anymore," Viviane says.

"But it looks so good."

Through the apertures of the hanging berries and twigs are rays of moonlight, its many beams penetrate a cluster of red smoke like lasers. The spectrum of red smoke illuminates off the beams of light to near perfection.

The night air sweeps away the red vapors only to surrender Robert and Jessica's location. Seth's teal eyes splash like crashing waves as he discovers their position. Roberts thoughts and emotions are overtaken with extreme panic leaving Jessica to be the voice of reason.

"They found us Jess. Run!"

"Baby, the book. Get the book."

Robert slams on his brakes, bringing him to a slide in the mud. Gooey slush packs into his fingernails and every wrinkle of his hand as he U-turns back for the book.

Seizing the book in his grasp, it erupts into a wiggling fit. Black smoke explodes out the center skull of the book, landing next to Seth, Ira, and Viviane.

"Looks like they pulled one over on ya," Seth says.

Death slides his cloak around his kusarigama. Its blade shines like glass. It is sharp enough to cut you even by looking at it. Chains rattle and cling as he un-holsters it from his belt.

"What do they say? An eye for an eye."

Death slings his chained kusarigama at Jessica. The cold steel chain wraps around her legs over and over again, and with a hard yank, she smacks her face along the ground, releasing a vicious groan and the axe from her grip. One pull after another, one huff and puff after another, Death drags Jessica closer and closer. The taste of grass and mud lingers on her lips and coats her teeth.

The red orb pulsates in Robert's pocket and shoots straight into his hands. "What?" The skin tone on his hands alters, appearing irritated, like a rash, while continuing to brighten and rise in temperature. Smoke ascends off his hands, abruptly combusting them into a flame.

Robert is literally holding fire in his hand! Oddly enough, what should be unbearably painful is indeed entertaining instead. Unintentionally, he propels a blast of fire in the Death Reaper's direction, catching the Reapers off-guard. The force drives Robert, sliding backward through the mud.

"Looks like someone's learning." The Death Reaper chuckles.

Sounds of rustling in the bushes draw the Reapers' attention, while Jessica unwraps the chain of Death's kusarigama from around her legs, she grabs the axe, and bolts over to Robert.

Sticks break and leaves crush under their tactical boots. The squishing mud sticks to their outsoles. Sleepy birds scatter the swaying branches as two police officers push their way through.

"I see footprints, Sarge. Do you think they killed those people and kidnapped that girl?"

"Question is, where did they hide their bodies? I'm just hoping that little girl doesn't end up being one of them."

The leading officer with his weapon aiming ahead of him also scans the woods with his flashlight. S

Approaching a group of bushes, the officer parts the twigs out of his way. An orange glow illuminates the woodlands in front of him. Coming around a sequoia tree the roar of merciless flames grabs the officers immediate attention. The officer clicks off his flashlight as he stands surprised at the blazing treehouse.

"My guess is right there."

"Shit, Sarge, we're not gonna find them now. They're nothing but dust in the wind."

The treehouse crumbles like a sugar cookie, leaving behind nothing but smoldering hickory and ashes. White smoke drifts toward heaven's gateway of navy blue like a mixture of melting blueberry ice cream with toppings of whipped cream and white sprinkles.

As they approach the flames, pieces of bone lie there amongst their ashes. The sergeant's face is dismal, emotionless, pale as a ghost at the thought of another maniac on a killing spree. His mouth can taste the plastic of his radio as it grazes his lips.

"205 to dispatch."

"Go for dispatch."

"You might want to contact the homicide detective and get them down here. I think I found more dead bodies."

"Copy, 205. Calling homicide.

"Bill, radio Jeff. Tell him to send that firetruck up here before this thing spreads."

"On it, Sarge."

Death can sense the two officers are close. With a deep inhale, he smells the sweat from their flesh and the anxiety rattling their bones.

"What's wrong, Master?" Viviane asks.

"Visitors," Death growls.

"Well, then, let's get the book and orb and get this party rolling before they get here," Seth says.

"Calm down there, Sethy-poo. We don't even know where my man is. I say we look for Tate and go after the book and orb later. It's not like we can't easily get it back."

"Master, the book's right there. They're getting away."

"Hush it, Viviane. Ira is right. We can't be seen right now. We split up. After Tate's found we meet at the rendezvous point."

POLICE

ELEVEN
SIXTH SENSE

The ambulance is a welcome sight. Its wailing sirens cut through the camp's driving path with an aggressive speed. It rocks and bounces, jarring around medical equipment in a rattling frenzy. Two chirps from the click of a walkie-talkie prevails over the cling and clang of medical equipment.

"Calling M and M, this is ambulance 719."

A disembodied voice blares through the paramedic's radio. "This is M and M. Go ahead, please."

"M and M, we have a priority trauma one for you, let me know when you can copy."

"I'm ready. Go ahead, 719."

"I have a female patient by the name of Amelia Crowe coming in, early twenties. Patient's having agonal respirations. Patient has Eosinophilic asthma. Sinus rhythm is 103. O2 stats is 88 percent. She's being bagged at this time. ETA, approximately fifteen minutes."

"Good copy, 719. We'll see you in fifteen minutes."

An oxygen concentrator pushes air that whooshes through a clear tube and into an oxygen mask over Amelia's face. She lies there on a stretcher, clammy and struggling to breathe.

"Kids—" Cough, cough. "Did they all make it out of here?"

"All the kids are fine Mrs. Crowe. Try and stay relaxed, okay?" the paramedic says.

"My hus—" Cough-cough. "My husband okay?"

"Try and stay calm."

The driver focuses ahead and remains completely oblivious of what is going on behind the ambulance. Tires shred through the mud, dipping in and out of the un-level path.

The rear view mirror vibrates, distorting Jessica's reflection.

She chases the ambulance down, jumping and waving the axe around, desperate to get the driver's attention. "Wait, wait, we need help."

Robert stops dead in his tracks, contemplating whether this is a good idea or not. He wipes the sweat off his brow while trying to catch his breath. "Jess, what are you doing? Emma's still out there."

She feels the lack of breath throughout her body. Her smoky lungs make her feel like she's drowning in the air. Squish, squish, squish, squish. Robert comforts Jessica, rubbing his hand along her back while the ambulance passes cabin one and makes a left, heading east into the avenue and exiting the camp.

Cough, cough. Jessica cries with overwhelming rage, dropping to her knees. She bloodies her pounding fists in the dirt path against the gleam of red-glowing brake lights as they fade off in the shadows of the camp's exit.

"There goes our chance."

"Our chance for what?"

"For getting out of here. I don't know how much longer I can take this."

"You got to take a breather. Emma needs us right now."

"I know. I know. But what if that was our only chance? Them crazy psychos may never let us leave."

Jessica stares at him vulnerably, her hands pressed into her head, ruffling clumps of hair between her fingers. Tears roll down her face, her heart is broken into pieces. Her wet amber eyes blossom like heavenly flowers, but they are rudely interrupted by an overbearing voice and the reflection of two individuals in her eyes. The voice conveys authority, feeling like the smack of a hammer against a nail.

"You got that half-right. You will be leaving but in the back of our police car. Now, hands in the air!"

Robert aids Jessica to her feet. Blood rolls off her knuckle and drips onto her burnt leg. They lock eyes anxiously, raising their hands in the air arguing with one another in a whisper.

"See? We should have gone back when we had the chance."

"We didn't do anything wrong, Jess."

They are held there at gunpoint by the two officers. The leading officer is a sergeant, much older than the other one. He's in his forties, fifties maybe, with stubble on his face as course as sandpaper. He stands firm and tall, impossible to move, like a statue. Every part of him screams power and valor. He holds a shotgun, motioning the younger officer forward.

The other officer, who's his junior by at least a decade or two, keeps his training manual available in his pocket. He wears a crisper uniform, its edges thin as paper. His clean-shaven face and ready-to-go attitude speak loudly on a resume, but his indecisive choices are far from wise. Steadily and cautiously, the officer moves forward with his handgun drawn at them.

"Don't you dare move. Keep your hands up. Turn around, lady, arms out, and widen your stance. Pat them down, Bill."

"What's your name?" the sergeant demands, holding the barrel of his shotgun at Jessica while Bill pats her down.

"I'm Jessica Hill, and he's Robert Lee, sir."

"Okay, now shut your mouth. Keep your head forward and don't move."

"Sorry, Officer, but we did nothing wrong."

"Yeah, that's what they all say, lady. Ohhh, what do we have here?" The officer spots the red axe at Jessica's feet. He gawks at it with a glint of pride in his eyes. He waves it like a proud puppy at the sergeant who retrieves their toy.

"What were you using this for? Don't tell me you're chopping wood at four in the morning. You haven't killed anyone with it, have ya?"

"Nobody. I swear, officer. Look, there's no blood on it."

"Doesn't mean nothing. You could have wiped off the evidence. Let me see that, Bill."

"Here, Sarge. Now, hubby, it's your turn. Spread those legs. Don't be shy now. What you holding there?"

"Don't take that, please. It's important."

"Don't take that book, it's important," Bill blurts sarcastically.

"What's so important about the stupid book? Are you guys in some sort of cult or something? Did you murder those innocent men with your witchcraft shenanigans?"

"No, of course not. Jessica and I are harmless."

"Look, Sarge, darn things empty. Not a single word in the whole thing."

"Just toss the darn thing. It's useless." Bill gives the book a toss, and it lands only feet in front of Robert and Jessica.

"Sir, I'm a teacher at Happy Oaks Middle School and there's a girl, she's one of our seventh graders. Her name is Emma Moon, and she's been kidnapped."

"So, you're a teacher who murders people and kidnaps children. Wow, looks like you'll never teach again."

"In prison, maybe."

"Good one, Sarge."

"See, the police officers here in Grym has a pretty good reputation. We don't want to ruin that by having the F.B.I involved, but we will if it means finding that girl you two are hiding."

Jessica sighs with full understanding that the officers aren't going to believe anything they say. Who would? The recent events that have taken place on what is most likely the worst day of their lives are considered a lie, a dream, and make-believe.

"It was Tate that took her," Robert blurts out.

"Who's this Tate fella? You're not making him up, are you?" Bill asks.

"He wears a red cloak and can manipulate fire, okay? Now, can you let us go?" Jessica says.

A sudden glow comes from Robert's shirt pocket. Jessica notices the glow and glances over at him, making subtle eye gestures to warn him of the glow.

'Manipulate fire.' Haha. That's a new one. Let me guess. He can fly, too?" Bill giggles.

"Actually, yeah, he can," Jessica says.

"All right, Jessica, enough of the ridiculous fairy tales. Arms out, Rob, and widen your stance. Manipulating fire—that's the best story I've ever heard." Bill performs a pat-down on Robert, first sliding his hands along his sleeves.

Robert bites his lips, slamming his eyes shut.

The orb may be his way of saving Emma. If the officer takes it away—or, worse, if they go to jail Emma could be lost forever.

The pat-down seems to last forever. Robert can feel beads of sweat rolling down his forehead as Bill's hand approach's his shirt pocket.

He slides his hand across Robert's shirt pocket, stopping as his fingers bump into the orb. "Well, well, what do we have here?"

"What is it?" the sergeant asks.

"It's a useless stone. Ah look there's a little bulb in it to make it glow."

Bill walks the orb back to his sergeant, and they hold a private conversation. It's quiet not a sound but their racing hearts, the orchestra of crickets chirping, and the grass and branches rustling in the wind. Jessica and Robert glance at each other out of the corners of their eyes with nerves too anxious to turn their necks.

"What do we do, Robert? We're not going to jail, and I need a shower."

"We can't do anything."

"Shut the fuck up. Stop the damn whispering," demands the sergeant.

Pieces of burning ash light up the sky, a remarkable sunset-orange traveling like migrating butterflies and nesting in a pile of leaves that rest on the edge of Wolf's Eye Den. The jumble of leaves becomes a burn pile before Robert and Jessica can react.

"Officer, you gotta turn around!"

"Officer, listen to him, please look!"

"I thought I told you two to shut the heck up," the officer demands.

A breeze snakes, through ruffling the grass where the book lays. A tremor befalls the book, and its front cover thrusts open. Its pages heave one way to the next.

"Babe, look."

The episode of supernatural hocus-pocus ceases at the book's middle page. Robert leans in, careful not to draw any attention to himself.

"What's it doing now?"

"Shit, Bill, this thing's got to be worth some money. Looks like I'm getting that boat after all. What do you want?"

"Our house could use central air."

"Out of all the things you can buy, you want central air? That one's almost as good as those dumb bozos claiming their innocence."

Bill faces his sergeant, his eyes expanding like a balloon reaching its limits. His blood boils, his face twitches, and his jaw smacks the ground while Jessica and Robert are frozen to the ground, stuck in fight-or-flight syndrome.

The sergeant gasps for any ounce of oxygen, making the most chilling gurgling sounds. His face shifts colors to cherry red as his hand lunges for the four bony digits that wrap around his neck.

POW! The sergeant dispenses a round from his shotgun, a mere warning shot as the Fire Deaders scorching hot fingers melt through his flesh. Blood bubbles out from under the Deaders grasp as he collapses to the ground.

Bill aims his 9-mm Smith and Wesson at the head of the Fire Deader, unloading multiple rounds with a war cry. One round gouges its skull digging deep and expelling bone fragments like a saw blade.

The second and third rounds miss, while the fourth round runs clear through its forehead. One orbital hole is interwoven with cobwebs and a family of fire ants and sun spiders that burrow into their new home inside the bullet hole.

It lowers its skull, unveiling a menacing aura that penetrates his nerves with a shuddering stare that could eat a person's soul. Like the flick of a lighter, the Deader combusts into a flame.

Robert hunkers down. One knee at a time, he creeps toward the axe that lays snug against the sergeant's bleeding corpse.

"Robert, get back here. Are you crazy?"

Bill lowers his aim toward the red glow, and with the pull of his finger, the bullet propels at the Deader, ceasing before the flames. Its brass gets red-hot bringing it to a bubble. The round melts like cheese coming to a sizzle as the brass strings dribble into the puddle of dirty rainwater.

Bill gulps, beads of sweat sliding down his cheek. He can taste the sweltering flames on his lips. Adjusting his grip, he switches hands to tolerate the steel handle's blistering heat.

Jessica scans the area for a way to help her fiancé first the sergeant's dead corpse, then the shotgun lying next to him, a puddle, and the axe in Robert's grasp.

Light on her feet, Jessica maneuvers over to the sergeant's shotgun. Swift as an eagle, she scoops the shotgun up, cradling the warm steel barrel against her chest as she stops alongside Robert.

Ready with his axe above his head, the fine tine steel blade facing down, Robert drops his shoulders and lowers his elbows. His grip loosens around the wooden handle, lowering it with a *thump* into the mud.

The Fire Deader jerks its head at Robert and Jessica, revealing poor Bill burned crisper than a burnt chicken and collapsing to the ground, breaking chunks of charred flesh that crumble around his fried corpse while holding the fire orb between his melted fingertips.

"Shoot it, Jess."

The shotgun rattles under her trembling grip. Her bangs dangle in front of her eyes as she tries to focus through the blur.

She remembers what her father taught her years ago when she was a little girl.

> *"Hold this end tight against your shoulder, take your safety off. Aim the sight at the target. When you're ready...fire. Don't forget to cock it after each time you pull the trigger," Jessica's father says.*
>
> *"Like this, Daddy?"*
>
> *"That's right. You have to stop shaking, though. Stay very still."*

The voice of Jessica's father drifts away like a dust cloud. Her trembling hands become steadfast, folding her fingers around the shotgun's grip to cease the gun's rattling parts. Her golden hair slow-dances like ballerinas on the ballet barre, kicking in the air one moment and back down the next as a huff leaves her lips.

Her vision is a smear, like a blurry oil painting of colors running together, searching for their rightful place. A consuming velvety black surrounds four glowing crimson smears that merge into two, and glaring as bright as brake lights.

It's two Fire Deader's. Both have red smoke circling around their red ectoplasmic hearts. Jessica squeezes the trigger, but she's unable to steady the gun its force flips the barrel upward, sending the round in a spiraling trajectory over the Deaders' heads.

"You missed, Jess. You gotta cock it."

"It won't do it. I can't pull the fucking thing back," Jess babbles slamming the pump toward her as hard as she can neglecting to press the slide release button.

One Deader nods to the other, and they split up, circling around them like wolves circling their prey. The axe slurps as Robert pulls it from the sloppy mud. The Deader on his side gets a little too close. The axe comes down with enough force to drive it into the Fire Deader's skull. The flames are like many hypnotized cobras, swaying back and forth, licking under his arms. He releases the axe in sheer pain, leaving it in its skull.

"Ow, dammit. Jess, give me the gun."

Click, clack. "I got it," Jessica blurts out as she cocks the pump back and forward. She pulls the trigger. The loud pow scares Robert into turning his head and closing his eyes. The empty shotgun case ejects from the loading port. Her eyes blink as the smoke drifts past them.

Flecks of burning ash trickle down over them, brushing along their flesh like an odyssey of landing phoenixes. The remaining Deader is rather close; Robert can feel the intense heat off its burning bones. Robert draws back as the Deader lunges in scaring Robert into tripping over his own feet and falling on his back.

One hand after another Robert pushes himself away from the Fire Deader with the book still in his grasp. His hands shuffle in the slippery mud while crab crawling away from the menacing dead freak.

The books cover flings open fluttering its pages stopping towards the center like some weird sinister magic trick. Robert's eyes feast down over the still pages. The word 'Transvoro' flashes on the page like an even better magic trick. His eyes widen sparking an idea in his already cluttered mind.

"Say it and the orb will absorb its flame." The book whispers.

"Jess, throw me the orb."

Jessica hustles over to the dead officer, peeling the orb from Bill's sticky flesh. With a toss Robert catches the orb. The Deader lunges in the air at him, and before the Fire Deader lands on him.

"Transvoro," Robert commands, closing his eyes so tight his eyebrows tickle his cheek.

Robert evades the leaping Deaders vicious attack. Its flame condenses to a burning ball of light with an iridescence of every fiery color. It spirals in pulsating beats like the ball of fire is fighting against the orbs pulling force. The orbs power is too much for the fireball as it draws it in with a beaming flash.

The flameless deader is very upset its fire is now quenched by the orb that it charges toward Jessica with a shaking rage.

Click, clack. Jessica racks the shot gun. Boom! A confetti of ash sprinkles down over them. A disbelief in the moment. A moment of peace within their minds is rejected by the their trembling bodies.

Robert can feel tiny pecks like snowflakes kissing his skin. Smoke escapes the barrel, whirling out of existence with each relieving breath. Jessica's eyes roll left, verifying Robert's condition. She releases a breath of relief that blows smooth as a gentle breeze. A smirk springs upon her lips as Robert opens his eyes. The fall of a million specks of burning ashes glide over them delicately.

"Wow, look at us. We're a mess."

"I know. We're covered. Can this night get any worse? All I want is a shower and a change of dry clothes. Is that too much to ask?"

The blur of flashing red lights float up Wolf's Eye Den, bringing to light the silhouettes of the trees.

A thump from a firetruck door is followed by a rush of panicky firefighters scrambling to their hoses and advancing toward the blazing cabin like knights amidst a battle with a mighty dragon.

A loud, anxious, and hoarse voice catapults across Wolf's Eye Den and over by the walking trail's tree line, where Robert and Jessica are.

"We can't keep up with the fire. The truck's out of water; there should be a lake we can siphon from just east of here, but we have to hurry. The fire's spreading and getting out of control. Call for another truck."

The burning cabin smells of a bonfire. The earthy aroma of hickory wood mixes with a sharp acrid smell of melting plastics. Glass crashes like tiny explosions in the middle of a battle that travels past them like whizzing bullets.

The cabin's smoke rises toward the somber nightly kingdom. The moon is the queen of the night, dawning her luminous crown of vivid orange, peering over the clouds with the gleam of her harvest eyes. The villainous clouds retreat from the velvety black battlefield and the burning cabin's rising smoke below.

You hear that Jess? We got to go. There are two dead officers here, and we can't be here when they show up. If we are, we're done. Now, come on, they'll be here any minute."

"So what? We can't just leave them here. You're a better man than that."

"What you expect me to do? Let the firefighters handle it."

"Use their radio, call for an ambulance. Something. I can't believe the shit we're doing. I never thought in my wildest dreams. Uhhh." Jessica stomps her foot, glancing at Robert with hopes he'll change his mind. "Fine, just know I think this is horse shit."

She searches the sergeant's pockets, pulling out shotgun rounds and lint. Full of guilt and maybe regret, she drops the cold brass shotgun rounds into her hand. Robert takes note of the resilience in her eyes as he makes his way over to Bill's dead body.

"Good idea."

Robert takes two extra magazines from Bill's duty belt. Jessica reloads three rounds into the sergeant's shotgun, racking the pump into place.

"Look, Jess, I know you're worried, but we have nothing to worry about. We didn't do anything; we're innocent here. We can't go to jail if we've done nothing wrong."

"So, what about Emma, Mr. Smarty Pants? How are we supposed to find her?"

"Sad thing is, we may never find her. I hate to say it, but it's up to the police now. With the ambulances gone and more police on their way, we should make our way to M and M hospital ourselves. We cut through the trails. We can stay better hidden that way. The police see us, and we're done."

"I just can't leave her out there. She's gotta be terrified."

"I know, Jess, but there's no telling where she is. There's not much we can do."

"Well, don't forget that dumb book, Rob."

The ground grumbles like a starving lions gut when he's ready to feast. The dirt recedes to loose particles swallowing both officers into the ground like quicksand.

A drawing appears on the book's page, showing the Impossible cemetery again, and its entrance-archway reads, *The Ones Who Tried.* Two new caskets emerge from the ground in black ink. One reads *Officer Bill Watts*, while the other reads *Sergeant Pat Peterson.*

"Take a look at this crazy shit," Robert says.

"Is that those cops? Creepy. Come on, we have to go. They're coming," Jess says.

Robert grabs the book as they make their way into the forest toward the trails of Heaven's Willow before the firefighters can notice them.

The forest is dark and dense, with little light passing through. Robert and Jessica's legs are moving with caution, unsure of what exactly their feet are crunching on. Their eyes wander in all directions searching for a touch of light. The extreme eeriness is enough to make their minds conjure up the most absurd thoughts of horror. Are the trees alive? Will they grab them with their creepy long fingers? What kind of creatures are out there stalking them, ready to tear into them at any moment?

Cedar trees are a coffee-brown with bark like moldy beef jerky. Their overhanging limbs shadow the forest with little space for the moon's light to shine through. A separate light in the far distance swoops and curves around the forest like Wonder Woman's lasso, but they first must make it through the void of the forest.

"I can't see anything? You don't have a flashlight do ya Rob?"

"No, not with me."

"It'll be very helpful if we had one."

"I know, Jess, but the closest one is a mile that way in the shed by cabin one. I'm not going out there for that."

A crisp ethereal voice as light as a feather speaks out from the book. "You wouldn't need a lighter if you knew the right command. It's obvious the orb likes you."

"Crap. What the hell? You gotta stop doing that, or at least give us a warning." Jessica shrieks, remaining vigilant of its spastic antics.

"Sorry, my bad. I don't get much opportunity to talk to people," the voice says.

"Who are you, anyway, and how are you doing that?" Robert asks.

"It's not beneficial for me or you to know who I am. I don't really feel like explaining it. We would be here all night. Anyway, you and I have the same goals. I think we should focus on them. First off, did the orb glow for you?" the voice from the book asks.

"Yeah, it's fully glowing right now," Robert says.

"That means it's fully charged. The slower the glow pulsates, the closer to powerless the orb is, until there's no glow at all. This means you're out of power. The orb will charge itself over time, so you don't have to worry about being out of power for too long."

"So how do you use the orb?" Jessica asks.

"How to use the orb? There's really no way to answer that. The orb has a mind of its own. There are commands, of course, but I don't know all of them. Oddly enough, the orb knows. If the orb likes you, it forms a bond, I guess basically reading your thoughts, so the commands aren't needed, but it's difficult to do. At least, it was for someone I know. Well, at the beginning, anyway," the voice instructs.

They patiently wait for more advice, but there's nothing else, not a single sound but the chirping crickets and the rustling trees.

"How am I supposed to cast a light out here? Speak, dumbass," Robert demands, tapping the orb onto the book's front cover.

"That's not gonna do anything," Jessica says.

"Hello, can you hear me? Could you please light the way for us? Hello?" Robert asks.

"The actual command is lux via, if that helps. I suggest you stop the name calling. I am helping you, by the way."

"Lux via." The flesh on Robert's hand burns red, like a sunburn.

His hand hair sizzles, combusting into a scorching flame. The surrounding shadows scurry like rats, cowering behind the trees, waiting for the flame to go out.

"How does that not hurt?"

"Weird, huh?" Robert stands there, amazed, rotating his hand around to capture its burning glory.

The ball of flames illuminates the forest with its aurora of orange light. The light is dim, but there is enough of it to pave the way to the trails ahead.

Jessica gives Robert an elbow nudge and a point at the most picturesque landscape they've ever seen. Several scattered solar lanterns line the walking trails. Their wooden posts support a mantle resembling a cabin.

"Whoa. I forgot how beautiful it was here. I haven't seen this part of the camp since you asked me to marry you." Jessica beams with a sparkle in her eye.

"I guess I never took the time to really enjoy it. My dad sure had an eye for this stuff. The heart of Heaven's Willow, the place I proposed to you, is north of here. We're taking the trails east."

Jessica lashes out in a coughing fit. She gags and gasps like a car that won't start. She hunches over, fighting for air and hacking up blood.

"Jess, Jess. What's wrong?"

'm okay, Robert. I'm fine." Jessica wipes the blood from the corner of her mouth as her lungs inflate and deflate to normal rhythm.

"C'mon. If we keep moving east, we'll reach the camps entrance sign in thirty to forty minutes. We can get to the main road from there."

As Jessica and Robert continue their journey through the lit trails of Heaven's Willow, Robert continues to light the way with the ball of fire consuming his hand.

Open and aware of their surroundings, they take each step with caution. A steady rainfall begins to drip from leaf to leaf, creating beats to a majestic melody, which is rather soothing and peaceful.

Robert's feet feel heavy, crushing the twigs under them with random steps. He takes a breath, and the musky smell of saturated bark from decrepit hollow trees alters into a cringing groan and shriek that is as threatening as the venomous arachnids inhabiting within there.

"Emma! Emma!" their voices call out, splitting the night's earthly air.

"Emma. You can come out. It's Ms. Hill and Mr. Lee, honey."

The majestic melody of the rain's tempo begins to pick up. The forest is dense, much thicker than it was. Pine trees begin to line the trails on both sides.

At their feet is the reflection of them in a puddle, distorted by the many raindrops coming to meet it and a splash that dissipates, subsiding into a rippling effect. The distorting reflection veers away when bony phalanges emerge from the puddle.

"Emma, please come out. We want to take you home."

Jessica stops dead in her tracks and looks ahead as Deaders rise from different puddles all around them. "Robert, are you seeing this?" Robert is certainly unaware until one's bones crunch under his foot.

The tall grass camouflaging them made it difficult to notice their existence. He mistakenly takes a whiff of the putrid air. The foul odor of molded bone and beyond-expired food stuck in between the crevasses of countless cavities merges with the mildew and fungus that populate the vines and moss wrapping around them.

"They can't be Fire Deader's," Robert says, holding the book at his side while his other hand remains in flame by at his chest. A breeze passes through like a distant memory blowing out the flame in his hand.

"What do you mean?" Jessica asks.

"They look just like them, but where's the fire at?" Robert says.

The Deaders around them all take on the same appearance, but instead of being covered in fire, they are soaking wet, with layers of vines and moss burrowing into their rotten bones, fusing together as if they are one with each other. Some of them have pulsating teal orbs glowing in their sternums.

"Hey, person in the book, we need you. Now's a better time than any. Fine we'll just call them Water Deader's if that's what they even are." Robert shakes the book with a last-ditch effort for some needed support.

"Very good. You know you're lucky you have me. Whatever I can do to help. These Water Deader's come from the water; they're covered in moss and vines, which are very dangerous by the way. Unlike the Fire Deader's red heart some of them have a teal heart. These are more powerful and much harder to take down," the book says.

"We get it. So, how do you kill them?" Jessica asks.

"How did you kill the Fire Deaders?" the book asks.

"Well, I have this bad boy. You have your gun. And did I mention the fire orb?" Jessica says, holding up her shotgun.

"I guess that will have to do. Are you ready?" Robert racks the slide back on the dead officer's 9 mm handgun. Their backs press up against one another like wanted gun-slingers ready to take out the evil mob of Water Deaders.

Jessica racks her shotgun. "Let's crack some skulls." She dashes forward, gun aimed at the nearest Water Deader's' head. She pulls the trigger as each full rotation of the twelve-gauge round propels toward the Deader's head.

The skull shatters and a nasty green water-like algae oozes out the Deader's head. Jessica moves ahead a few steps. Clink clank. She takes another shot at the same Deader. Water splatters in Jessica's face from its wounds, driving it off its feet and sending it flying backwards into a gathering of bushes.

Robert marches forward with prominence, dispersing three rounds at the closest Water Deader, tearing off its jaw and shattering it along the ground. The next round lands dead center in the next Deader's blackened eye hole and exits the back of its head, giving it no chance as it cracks its skull on the ground.

More Water Deaders come at them from all directions. All they can do is back up one step at a time, reserving every moment of their lives. Their shoulders bump into each other like mad rams slamming their heads into anything that steps on their territory. They jolt forward, spooking the bejesus out of each other.

"How did you do?" Robert asks.

"Besides my hair being a mess, I'm doing well so far. How about you?" Jessica asks.

"Actually, it was too easy," Robert responds.

The three Deaders they shot ease their way up to their feet, leaving behind a shattered jaw and their bone fragments as they creep back into the circle of Deaders.

"What? I shot it through its eye. That should have killed it!" Robert declares.

"Guess not," Jessica says.

"Now what, Jess?" Robert asks.

"We keep fighting. We don't give up on each other," Jessica pleads, loading three rounds into her shotgun, loudly racking the pump back, making a sharp ratcheting noise.

Thunder rumbles in the gloomy skies, summoning back the gloomy clouds to plot their revenge against the shimmering stars.

The clouds attack with a flash of white light that strikes the reflection of stars in the puddle ahead, scaring both Robert and Jessica to their knees. The black fades as they uncover their eyes, staggering back to their feet. It intrigues them to witness two Deaders with white light that bolts through them like flickering Christmas lights.

They poof into a splash of wet ash, pitter-pattering along the mud below. Their ashes descend into a tango onto the Water Deaders' remains setting sail across the newly formed pond.

Robert thrusts forward, scrambling to keep his balance. His feet paddle with urgency as if he is drowning. He can smell the woodsy citrus as he nearly falls onto the fallen trunk of a cedar tree.

A Water Deader tackles him to his back, knocking the gun from his grip. Sloppy mud squishes along his back as he and the Deader tussle on the ground.

Putrid saliva spills out its mouth, sopping Robert's face. With one eye squinting and the other peeking into its darkened sockets, he clenches its forearm, thrusting it away from him.

"Get off of him." Jessica fires a round through the Deaders skull, knocking it off of Robert and sending it tumbling down the hill. "Are you okay?" She rushes to his aid, reaching in to help him up.

They lock hands; he's covered in ooey-gooey mud squishing between his fingers. He reaches for her, but the hill's edge is so slick their feet can't steady themselves in the sludge as they fight to find an ounce of grip.

Slippery as ice, they tumble down the muddy hill like a turkey on a slip 'n' slide and splashing into the canoeing lake below.

Leaves and lily pads float along the pond, which is heavily populated with crazed gnats. Frogs croak, camouflaging themselves under the duckweed. The head of a bullfrog lifts briefly above the surface, scaring it back into the murky water at the sound of Jessica and Robert bursting out of the water with heavy gasps. They stand with the water at their knees.

"Eww, I hate the water. This better be the last time I step in a pool, a pond, a lake, or the ocean. Ohhhhh."

"I'm so sorry," Jessica giggles at Robert's expense, the cold silver engagement ring embracing her ring finger, lays against her chin as she covers her mouth.

"Sorry, Jess, I'm just terrified of water."

"I know. You're so cute when you freak out. Ohhhh, look at us. We're a mess. Come here, babe. Let me clean off your face."

She slides her hand along his brow, smearing the mud across his face. She tickles his nose for a giggle knocking tiny clumps of mud off its tip.

The harvest moon peeks above the gloomy clouds, beaming its smiling rays of orange upon them. Thunder gently massages the dark somber sky of gray, black, and white, the hour whence dreaming begins.

A fall breeze blows Jessica's luscious golden hair into artistic swirls as Robert braces her cheek. The blushing stars bury themselves behind the murky clouds, shining their heavenly light so bright it escapes their puffy edges.

He lowers his lips to hers, caressing her mouth in a lingering but gentle kiss. He lowers his hand around her waist, pressing her body closer to his. Their lips separate and their eyelids slowly lift, unveiling the whites of their eyes, and in the reflection of Jessica's eyes are two Deaders.

"We're not done, Jess. Look, up top."

Both Deaders tumble downhill, their bones thudding and cracking along the dirt's decline, ending with an inevitable splash in the lake behind them. It's quiet, with not a single sound but the rush of blood flowing in their ears. Even the croaking frogs cower at the bottom of the lake with their mouths sealed.

"Oh, shit."

"What is it, Jess?"

Jessica searches frantically around the bottom of the water for the shotgun. "The shotgun. I had it. I must have dropped it when we landed in the water. Looks like you lost the book too."

Robert stares at his bare hands with astonishment. He gazes at the water, wanting desperately to dive in and search for the book, but the threat of the Deaders grows by the second.

"Come on, forget about it. It's not safe here anymore. Let's get out of the water."

The water splashes around them and onto the canoe's dock with each driving thrust forward, exhausting every ounce of endurance they have. Their legs feel heavy, like they're submerged in concrete.

Splash after splash, they make it to the lake's shoreline with the Deaders on their trail. Water pours off their bodies, their hands brush through the algae stuck to their clothes as they stagger away to create distance from the Deader's.

Their hands lose strength, their muscles ache and burn, and they begin twitching like pounding drums. Their arms soon buckle under their weight, collapsing to the ground like bags of potatoes.

The recent tumble downhill has left fractures in the Deaders' radial and fibula bones. They jitter and rattle as they shuffle their way closer and closer to them.

Lightning expresses its anger in the night's void, shaking the Water Deaders' rattling bones into a split-second decision to liquefy into a crashing wave. Their faces take shape in the rushing waves, rising higher and higher, ready to consume their bodies, never to be found again. Robert and Jessica crawl backward alongside the wooden dock in the shallow lake to escape its wrath.

A bright flash paints the camp white before lightning whips a bolt into the lake. Voltage zigzags across the lake, zapping through the wave of Water Deaders, dissipating droplets of water and wet ash back into the lake.

Rolling to their backs, the feeling of relief immediately encompasses Robert and Jessica while they release a sharp exhale and a welcoming giggle that alters into a nervous laughter.

Another Deader in fact, the first Deader Jessica shot down the hill creeps out of the lake. As stealthy as a navy seal, water dribbles down its cracked skull, pushing fragments of loose broken bone down its cheek and silently into the lake.

Revenge lingers on its algae-covered skull with evil in its blackened eyes, which are potent as venom. The Water Deader smirks as it makes its stealthy descent back into the rippling waters.

"I can't believe that just happened."

"Tonight is a little overwhelming. I'm starting to regret even coming here."

"Well, we can't stop now. I just feel so bad for Emma and what she must be going through right now. You don't think she-"

"Don't say it, Jess. Today's already been really hard. I can't fathom the thought of it."

The Deader's cold, bloodless fingers re-emerge to the surface like a lethal shark, and it lurches its vicious grip onto Jessica's leg, dragging her inch by inch back into the water.

"Robert!"

He flips around like a canoe in the rapids, lunging for her hand, but all he can catch is the air between his fingers. Vines and moss grow off the forearm of the Water Deader at an impressive rate. The vines and moss pierce Jessica's leg, digging deep into her flesh. She stiffens her limbs as the vines twirl around her bones, pinching her nerves. Fear paralyzes her vocal cords while sheer horror hinders her airway.

Forearm over forearm, Robert fights through the sloppy mud, crawling closer and closer to Jessica. Before the Water Deader can fully drag her into the water, he lunges forward, sliding through the sludge. Tiny rocks wedged into the ground scrape his mud-smeared forearm as his hand slips into hers, holding her on the shoreline.

"The vines. Get them out of me!" Jessica's eyes bulge out of her sockets, fighting to find the air to scream.

"What's wrong?"

"My leg!"

The pain is agonizing, and her screams intensify like an approaching train horn. Robert lifts his leg up, kicking and thrusting his Brahma boots into the Water Deader's skull over and over again, breaking its grip off Jessica's leg and knocking it into the lake.

Robert doesn't see the very awkward situation taking place at the tip of Jessica's nose neglecting to recognize the dull shades of gray expanding across her face like a withering flower.

Robert manages to gain the win on the tug of war match, and with a firm tug, he pulls Jessica out of the shallow water. The vine in her leg wriggles like an angry snake, wrapping itself around her leg, and begins to squeeze.

"Hurry, Robert!"

The overwhelmingly intense pressure of survival leaves Jessica desperate for an answer. Her mind becomes a slideshow of flashbacks, leading to a very important one.

Back at Wolf's Eye Den, she was pinned down with the Fire Deader over her. Jessica gazes into the void of the Fire Deader's eye hole as she over powers it, pivoting the axe's handle and pick under the Deader's heart.

With murder in his eyes and confidence in his walk, Robert gives it one final message. "Ashes to ashes, dust to dust." The axe's pick impales the Fire Deader's heart as Robert thrusts his foot into its spine, and immediately, it combusts, disintegrating to burning ashes.

"The heart. Shoot it in the heart!" Jessica yells.

He slips his hand toward his waist. The cold steel handle of the handgun grinds like sandpaper against the webbing of his hand as he firmly grips it.

He rips the handgun from his waist, trying to pick off the Deaders' glowing teal heart. Waving the gun around is easy. Hitting a moving target is not so much. Pow, pow, pow. The squirming Deader is too hard to hit.

The 9mm's sight stares deep into the teal ectoplasmic heart of the Water Deader, and with a deep inhale, Robert pulls the trigger. POW, POW. Both rounds propel through the Deader's heart, bursting it like a balloon and spreading a burst of wet teal ash pitter-pattering along the lake. Robert can't help but to peer intently at Jessica.

"Why are you looking at me like that?" Jessica blurts out, tilting her head quizzically.

"Your face. It's it's." Robert ventures as if he's afraid to finish his sentence. He blinks quickly, shaking his head, hoping to ward off the cruel tricks his eyes are giving him.

Jessica winces with a groaning cry. "My leg still hurts. Can you get it out?"

Part of the vine still protruding out from her leg, slinks around like a water snake and continues to seep out blood. Robert takes a grip of the slimy vine, also wrapping it around his wrist. Jessica bites down on a nearby twig, tasting the bark sticking between her teeth, chomping down hard enough to crack a tooth.

He grips the vine with all his might. He tugs and tugs and tugs, but the pain is too much for Jessica to bear. She screams and groans. Each tug is as unbearable as a blade piercing her flesh.

The orb pulsates in the pocket of Robert's work shirt. The vibration gathers his attention, and he thinks of how they were lit in the first place. The command Lux Via echoes in his mind, and his hand glows a bright orange, as hot as lava. The heat makes his forehead sweat. The vine is squirming like a cowering snake to get away from the scorching heat.

Its green skin chars to the darkest black, forcing it to retreat out of Jessica's leg, bringing about a pool of oozing blood.

"Ewww, so-so-so gross. That's a lot-lot-lot of blood," Jessica stammers, dropping to her back to conceal her eyes from her leg wound.

"This is going to hurt."

"What are you going to do Robert?"

"Stay still, I'm going to try and cauterize it."

"The hell you are!"

With the point of his finger, Robert moves closer and closer to Jessica's seeping leg wound. She bites down on the collar of her shirt, digging her fingers into the dirt in an unforgiving squirm.

Her flesh surrounding the open wound reddens to a blister. Blood boils and sizzles as she lurches in a blood curdling scream.

"I'm done, I'm done. You're good, Jess. You okay?"

"Ow, Shit. Yeah, I'm good. Thank you thank you." Jessica groans.

Robert tears off the bottom left side of his work shirt, wrapping it tightly around her wound.

"Here, this should help."

"Thanks, babe."

"Come on, darlin'. Let's get you cleaned up."

Robert assists a limping Jessica over to the lake, where they wash up. Cupping the cold water in their hands, they slurp till their thirst is quenched. The taste of bitter water lingers on their tongues and dribbles down their chin. Soaked towels scatter around the shoreline, while life jackets left out by the last group of irresponsible teachers waft across the rippling waters.

Subsequently to a series of burbles, the lake regurgitates the wordless book. The moon's gleam over the book shimmers like a spotlight over the mirror-like lake. The gentle ripples glide the book over to Jessica and Robert, who are unaware it is sailing in their direction.

The book knocks into the canoe that's tied around the dock before skimming into the shoreline, flicking the grass as it anchors down next to Jessica. Her eyes close, using her shirt to dry her face.

A soft voice lingers like a gliding leaf, wafting as if gravity doesn't exist. Its words come delicate one second and piercing your eardrums the next. "They're coming."

"Did you say something?" Jessica asks.

"No, that wasn't me," Robert responds.

A gust comes as a warning, soaring down like an eagle and zips past the book. The front cover explodes open, slinging the pages from one side to the other like shrapnel.

"Robert, you seeing this?"

"I thought it was at the bottom of the lake."

"Looks like it found us."

"What are you trying to say? We know you can talk. Speak, you stupid book."

Ink forms while they try and decrypt the mystery forming on the page. Their eyes squint, and Robert scratches his head as Jessica rolls her lips. They pry their eyes open as the picture becomes more recognizable. It's a perfect snapshot of Robert and Jessica.

"Wait a second, Jess. Is this us?"

"What is that above us?"

Above them are two smoke trails arching over their heads like rainbows. Apprehensively anxious, their heads turn around leisurely, like a curious owl. Fear boils in the pits of their stomachs like sizzling grease, popping like popcorn through their veins.

Unaware and a few feet away, a single strand of grass standing tall and proud loses its green color, which fades to a dull gray, shriveling to non-existence.

Thunder shakes the cloudy night skies, giving light to Seth and Viviane zooming over them like rockets, unaware of Robert and Jessica below them like the picture predicts.

ra found Tate. Off to the rendezvous point," Viviane says.

"What's a rendezvous point?" Seth asks.

The teal and purple smoke vanishes into the shadows of the wooded trails ahead of Robert and Jessica. Following the reapers disappearance is a clap of thunder and a hammering rainfall. Both Robert and Jessica gander up at the sky as if they can somehow tell the rain to stop.

Come on. Let's get out of here before another one of them sees us."

The drawing of them fades away, and on the opposite page, a different ink drawing emerges. This one is of a Water Deader. Its ink dissolves to ash, swirling into the air taking a nosedive for the lake.

A flashing teal glow illuminates the lake and canoeing area, expanding at an incredible rate. Tucking their heads into their shoulders, they slam their eyes shut to shield them from the blinding light, which quickly dwindles back into the darkness. A slight touch of dizziness latches onto them like a blood-sucking mosquito.

"Jess, Jess."

The pressure in her brain feels like a bomb that's about to explode. Robert, her dear Robert, yells at her, but the volume is barely recognizable. Although his voice is quite faint, the noise drives her insane. Each word makes her body ache. She closes her eyes and counts to ten.

"I got the book. We're safe now. Seth and Viviane are gone. We have to find shelter. It's pouring out here."

Her chest rises with a deep inhale. Both lungs go to work, like a train engine chugging along the steep incline of a mountain. Her fuel is running on its last drop as she fights for more with a wheeze.

"It it's. har hard to breathe."

"You all right? Are you able to walk? There's an empty cabin up ahead. Can you make it?"

Reading his lips is no longer a need. The sweet sound of his soothing voice gently enters her ears like a fall leaf drifting onto still waters. Her eyes scream with agony as her head bows, letting her sopping-wet hair screen her eyes. She holds her ribs, taking in deep breaths; the oxygen flows into her airway and bloodstream, jump-starting her lungs into full power. She answers with a nod, wrapping her arm around his shoulder.

"Okay. Okay. I'm okay. Let's go."

"Come on, let's get you out of the rain. Maybe I can find something to rewrap that leg of yours."

A skull rises out of the lake, followed by many more. It looks like the graveyard of many fleshless drowning victims. Their eerie blackened eyes are nothing more than ominous as they remain furtive, wading their way over to the shoreline. Their long white bony fingers creep over the lake's shoreline, pressing deep into the squishy mud.

The shadows of the canoeing area vanish in the golden halo of the front entryway's street lamps. The coarse dirt scuffs the bottom of their shoes as they hobble across its golden grit.

"What are you doing? Cabin one's over there."

"I know, but people may still be here. We haven't seen any-one leave yet. We shouldn't take chances. We can't trust anyone right now. Plus, we would be putting them in danger. We're heading somewhere else more secluded."

The entrance sign is the spirit of the camp, arching proudly over the camp with all its love. Facing the camp's exit, it reads: Thanks For Visiting. See You Soon.

The shadows of the eastern woods running parallel to the camp's entrance avenue swallow Jessica and Robert in one gulp like a colossal sea beast. With each aching step, from one bounce to the next, Jessica's leg grows too sore to bear weight.

"It's okay; we're almost there."

A cabin to the north, not listed on the map, reeks of desolation and neglect which is a simple case of mother earth reclaiming what's hers. Its rustic character exudes a kind of charm, whispering tales of way back when. Moss scales the walls and roof, a mere cushion for the fallen twigs, and home to the moss mites.

Besides the burnt-down appearance and the missing front door, the cobwebs and creepy crawlies are a testimony that this place hasn't been up to standards in quite some time. Robert assists Jessica over to an un-sturdy couch reeking of mold and mildew.

"I'm not sitting on that thing. Look how filthy it is."

"Hang on, are you okay to stand?"

"I'm fine."

"Lux via." With a wave of Robert's hand, the fireplace lights up. He lays the book on the fireplace's mantle. "Here, this will keep you warm."

"That's perfect. Try and hurry. I don't know how long I can stand here for."

He searches around the cabin for something decent enough to drape over the couch for Jessica to lie on. Sneaking down the hallway he brushes away the cobwebs from the corner of the kitchen entranceway. A corded phone lies broken on the kitchen floor. Surrounding it is a puddle of water and fallen ceiling debris.

Wooden floorboards crackle and groan with each careful step as he continues past the kitchen and into the living area. A separate groan, one not caused by his own weight, but by the weight of age and ware of the balcony up the stairs caves in.

"Arghhhhh!"

"Are you all right?" Jessica yells from the living room couch.

"Yeah, I'm fine." He chuckles. "It scared me, that's all."

Robert continues up the squeaky and unsafe steps with great caution. There is a great possibility he could fall through the floor at any moment. The creaking wood bows to its limits. There is one way to go, and that is the first room on the left. One subtle squeaky step after another, a slow, gentle creak of the bedroom door opening leaves an eerie feeling at the bottom of his gut.

"Lux Via." The words drift out of his lips in a murmur against the chilling air. The utter darkness of the room takes light when his hand goes aflame.

The room reveals itself amongst the retreating shadows. It appears to be a child's room, judging by the amount of toys and clothes on the floor with layering years of dust and abandonment.

The rather-large hole in the wall to the right leads to a bathroom with a tub full of dirty water. Rummaging through the medicine cabinet, clinging the empty perfume and cologne bottles together, Robert finds a half-used roll of gauze wrap.

"Awesome." He slips out of the hole of broken drywall and back into the bedroom.

The moon's lustrous harvest light welcomes itself into the bedroom window, beaming its lunar golden rays over an unmade bed and a cluster of toys scattering along the floor. Robert shakes off the flame in his hand. The time worn sheets reminds him of the aroma of his bedding as a child.

The white sheets smelled of fresh orange blossom, like a garden in bloom, thanks to his dear mother, who worked most of the sunlight to keep their place in order.

His mother would wake him up to the sweet smell of sugar toast. Layered to perfection, the melted butter spread over the oven-toasted bread is adorned with sugar glittered atop its golden goodness.

Robert takes in a deep breath, the musty smell of dirty sheets enter his nostrils, prevailing over the sweet aroma of sugar toast and the fresh orange blossom sheets. He wakes right out of his daydream, giving him depressing vibes as he ganders over his quiet and dark bedroom.

"This ought to work."

His fingers curl around the wrinkle of the blanket, and with a tug, he snatches it off the bed. A myriad of dust particles toss about into a trickle through the rays of light, displaying much neglect over the years.

Returning to Jessica, Robert lays the blanket over the old worn-out couch, assisting her onto it. He gently lays her injured leg over his lap.

She bites her lip to tolerate the forthcoming pain; her body lies stiff as a board, and her eyes squint, anticipating the blood that's about to ooze out.

The torn cotton shirt adheres to her leg like a gooey paste. Robert peels it off her flesh one slimy string at a time till it spills blood out of the open wound. Jessica rears back in pain while Robert re-wraps the hole in her leg.

"There ya go. How's that?"

"That's good. Thanks, babe."

Nestling in the cushion of the couch is a brown wooden picture frame. Pulling it lose from its pinch, Robert humbly takes possession of the frame. He slides his finger against his lips, tucking his thumb under his chin.

"This looks like you and your parents."

"It is." Robert nods with watery eyes, gazing deeply into the photo.

"I'm sorry, I didn't realize it. You're so cute here. Whatever happened to you?" Jessica smiles, slipping her hand into his.

"Funny. Don't worry about it. Oh, I sure do miss them. I was five here, I think. Mom and dad died the following year. This picture is the last one we took together."

"Where was it taken?"

He rolls his eyes from one side of the room to the other. "We're in it. Actually, it was taken over there on the front porch. This cabin is my home. Was my home. My dad used to tell me stories about when he and mom were our age. This was before I was born. I remember him telling me this cabin was special. When they were digging to lay the foundation, they realized they dug into an abandoned old mineshaft."

"Whoa, that's kinda scary. Did your mom and dad explore it?"

"He never said he did. Probably too dangerous. Anyway, this is where dad's dream all started. He built this place with his bare hands. He loved the camping life. The woods, the nature was his thing, so he bought the land and began making his dream a reality. After they passed away, there was still so much more to do. So, I finished. We finished what my dad started. I wish he was here to see it."

"He would be so proud of you."

"Yeah, he would have been. Now, those bastards are going to destroy this place. And I let it happen."

"Babe. None of this is your fault."

"Maybe we can go back to the Impossible place and talk to the old man. He may be able to help us."

Robert pulls the orb from his pocket, showing its dull lifeless existence. "I couldn't go there, even if I wanted to. Look, it's not glowing."

A small thud breaks their conversation, and a fleshless hand pounds at the window. Unable to suppress the fright, a scream escapes Jessica's lips.

"Jess, get down!"

She falls off the couch, banging her injured leg on the floor. She winces in pain, refraining from yelping with her hands over her mouth.

Robert crawls toward the window, peeping out the bottom with one eye. His heart pounds out of his chest at the horrific site of the herd of Water Deaders creeping toward the cabin. The calming night of rustling leaves, the pitter-patter of pouring rain, and the whistling wind knocking loose shutters against the cabin is overtaken by the moans and groans of the approaching Water Deaders and the clinking of the Deader's hand against the window.

"What's out there?"

"More of the fleshless corpses."

A muffled scream from underneath them jolts their nerves,

bringing Robert to his feet as if someone lit a fire under him. They are happy, nervous, and scared at the same time.

"You hear that, Jess? Grab the book," Robert says, reaching down for her hand.

"Sounds like Emma. I got it. I can make it up on my own."

Robert reaches into his waistband, gripping the cold steel of the officer's handgun. He draws it out, keeping Jessica close behind him. The distant screams muffle the exceeding sound of thudding bones against the cabin. CRASH! The glass breaks, sending the Water Deader tumbling into the living room.

"Forget about them, Jess. Come on."

They make their way toward the kitchen door. Thunder rumbles in the skies. The wind throws a fit of rage. Rain comes bucketing down smacking violently against the roof. The sound of the rain is like the musician, while the wind is the vocalist, singing in perfect harmony, but the spine tingling growl of the crawling Deader taints its purity. The roof springs a leak, shedding tears at the progressing threat approaching them.

"Jess, can you open the door?"

She limps, but makes it to the door one hobble at time. He has his gun drawn at the Water Deader and is ready to fire at any moment.

"Don't waste the bullets. Dang thing's moving slower than I am."

Jessica snatches the door knob using it for support, her eyes lock with his waiting for his directives. He gestures with a gentle nod, and she shoves open the door. Nothing is on the other side but darkness and concrete steps leading to a dark and spooky basement.

"Can you make it down the steps?"

"Yeah, I think so."

The steep, old, and narrow concrete stairs give way to a brick wall and a leaky plaster ceiling. Jessica slams the door shut before the Water Deader can scoot its way to the door. Cold chills run up Robert's spine as he makes his descent down the creepy stairs.

"Here, hold onto me. You're not falling on my watch. Too bad I left my cell back at the cabin. The flashlight would have been useful."

"You're not getting it back now."

"Nope. That thing is nothing but ashes."

"What about that orb?"

"Won't do much good. It's not glowing."

Wanting desperately to turn back, Jessica stands at the threshold and tries to wriggle herself out of the grip of fear.

One step at a time, she makes her dreaded descent down the steps. Her hands brace against the moist gritty brick wall. Cobwebs stick to her hands as she approaches the basement.

They are approaching the bottom of the steps when his foot slides forward a little. Moving his foot out of the way, he stoops over, picking a small object up with a pinch of his fingers.

"What's this?"

The layers of dust feel gritty between his fingers. The smooth white texture spikes his curiosity. He flips it over, blowing off the layers of dust. He raises his hand toward the moon's beam of silvery light to reveal a picture of a man and his girlfriend.

"That's strange."

"What is it?"

"Here, have a look yourself."

"Ah, that's going to be us someday."

"Look closer."

Jessica takes a closer look at the picture, searching as if it is a puzzle. "What, I don't see anything."

"Flip it over."

Jessica flips over the picture and reads what it says. "'The only fire you can't put out is the one you started in my heart. To the beautiful Ira.'"

"Is this the same Ira as the Reaper in the white cloak?"

"It seems that way. I mean, how many people do you know by the name of Ira?"

"That's true. Ask the person from this book. Maybe they know. We need your bookbag. I'm getting tired of holding this thing."

"It would definitely come in handy, but I left it back at cabin seven. Actually, if I remember right. Aha! Look at this."

Wooden shelving made from plywood and two-by-fours edge the left side of the basement, holding random junk including a plain Jane black bookbag. Robert wipes off the dust with a swipe of his hand, blowing off the remnants with a single breath.

The unzipping sound is more like a growl as the zipper fights through the dusty brass. Jessica tucks the old photo inside the book and slides the book into his bookbag, zipping it back up for him. He throws the strap over his shoulder, forgetting how long it's been since he wore it.

"Oops, I forgot how long it's been since I've worn this thing."

He loosens the straps for a relaxing fit, and a distant murmur echoes in the basement, as quiet as a crackling campfire.

Every square inch of their guts and muscles twists and turns. Their skin is pale as turkey flesh.

"Leave me alone," bellows an innocent and familiar voice.

"Is that-" Jessica says.

"It's Emma. It has to be." Robert stealthily moves toward the voice.

"Hold up. You hear that?"

A hissing noise, like the sound of sizzling meat, is venomous as a snake, it's teeth constricting his ear canal and piercing his eardrums. What is it? Better yet, where is it?

The sound grows louder and louder until they approach the corner of the basement, halting in their tracks at the sight of three massive shadows. They take cover behind a wall, taking a peek at what is creating the towering darkness. One shadow is less overbearing than the other two.

A flickering orange sputters like a strobe light, bringing about that sizzling noise again. Sparks fly, parading their campfire orange, shining brighter than a herd of traveling phoenixes.

The chalky smell of concrete dust permeates their nostrils as the expanse irritates their throat to an uncontrollable coughing fit.

Jessica clamps her teeth onto her shirt. She holds her breath, sliding further down the wall to avoid the possibility of lung damage if she doesn't have some already.

Robert fights the urge to cough with his hand pressing firmly against his mouth. He is taking another gander through the thicket of dust when a sizzling bright blue light cuts at the concrete wall like a plasma gun. Robert and Jessica jolt, hunkering toward the floor at the explosive boom as the concrete wall tips over, shattering along the floor.

Three images as blurry as frosted glass come into a clear view, displaying a hodgepodge of colors of red and white.

"What was that?"

"It's too smoky to tell. Wait, it's Tate and Ira."

"Is Emma there?"

"We must go to the coalmine entrance. He's waiting on us there. We commit to the plan and after …" Tate says, but before he can finish, he's cut off by a girl's scream.

"Help me!" a girl's voice cries.

"That was Emma. How are we gonna get her out of there?"

"I don't know. I'm thinking."

"Oh, boohoo. Enough with the crying. As soon as Death gets ahold of you…"

"Easy, Ira. Death wants Chris docile. We don't want her too anxious, now do we? It'll make things more difficult."

"Ah, sorry, kid I guess I'm the most horrible person in the world," says Ira.

"Hush it, you clown. When my teacher gets here, you're gonna be sorry, you you evil witch."

"Kids." Ira smiles with a giggling gaze into the void of Tate's hood.

Jessica's nose begins to wiggle following a flare. Dust particles tickle her nostrils into a twitching fit. "Achoooooo!" Her mouth drops slightly and her eyebrows rise in shock, with not a movement but the air that glides off her lips. Did they hear it?

Light on their feet, Robert and Jessica tip-toe away from them with their backs firmly against the wall. Their faces wrinkle, eyes stuck shut, grinding their teeth to the gums.

"They heard it; I know they did. We're screwed, Robert."

"Shhhh! Did you hear that?"

"What?"

Robert stands still, unsure of whether or not he should stay or take off with Jessica and run for their lives. His knees begin to quiver. The concrete starts to warm up his back. The heat draws beads of sweat, dripping down like a leaky faucet. It's so oppressive, even the shadows are looking for shade.

"Rob, what's wrong?"

The heat takes the breath from his mouth. His heart hammers in his chest. He no longer has control over his trembling hands as they shake in an abnormal cadence. Before his next breath, two arms explode through the concrete wall, dispersing concrete fragments that scatter like gun powder. It's Tate's arms, and they begin to strangle him. Before Jessica can limp to his aid, ice forms along the concrete wall in a crackling expanse up to the ceiling.

From out of the darkness, the white of Ira's cloak emerges in front of Jessica. Lingering around Ira are concrete dust and snowflakes that are as still as the hands of a dead clock. Ira's head calmly raises exposing her ice crystal eyes and diamond-dust cheeks. With a wave of her hand, Jessica slams through the ice-covered wall, shattering it into countless pieces.

Running down both forearms of Tate is lava, sliding its thick blazing ooze of liquid rock to the ground, melting the snow into vapor.

The hot concrete wall takes on an orange hue that becomes

brighter by the second. Steam rises from the searing hot wall. Robert can feel his flesh redden, as hot as a sunburn. His clothes begin to swelter with steam.

Tate's grip around his throat is relentless. He coughs and gags till he's blue in the face. His body goes limp like a hotdog. Both hands slip and drop to his side. He is fighting to keep his eyes open when …BOOM! The glowing orange wall around him explodes, driving him backward, landing on its remnants. He grabs his throat, gasping for air and fighting for oxygen till everything goes black.

"Mr. Lee!" Emma peeks around the corner of a hole in the wall, which appears to be a tunnel entrance.

The spirit of hope springs out the sparkle of Emma's eyes a look as bright as a beacon of light from a lighthouse and as brave as the fiercest soldier.

Jessica lifts herself to a sitting position; a thick glaze of concrete dust covers her. Her beautiful amber eyes are lathered in sprinkles of concrete dust that scrapes like sandpaper, putting them in a permanent squint. Her hair is dry and stiff as a burlap sack.

A cough forces a wisp of dust out of her mouth like a screaming locomotive barreling past the railroad crossing. The residuals are shaken off before she can struggle to her feet.

Jessica waves her hands around the dust-covered area, searching for Emma, Robert, and any sign of existence in a world seeming vacant.

"Emma. Emma. Come to me, sweetie. Hear my voice."

Blood dribbles down her leg as she drags her dead limb across the floor. Smoldering remnants scatter across the floor, while tiny pieces crunch under her shoes.

"Emma, are you okay? Emma, where are you?"

"Over here." Emma coughs.

Jessica's unaware of Robert, who lies still on the ground close by. She sighs as she approaches Emma through the haze, which is starting to clear up. She becomes upset when she's close enough to realize Emma is frozen like a popsicle.

"Emma, what did she do to you?" Jessica mutters, reaching a hand out to touch her face when the cold of Emma's face absorbs into Jessica's skin, giving her a spine-jolting chill.

"Ha, ha, ha, ha." Ira and Tate's laughter sends a shiver up her spine. Through the darkness of her hood, Jessica can sense the smirk growing across Ira's frostbitten face.

"You bitch."

"Sticks and stones may break your bones, but a bitch I sure am. At least I'm not dead. Ah, wait a second. I am. Ha, ha, ha, ha."

Jessica can feel her lungs collapsing as she goes into a coughing fit, becoming weak in the knees as she drops to one of them.

"Ira, why don't you clear this mess up? It's hard to see her suffer."

A breeze kisses Jessica's cheek, whirling the dust around her and crashing out the window. It's clear, with not a dust particle in sight. Jessica inspects the room and looks for Robert, finding him lying unconscious behind her. She observes his chest rising up and down with each breath he takes.

A glint in her eye is followed by a smile of relief that crosses Jessica's face at the knowledge Robert is still alive. Her nostrils flare, and her eyebrows slant, shifting her expression to fury and a raging charge full sprint at Ira.

With a wave of Ira's hand, she sends Jessica flying backward in a slide, landing next to Robert. The handgun is held in his motionless fingers. Jessica eyes it with a sneaky glance. Well, she thinks her glance is secretive.

"Are you serious? Those little bullets are no match for us. I'll melt those little bullets into nothing."

Careful not to draw any attention to herself, Jessica slides her foot across the tiny pieces of concrete and toward the gun with both eyes glued on Tate and Ira.

"Unfreeze the girl, or…"

"Or, what? How about I unfreeze her when you give Tate back the other half of the broken orb?"

"Or, better yet, how about if you don't give it to me, I'll break her into a million little pieces?"

Tate stoops down, picking up a broken piece of concrete. His hand is a-blaze, glowing bright orange like melting steel. His fist tightens, crushing the concrete in his grasp as he places his hand over Emma's frozen body.

The liquid rock oozes between his fingers like the mouth of a drooling dog, stretching like a string of melting cheese, dropping faster the longer it gets.

"Wanna give it back now?"

"Okay, okay. I'll give it to you. Just stop. Give me a second. Robert has it, I think."

The string of liquid rock slurps back into Tate's fist while Jessica pretends to be searching for the orb with her back facing Tate and Ira. Robert's eyes flicker like a bad bulb. Jessica places her hand over his mouth as he comes to. He gasps, and his eyelids seem to flee from his face. His yelps are muffled under the seal of her hand.

"Shhh. I have an idea. Pretend you're dead. Stop moving. You'll get us caught."

Under the scrapes of her knees, the handgun is leaving a irritating red impression of itself on her flesh. Her hand slips around the scabrous rubber grip, hooking the trigger with her finger. She inhales deeply.

"So, where's the other half of my orb?"

"I got your orb…right here."

A rush of air swoops through Jessica's hair, kicking up a layer of dust that wraps her body in a cocoon of dust particles. While swinging around and aiming the gun out in front of her, both eyelids roll down, but before she can open them, sparks fly like fireworks and something solid hits the gun from her hands.

"Nice try, but guns don't scare me. It's dumb blonds that really crack my frozen nerves," Ira says as the boomerang whips back into her hand.

Ira unleashes a gust of wind at Jessica, which sends her smacking into a wall, then unleashes both boomerangs, which hurl into both sleeves of her shirt, pinning Jessica against the wall.

Tate eases his head toward Ira, giving her a nod. "But only after."

"Yes, of course only after. Take out Robert. He's still breathing."

First, Ira marches toward Jessica, while Tate eases out both of his axes. With his size and stature, he towers over Robert, blanketing him in his shadow like a kneeling mountain rising toward the heavens.

Symbols materialize along Tate's red velvet cloak, visualized by a wave of embers that sweeps across it entirely. He raises his axes high in the air, smacking them together with a blinding combusting flame.

A vibration from inside Robert's bookbag gains his attention. "Calefacto. Say it," the voice whispers from within the wordless book, as soft as a flower's kiss.

"Calefacto," Robert mumbles, and the ice begins to melt off Emma. The melting outer layer runs down her arms and drips off her fingertips.

Before Tate can thrust his axes into Robert for the kill, he pulls out the broken and glowing fire orb from his pocket bringing Tate to an immediate halt.

"You want it you big red bitch? Come and get it, big boy."

He's on his feet in a flash as he charges into the tunnel as dark as a black hole. Its void swallows him from existence. Red smoke emits off his flesh, transfiguring him completely into smoke as he whizzes down the tunnel.

"Cool, Mr. Lee can use the orb too. Go, Mr. Lee, go!" Emma cheers, jumping for joy and slinging water droplets all around her.

Tate and Ira geo leap after him in a deadly chase of cat and mouse. The memory of Tate's words dances on the tip of Robert's tongue from their first encounter with each other. He can feel the flames circling around him and Jessica back at Wolf's Eye Den. The mixture of cedar, burning grass, and moisture from the on-coming downpour irritates his nose. It's another memory from this awful day he wants to forget, but what word did he use to trigger that ring of fire?

He perks his head up in the mass of red smoke that surrounds him with a gasp and a smirk, his lips spread in a sly roguish manner. He extends his arm into the trail behind him.

"Incendia."

Fireballs explode out of his hand like a cannon, one after another in the Reapers' direction, catching Tate off-guard as one of them drives him backwards.

"I'm not gonna hurt him; I just wanna have a snowball fight."

Ira's hand freezes, crinkling into an expanding ball of ice that grows to the size of a bowling ball. Before she can connect with an uppercut, Robert dashes out of her way setting her up for the counter attack. She reaches behind her back for her darlings. Her fingertips brush up against the distressed leather of her boomerang holster.

"Damn, where's my darling boomerangs?"

Jessica's arms are pinned against the wall by the blades of Ira's boomerangs like a butterfly on a collector's board. With near-perfect timing, she's able to let the boomerangs support her weight to double kick Ira as she makes her way out of the eerie tunnel and back into the basement.

Not far behind, Robert zips back to Jessica's aid, yanking both boomerangs from the wall, freeing her before Ira can stand. He slips both boomerangs in Jessica's cold, fatigued grip, contradicting her personality at the moment.

"Here. You okay?"

"Yeah, just a little tired. Where's Tate?"

"I think I lost him."

"Let's get Emma and get the fuck out of here."

Emma is fully unthawed and wet as Ira's humor. She rises to a sitting position, shaking off the excess like a wet dog. Water runs down her forehead and into her eyes, making it tough to see through the blur.

"Mr. Lee, Ms. Hill, what's going on?"

They run to her, but before she can accept Jessica's warm embrace, Tate whips past the tunnel, geo leaping in between them interrupting the emotional reunion with the growl of his voice.

"Enough! I'm tired of playing your childish games and your ignorant and feeble minds."

"We're tired too. There's got to be something we can do. Look, we have the wordless book you wanted. I'll give it to you in exchange for Emma. We'll leave each other alone and pretend none of this ever happened." Robert reaches for his bookbag and is immediately halted by Tate.

"You call it the wordless book, huh? It's far from wordless. No good to me anymore. I got what I wanted from it. What I do want is the broken end of my orb. This is your only offer: the girl for my orb. Do we have a deal?"

"Rob, just give it to him, and let's go home. Come on, give it to him." Jessica encourages him with a gentle shove of her shoulder.

Robert stands there, unsure of what to do. His hand slips inside his shirt pocket, shuffling the fire orb between the tips of his fingers.

He remembers what the old man said about protecting the book and orb with his life. His wise words fumble around his mind like the orb between his fingers. He can hear the wandering crows flap their wings as they linger around the bell-tower walls. He shakes off the stench of rotten bones, swamp water, and boxwood bushes at the repulsive sound of Tate's searing voice.

"Well, then, I guess you've made your decision. I guess we're gonna have to take it from you, then."

"You got this, Tatey boy. I'm gonna rest here for a moment. These nails look like shit. Since hot stuff and I are an item, he gives me immunity to annoying people like yourself. Make it quick, pookie. Momma needs a makeover."

Sparks fly as Tate clings his blades together. "Come on, let's go." They kindle into a bright orange flame. Steam rolls off his lips, searing the oxygen around him as he hunkers down in position. With a dash forward, red smoke emitting off Tate expands toward Robert.

Tate cuts the air with his blazing axe. The flame licks Robert's ears and singes his eyebrows as he knee slides under the axe's unforgiving blade, nearly filleting his face off. His hand scrapes along the concrete. Crumbles of concrete dig into his hand, leaving burns in his palm as his fingers swoop up the handgun.

"You know how to use those, blondie?"

"Emma, run. Now," Jessica pleads, and Emma runs down the dark tunnel before Robert can get to his feet.

"Ah, goody, goody. I love this so much, my arctic blue wintry eyes might shed an ice cube or two."

"If you're gonna do it, then do it."

"Blondie, I can freeze more than that pretty face of yours."

Robert comes to his feet, aiming the handgun at Tate before

he can turn around. The crackling and creaking of ice stretches through the basement's entirety.

The room has a blizzard-blue filter to it. Jessica shivers, hugging herself for a little warmth. Her lips quiver as frost expands out her breath. The bead of blood trickling down her leg wound begins to freeze.

She stands awestruck to see that everything appears to be frozen including her fiancé. She whispers Robert's name touching his cheek, quickly jerking away to ease the pain of ice burn that penetrates her flesh like a thousand needles.

Ira and Tate circle her like hungry vultures. The crystals in Ira's eyes sparkle like light bouncing off a glacier, while Tate's burning irises smoke like coal that burns hot enough to give Jessica third-degree burns.

"Hot stuff, bring the girl back."

"On it, dear. Don't start the party without me."

Emma stops dead in her tracks. Her toes hang over a puddle of nasty water. She guards her nostrils from the putrid odor. She hears squeaks of something; maybe a rat as it scurries down the tunnels escaping the toxic smell.

"Eww, gross. What's that smell?"

Unstrapping her bookbag, she remembers something. Rummaging through the pockets of color pencils, coloring books, her brush, strawberry chap-stick, and random clothes and hygiene products, she sees a flashlight nestled at the bottom. She hugs the flashlight, holding it near to her heart.

"Thank you, grandpa."

The button clicks, shining a beam of white light down the tunnel. Emma shines the light at a grouping of flies hovering over a floating barrel. The barrel spins ever so slightly, exposing a label that reads: Flammable.

"What? Am I standing in gas?"

CAMP WOLF CREEK

Ira observes her broken nails. Icicles with tips as fine as ice shavings sprout out her nails, pushing away the old dreadful ones all but the one pinky finger, who is the runt of the bunch, and grows a tad too short.

"Ah, look at that. Let momma fix ya."

Ira's cheeks sink and her lips pucker, releasing a stream of frost that she aims at her pinky nail. The chilly air congeals to ice that expands her pinky nail to a length she desires.

"Ah, there you go, good as new. I should have been a hand model. Might have to freeze a few blonds along the way. Oh, speaking of blonds, what are you waiting for?"

Lacking confidence, Jessica gawks at both boomerangs, questioning her ability to use them and guessing to herself whose blood-stains are over the leading wing and razor-sharp blade of one of the boomerangs.

"What, blondie? Are you wondering whose blood is painted on my darlings? Don't worry, it's no one you know. Your blood will spill over the other one soon enough." Ira giggles like some sort of psychotic cheerleader.

Jessica draws the boomerang over her head, finding it hard to block out Ira's sinister laughs. She looks into the darkness of Ira's white hood as her ice-glazed pupils glance down at her orb.

Her eyes become narrow as the crackling sound of ice expands from her eyes to her face as her body reverts to its natural pale-blue color.

The dark and dreadful tunnel is close to vacant. Starving arachnids and scurrying rats seek refuge at the sight of Tate's hulking presence.

Embers diverge off his flesh, scaring away the tunnel's shadows. His scarred hands smolder like firewood smearing his charred fingers across the tunnel walls as he walks.

Emerging from the tunnels void is a swiveling light and the innocent echo of Emma's voice in the opening of a lonely song of The Itsy-Bitsy Spider.

"Lux via," Tate whispers.

His hand is engulfed in flame, illuminating the forthcoming passage. His pungent burning fleshy hand hisses like a snake singing in the night. His boot sloshes into the shallow puddle.

From overhead, the leaky pipes send cold water to plop and sizzle onto his grungy red cloak. Each step sinks deeper and deeper into the filthy water until the song ends. Click. The white beam of light disappears into the darkness.

"Emma, time to come out. I promise, no one will get hurt."

Ira's glowing orb changes to a dull pearl color. Robert's frozen nose twitches, cracking the layer of ice to crumbling pieces. The crackling retreats from the rest of his body, then the rest of the room. Frost emits from his mouth as his finger abandons the trigger at the realization of Tate's absence.

"Ah, look who's back. It's Sobby Robby. Don't cry."

"Hush your cold mouth, or I'll shoot it off."

"Go ahead, waste your ammo. If I were you, I'd find someone more important to shoot rather than little ol' me."

Jessica's eyes fixate on her own reflection in the blade of Ira's boomerangs. The dry blood stain coats one half of her face, unveiling the reality of her own mortality.

"Don't bother. I'll hush it for her."

With a thrust forward, Jessica almost releases one of the boomerangs, but ultimately, she is halted by the tone of Robert's voice.

"Can we just stop this? Look, I have something I need to show you," Robert says as he calmly slides the strap of his bookbag off his shoulder.

"Ah, your boyfriend's cute. He's about to give me flowers. Come on, cutie, do it already. Better hurry; my man tends to get jealous with all this flirting."

"My fiancé's not into flirting with dead people. What's wrong with you?"

"Blondie, I'm off my meds. I can be quite vexatious at times. Well, all the time. I love me."

Tate stops in his tracks. A stench swoops into his nostrils, pulling his head high like a starving dog sniffing out a trail of food. The skull's eyes on his belt glow bright red, and it speaks to him.

"Gassss," Natsu growls.

"Yeah, it's definitely gas, Natsu."

The skull on Tate's belt dissolves into ashes and embers, swirling like a dust cloud. Each burning piece takes its spot in perfect formation, taking the shape of Natsu.

"Careful with all the ashes and embers, Natsu. Let's try not to blow ourselves up."

Ira's wondering eyes grow more skeptical by the second. Each trusting moment is as painful as breaking off one of her frozen extremities.

"I'll tolerate this nonsense if you hand over hubby's orb."

"Fine, but humor me for a moment."

Robert reaches into his bookbag, pulling out the polaroid photo from the inner hinges of the wordless book. His body faces away from her blood-lust-chilled eyes. The polaroid photo's backside is covered in dusty fingerprints, while the front suffers from an orange cast and is faintly overexposed. With a scoff, Ira swipes the polaroid from Robert's fingers.

"Woot woot, hot couple. This nearly unthaws my evil frozen heart."

"I think that's you," Robert says, zipping his bookbag up and slinging the strap over his shoulder.

"I almost snapped a nerve there. Nice try, cutie pie, but I've never been like you. Ever."

"It has your name on it. Turn it around." Jessica hesitates to breathe, practically frozen in place at the sight of Tate's orbs illuminating.

Jessica's pupils dilate, and she blinks her eyes repeatedly locking them both onto Robert's as he follows her gaze to the glowing fire orb within his pocket.

"Ouch! Ouch, ouch, ouch," Ira says, hopping on one foot at a time.

Before Ira's frosted pupils can validate her name, she drops the photo onto her sopping-wet flame-covered foot. The golden ball consumes her foot, outshining the stars. The flame snakes its way into the tunnel. Ira glances down at her orb's white glow, which glistens off her polar eyes as an avalanche of icy death.

"I didn't have to give a command that time. Jessica, now!"

Jessica whips the first boomerang underhand. The twirling blades rotate like an out-of-control smoking exhaust fan 'spinning' off its bearings.

The boomerang penetrates Ira's chest when a flash of light drives everyone backward off their feet. Shards of concrete peg Robert's flesh. The taste of dust and grit dries his mouth, which then fills with blood. All he can do is spit it out to keep himself from choking. A willful desire for one drop of water to satisfy his mouth and quench his thirst is all he can beg for.

Robert struggles to stagger to his feet, fighting through

the dizziness. "Jessica." His ears feel like they are stuffed with cotton. The dust is thick as in a vacant chamber under an abandoned ghost town. "Jessica." Scattered concrete remnants crunch under his feet, and one particular fragment causes him to slip to his knees.

His hearing gradually recovers, pulling in spine-shattering sound waves of her groans. Jagged edges of concrete scrape the reddened palms of his hands as he crawls to her. Reaching for his beloved's shoulder, he says, "Jess. Come on. Get up. We have to get out of here." Robert can feel her limp body, dead weight as gravity rolls her to her back, exposing Ira's boomerang lodged into her chest. Her gray counselor shirt is saturated in blood.

"Jess! Jess!" Robert cries, shaking her still body. "Jess. Honey, please."

Her irritated eyes flutter against the dust. She springs to life with a sharp gasp, releasing a pool of oozing blood from the corner of her mouth. She coughs, showing her reddened teeth with a smile. A smile of happiness and relief that Robert is there with her, his hand slips into hers as gentle and weightless as cotton balls.

"Honey, you're okay."

"Emma."

"What is it?"

"Emma. Check on her," Jessica cries with little oxygen to push the words out.

As much as Robert wants to check on Emma, he can't just leave Jessica. Robert wraps his arm around her back, bringing her in close and holding her tight.

"Hold on. I'm gonna get you out of here."

He wraps his arms around her, and with all his might, he attempts to pick her up, but he isn't strong enough. The tears pour as the darkness begins to take her from him. Her fragile hands grow cold like the fire orb's glow amongst the surrounding flames as he comforts her with a soft caress against the warmth of his cheek.

"Jess. Jess. Jess. Don't leave me." The sound of his cries washes away like a distant wave.

A frantic look of terror across the room's eye watering gray haze, Robert can hear the cracking and popping of fire around him hissing a threating warning. The acrid smell of burnt wood lingers in his nostrils. He catches a motionless Ira whose still open fingers lay within reach of Tate and Ira's burning picture. The dwindling flame shrinks as the polaroid withers away to crumbling ashes.

Eerie whispers ascend from out of Ira's skull on her belt while she's lying in the gray haze, motionless, and appearing dead.

A frosty mist, white as foam and translucent as a veil rises out the eyes of Ira's skull off her belt and expands toward Robert and Jessica. Every floating icy particle from within the chilly fog glimmers off the spreading mist.

A spine-shivering shuffle sounds off within the frost. The identity of the noise is as mysterious as the world's most popular conspiracy theory. For a moment Robert forgets about the pending burning threat of his enviable death as the thumping sound grows closer.

A beastly paw the size of Robert's head shows its dominance by unveiling its mighty paw outside the mist. Its claws are sharp as ice cycles, its toes as round as a man's fists, though the rest of it remains a mystery. Concealing itself within the thicket of the mist, the beast roars with enough power to split an iceberg.

Robert's hairs stand on end, and his chattering teeth clamp down hard enough to stamp metal. His breath is as thick as cotton. He scoots back to create distance while holding Jessica. It is clear that whatever it is, it is definitely protecting Ira like a pet protecting its owner.

Robert bows his head to show, whatever it is that they are not a threat. His hands shake in hers as he holds her tight. Robert can't tell what is louder; its threatening grumble or his chattering teeth.

A shadow consumes Robert and Jessica like an eclipse. The smell of hunger and foul breath evades his face but he dares not to peek as Robert holds his breath. The mysterious beast snarls as it realizes Robert is not a threat and steps back into the dense frosty mist as Ira's skull consumes it like a vacuum.

The basement is on fire in every direction, wrapping around them like curtains ready to burn them till their dust of the earth.

Robert gazes around the room for a way out. The fire has taken all it can but yet the cabin still stands. There's no place to go and no place to hide.

It is all being taken from him. What was once his home, his safe place, what kept him dry on the rainy days will no longer be there to keep him dry. The place he can go to re-live the few memories of his mother and father is now merely a memory itself.

Robert cradles Jessica's dead body in his warm embrace while the familiar-but-horrific scene reminds him of risking his life to save Jessica the first time she was surrounded by the blazing flames in cabin eight.

He holds her close and tight. The blood from her perforated injury drips off Ira's boomerang and onto his thigh.

His soft and gentle moment with Jessica is disrupted by Tate who explodes through the flame covered tunnel entryway. Tate transcends into red smoke with rising embers that meet the charred ceiling, geo-leaping through the expanding grey smoke and over to Ira's limp body. A twitch of Ira's hand, followed by the furl of her fingers, and the blood covered boomerang that penetrates deep into Jessica's chest rips out her flesh with a whirling whoosh, cutting through the smoke like a hot knife and into Ira's hand.

"If she dies, you'll be the ash under my feet, if you don't burn in here first," Tate blurts out with a point of his finger as he scoops up Ira and throws her over his shoulder.

"Don't worry, I'll find a way out," Robert promises.

"I don't see how that's possible. The other half of my orb is not glowing. I'll be back for it soon. Right now, she's more important. Good luck getting out."

Red smoke consumes Tate and Ira, who burst out of the basement, parting the dreary haze and whipping through the raging flames and into the tunnel's entryway.

Robert's irritated eyes are dry and itchy from all the smoke that has been filling the room. Time is running out for Robert as the smoke crawls closer to him. Red bumps form up his red, dry skin. His lips bounce off her forehead as he lowers her body gently on the concrete floor. He closes her eyes with a swipe of his hand as he fights back a pool of flowing tears.

"Rest in peace, my love."

A brief tugging sensation from behind him, followed by the sounds of soft and subtle sobbing, catches him off guard. It's innocent in nature with a voice that is recognizably bittersweet.

"Emma. Thank heavens you're okay. We gotta get out of here."

"What's wrong with Ms. Hill?"

"Sorry, sweetheart. She didn't make it."

"What do you mean, she- she-" Emma releases a round of coughs that speeds up the clock on Robert's hurry meter. "Didn't make it?" A single tear escapes her eye as Robert fights to hold back his own.

"We'll discuss this later. We have to find a way out of here. I'm taking you home."

Robert knows now he must focus on Emma. Jessica would want him to. They search around for a way out but there is none. Every direction is a blazing inferno.

He takes the broken fire orb from his work shirt and places it in his pants pocket. The heat is too much. He takes off his work shirt, placing it in his bookbag and leaving on his white T-shirt, which is soaking in sweat.

The flames and shadows dance like demons, climbing the walls like a bobcat after its evening meal. Poisonous gasses from burning fixings drip down the walls. The ceiling buckles, spitting out charcoal remnants and flashing orange embers like pixie dust.

"Mr. Lee, look! I can see a way out."

Robert feet are stuck in place, gawking at the ceiling, when a continuous crack slithers across its center. Emma's hand slips from his, separating them more than he wants leaving an agonizing hole in his heart.

"Emma, come back to me. It's not safe."

Pow! The ceiling falls, scaring Robert and Emma to the ground and separating them from each other. Emma, who is on the other side of the debris by the tunnel entryway cries out to Robert.

"Mr. Lee. Mr. Lee. I can't see-" Emma grunts releasing a flurry of coughs that can wake the neighborhood if it weren't for the roaring flames.

He can faintly hear her cries as it would be easier to speak to a stranger in the middle of a screaming crowd at a heavy metal concert. He remains on his hands and knees, as the temperature and breathing are a little more bearable. He pants faster than his heart can beat. The lack of oxygen makes him dizzy, and he's finding it hard to keep his balance.

All sounds become echoes that are more distant by the second. There is no way out. It is hard to fathom, but Emma is on her own. Through the wave of orange flames, he can barely can make out his dear Jessica, who lays next to a pool of her own blood.

One hand and knee after another, he wobbles slower and slower to Jessica. The smoke that fills the room leaves him breathless. He gasps, fighting for even a pinch of oxygen. His eyes are red and itchy, with not a single drop of water in his entire body. The creaking and crackling of the remaining ceiling above brings a gust of embers over him burning holes into his T-shirt and scorching the back of his neck.

The sudden rush of adrenaline languishes in sync with

his sluggish heart. He's completely paralyzed, falling to the ground, face-planting into the pool of Jessica's blood, which forces the fire orb to roll out of his pocket and come to a halt within arm's reach.

In the translucent glass-like orb lies the reflection of Emma, struggling to keep it together. She's terrified and begging for Robert to wake up. Poor Emma's life depends on it.

FIFTHTEEN

APIPHOBIA

Don't be dead, Mr. Lee! Ms. Hill! Please, don't be dead!" Cough, cough, cough. "Please, don't be dead."

Emma can't see Robert through the fallen rubble of plaster, hickory wood, and the upstairs recliner. Her knees buckle. "COUGH, COUGH. I'm so dizzy." Her eyes widen to hopefully regain some focus. She can somewhat make out a shinny red thing through the debris. Emma reaches under the broken hickory and plaster as hard as she can, trying to feel for it. Her fingers roll over its glassy texture as she pushes it further away from her reach. "C'mon, c'mon." She leans in stretching with all her might.

"Ah, got ya." She admires its translucent beauty. "You look like the orb I pulled from that book. It's all my fault. If I left the orb in that dumb book, none of this would have happened. Stupid, stupid, stupid," she says, slapping her head repeatedly.

She can't help but to remember what the fire guy kept repeating back in the tunnel before the explosion passed through him. What was it?

"What did he say?"

Emma remembers the toxic smell and the darkness of the tunnel she was in minutes ago, sitting against a wall and hiding from Tate and that scary three-headed monster.

They were on her trail as they hunted her down like she was their food. Its three mangy snouts sniffed in three different directions, growling at the hint of her scent.

"Did you find her, Natsu?"

"Indeed," Natsu growled in a full sprint down the tunnel.

Emma quivered under the spine-chilling gallop of Natsu's approaching presence. Caught by surprise at the beast's rather speedy arrival, Emma stumbles to the ground quickly gaining her balance and footing as she returns to a dead sprint down the tunnel.

Natsu stomped on his brakes, sliding past the corner and slipping on his side. He scurried to his feet, commencing a game of cat and mouse.

She ran along some railway tracks, approaching a number of connecting mine carts full of coal. She clinched a cart's rusty edge for a tough push on top the loose coal. Natsu leaped reaching out his beastly paws, missing Emma's leg by a hair and instead sinking into the cart's corroded steel wall.

His railroad-spike claws cut through, serrating the steel with an ear-piercing screech.

Her feet slid one way to the next, kicking up coal dust as the coal rolled from under her feet. From one cart to the next, she made her way, opening the gap between her and Natsu.

The three-headed beast jumped onto the first cart, slipped to his stomach as his legs slip out from underneath him. Coming to his feet, he bellowed with a snarling fit of rage. Hot steam and flames sprayed from his mouth and nostrils as he huffed and puffed. His steaming beastly paws brought the coal to a slow burn as they ticked and popped from under his feet. Emitting embers, his decaying flesh greeted the lingering coal dust, combusting each coal cloud like firecrackers that popped all around him.

From one cart to the next, Emma makes it to the last one, leaping off the final cart, missing a withering ball of fire as she lands on the ground.

The smell was like grandpa's grill and if she doesn't move she may be the dogs steak dinner. A crackling sound grabbed her attention. She glanced up at the second set of coal filled carts as each one burned an earthly scent similar to a campfire.

Her only option was to crawl underneath them or to go around. The worry of Natsu catching her was likely if she choose to go around.

Emma came to her stomach, digging into the

dirt till she is under the first cart. It was dark. The shadows expanded to the walls on either side of her, and were met by orange scintillating the walls and ceiling with a flicker.

One arm after the next, Emma dragged her way to the middle coal cart as a menacing shadow lurked amongst the orange hue. She held her breath as the shadow eased closer and closer.

She held her breath, and with a blink of her eyes, the shadow was gone, vanishing without a trace. Emma held back the tears, pushing the emotion deep down within her gut as a soft whimper escaped her lips. She searched up and down the tunnel for the shadow.

"GRRRRR." Natsu released a hair-raising growl on his hunt along the coal carts.

His three snouts aimed toward the ground to track her location. Emma could feel his hot breath beating against her skin as he got closer. Natsu lowered himself, opening his eyelids, exposing the whites of his evil black eyes, which pierces her like daggers.

He snorted and growled slinging lava out his mouth as the hostile beast gnashed his teeth at her. One of his heads reached under the cart, swatting his behemoth-size paws at her. If one of those claws were close enough to reach her, Emma's life would be over with.

Her bravery pushed her forward, paying close attention so as not to get too close to Natsu's swatting paws. Emma knew she could only go forward safely for so long before she cleared the coal carts and was out in the open where Natsu could kill her.

She was still, searching for a way to escape the beast, when Natsu's paw nicked a lever separating the back two carts from the remaining four. They rolled back into the carts of burning coal behind her with a clang.

Emma could see the feet of Tate and Natsu from under the coal cart as she suppressed a cough with her hand over her mouth. Natsu's mangy paws dissolved to whirling embers, spiraling upward, leaving Emma curious enough to lean her head a little closer to the coal carts edge.

The whirling embers transfigured into a skull that attached itself as a buckle onto Tate's belt. Emma continued to crawl farther down the coal carts before Tate could peek under to find her.

"Chrissie, I know you're under here. You don't have to be scared of me. What's the use of trying to get away? You can't outrun me. Come on, Death just wants to talk to you. I guess I'll come to you, then." Tate transfigured to red smoke, rolling in behind her steadily like morning fog.

Passing under the last coal cart, Emma came to her feet, running for her dear life from Tate, who taunted and toyed with her, lurking in the shadows not far behind her. The farther down the tunnel she ran the darker it got as the shadows be-

gan to swallow the light. Its distant flames swayed in the air like the inflatable tube man at the ice cream shop.

She came to a stop at a blocked entrance-way of broken boards and debris. The boards squeaked and creaked as she pushed them to the side, giving her enough space to slide through.

Breathing seemed to be better with all the smoke behind her, but the smell of gas burned her nostrils. Winter's chill coated her skin, giving her goosebumps across her forearms. A literal light at the end of the tunnel made her smile. The moon's gleam beamed through a window, giving way to the basements entrance.

"Mr. Lee, Ms. Hill."

Emma ran, sloshing her feet in the watered-down gas. She could see Ira talking with Mr. Lee and Ms. Hill when a dark deep menacing voice crackled like flames from behind her.

"Chrissie, why do you keep running? Just give up. Your impending death is…inevitable. Give up. I'm sure Death will make it quick."

Emma remained brave. While easing around, she looked into the darkness at Tate, warming her chilled arms with a rub of her hands.

"I'm not afraid of you," Emma said. The whoosh of water drew her attention to Tate's foot, which was submerged in a puddle of water and gas.

Tate's face lit up like fire emitting embers that

burned out in the chilled air. He leaned in, lathered in darkness except for his lit face.

"You should be. It's about to get hot in here. Fiet unum," Tate said as his head and arms transformed into a flame.

The flames ran down Tate's chest and stomach, approaching the gas-filled puddle below. Emma gasped, and her body vibrated with anxiety while her white pale face drained of blood. Paranoia locked her in place till…

"JESSICA, NOW," Robert yelled with an echo that ricocheted down the tunnel, along with a trail of fire, crawling out from the basement and toward Emma.

Robert's scream awakened Emma from her episodic paranoia, sending a rush of blood back up to her face and extremities. She took off like mad, darting toward the basement entrance and leaping behind a wall that stuck out and shielded her from the explosion.

It's pitch-black. The sound of roaring flames rush into Emma's ears. Her eyes flip open to a room surrounding her in flames and smoke. Robert and Jessica lie dead at her feet. She coughs, opening her fists to Tate's broken fire orb, glowing bright through the thicket of the smoke.

"Oh, ya. Fiet unum."

A warm feeling comes over her. Red splotches form like a sunburn on her arms, but it doesn't hurt. The splotches travel up her arm covering her entire body as if she is burning from the inside out. Her hands tremble as she looks down on them, and a combustion in her fingertips travels up her arm. She desperately tries to pat out the flame, anxiously shaking her arm as the flame inches its way toward her shoulder.

In a flash, the fire consumes her. She can't help but marvel at herself, wondering how and why she isn't in pain or even dead yet, or even how she's breathing through all the smoke. She sees her reflection in a small puddle on the ground, only to realize how horrifying her appearance looks. Then she feels a rattling in her hand. Her fingers uncurl to a pretty orb glowing brighter than her grandpa's flashlight, which is back in her bookbag.

"It's the orb." Emma marvels at its brilliance. The flame covering her dwindles down as the orb flickers slower and slower. The tunnel's entrance is ablaze with color. White-hot flames shimmer through fierce yellow and into burnt orange as flames lick her hand. She jolts back, anticipating the burn with clinching teeth and squinting eyes. She's okay; it didn't hurt at all. The flame consuming her must be a protective force field. For a moment, she feels like a superhero.

An idea crosses her mind, but she must be brave. Looking away from the scorching heat with firmly squinting eyes, she eases her hand toward the fire covered passageway. The feeling of her heart pounding in the back of her throat makes her sick to her stomach.

She can feel the cool breeze against her fingertips as her hand passes through the flame-covered tunnel entrance. She gains a boost of confidence, peeping one eye at the other hand. The protective barrier is going away. It is now or never.

With every ounce of bravery in her, she dashes through the flames, releasing the kind of scream that goes unheard out of pure cruelty.

She's no longer a superhero anymore, since the flame consuming her burns out. The red orb's final glow comes to a stop. The golden fireball of the tunnel's entryway lights up the shadows with arms like tentacles reaching in toward the ceiling. She can't take the heat anymore so she takes a few steps back, happy to be alive and safe. If she could, she would go back in there and save them, but without the protection of the orb, it's impossible. Even then what can she do? So, she does the only thing she can do: survive. As hard as it is, she turns around and continues down the tunnel. Maybe she can find some help.

She takes the narrow edge, heading upstream back toward the cabin's basement. The flammable barrel still floats there, burning with the water. The orange hue gives enough light to read an old wooden arching sign fastened with rusty nails.

"Huh, Grym Hollow Coal Mine. Never heard of it."

The first thing she notices is the smell a mixture of rotten eggs and something dead. The rock walls are damp, and moss grows at regular intervals. The only source of light is the fire behind her, and that isn't a comforting thought.

It is darker than the night. She pulls out her flashlight from her bookbag. She reaches past her SpongeBob coloring book and coloring pencils grabbing her epinephrine pen first.

"I almost forgot about you."

With everything she's been through, she is relieved to see it isn't damaged. For a moment, the pen makes her feel safe. She places it inside her bookbag before grabbing the flashlight.

A steady drip from the moist ceiling above drifts away as she finds shadows of life in the form of abnormally large mice and insects as she eases forward.

"Help! Is anybody down there?"

She slides the flashlight button to the on position. The plastic rattles in her jittering hands while she's moving the beam of light all around her to spot any more icky creatures.

The light sways down the flooded tunnel, stopping at the shallow end, where water flows steadily over a railroad track. Her throat is dry and sore; every lungful of hot hair steals what little water is left from her body, though the raging flames drained most of it out already.

There is a pain at the back of her head, threatening to grow into a powerful migraine. As filthy as the water is she needs a drink. She doesn't care at this point if it was dirty or not. She is cupping the water in her hand, slurping down what little she can hold, when a loud bang echoes down the tunnel.

Emma cautiously comes to her feet, second-guessing if it is a good idea to search for the noise. It might be someone who needs help, or maybe it's one of those cloaked monsters. She is wiping the dribble of water off her mouth when she spots a light switch. She clicks the switch, not realizing there's a bee lurking under the light switch's cover. To Emma's surprise, it works. A line of pneumatic lamps runs the length of the tunnel, lighting the tunnel with a blanket of fiery yellow beating back the darkness. She holds her hand up to shield her eyes from the yellow light, and both eyes get acquainted with the coal mine's hidden tunnel. She clicks the flashlight into the off position. A constant annoying buzzing sound gurgles around the lamp lighting above her.

"Ah, great, bees."

One sting will put her in the hospital or, worse yet, she may die. She's been hospitalized twice before for a bee sting. The first time was the worst.

Emma was eight years old. Her grandpa was at work, while her grandma was outback watering the flowers. Emma, who was bored, decided to draw some pretty pictures on the sidewalk with the brand-new colored chalk she got for her birthday. She didn't get much done before she was stopped by a hissing sound.

Curious as she was, Emma crossed the yard, inspecting the neatly trimmed bushes along the way for the noise. She could still remember the smell of the freshly cut grass. Grandpa always took care of the yard. The hissing turned into yowling, which was what grandpa called it. She traced the noise to the only tree in their front yard.

This tree was so ginormous you couldn't fit any more trees in the yard. It was an Angel Oak tree, the most beautiful tree ever. Its branches were so long and curvy. Some reached to the ground and back up to the sky again covering the clouds and sun. This made it simple to climb.

Grandma and Grandpa didn't want her up there, but she couldn't resist when they weren't looking. Approaching the tree, she knew right away what it was. Her eyebrows raised, her forehead wrinkled up, her mouth hung open loosely, and her eyes widened. To Emma's surprise, it was only a stray cat. The kitty was so cute.

She wanted to keep the cat as a pet. If only she could climb up there to get it, maybe her grandmother would let her keep it. She checked to see what her grandma was doing and to her luck, she was still watering the flowers.

She pushed herself onto the only branch resting there, which practically touched the ground. The tree looked alive, like it was reaching its hand out, waiting for her to step on its palm to carry her away. She preferred walking up the branch with no hands. She thought she was a wizard at balancing herself, so up the tree she went, moving toward the tippy top. In that moment, she went face to face with the fluffy orange kitty.

Reaching over to grab the poor kitty, she placed her foot on a small twig. It creaked and cracked, snapping in two and sending Emma face-first into the branch. She caught her composure when she realized the kitty wasn't stuck in the tree all along. Behind the cat and around the trunk was a bee's nest that hung off the branch. The poor kitty was trapped. The branch below the bee nest was its only way down.

Emma slid as close to the trunk as she could, becoming more cautious the closer she got to those bees. She called for the kitty as she reached as far as she could when an idea crossed her mind: maybe if she could knock down the bee nest the kitty could get down. Snapping off a nearby twig she smacked the bee's nest over and over again, but she couldn't knock it down. She leaned into it this time and gave it all she had, but she slipped off the branch, catching herself with both hands.

She was so scared, but screaming for grandma was useless. She would never hear her. She was trying so hard to pull herself back up when an endless group of bees was all around the kitty. The cat was so brave it jumped from branch to branch, making it to the ground in no time. She was so happy to see the kitty was okay. Then it happened. A scary bee landed on her finger. It all felt like it was going in slow motion.

The sting hurt so bad, she slipped off the branch and fell straight to the ground. Everything went black after that. She only remembered waking up in the hospital with her gauze around her finger and an oxygen mask on her face. The doctor said it wasn't the fall that put her there. It was the bee sting, and she was lucky to be alive. That was the day she found out she was deathly allergic to bee venom. She carried an Epi-pen ever since.

That was the most terrifying thing to ever happen to her. Now, being down here, all alone in this tunnel with all those bees one sting and she'll die. Light on her feet, she tiptoes down the tunnel with one eye aiming at the wandering bees in the glare of the light while the other remains wary down the shadow covered tunnel.

"Hello. Anybody here? Somebody. My friends are in trouble. Please. Help. They may be dead. Hello," Her lonely voice echoes off the wet tunnel walls, drifting past a hungry spider who's in search of its next meal.

The tunnel seems to go on forever. The plip-plop of water droplets dripping off the ceiling only makes her more aware of how empty this place is.

Her legs began to cramp up as a tickle crawls up her neck. She tenses up, clamping her jaw bone tight as a vise, breaking out in a sweat.

"Be brave. Be brave. Be brave."

Stomping her feet, feeling icky about the situation, she slides her hand down her neck, knocking the bee to the ground. She wipes the sweat off her brow, super relieved to see the bee is now on the ground and away from her.

Emma breaks out in tears. Every shaky moment feels like it could be her last. Both of her knees buckle, sending her to the ground. Crawling is the only way she's making it past those bees. Irritating as nails on a chalk board, the buzzing lingers all around her. They whip past her from one direction, then the next as she stiffens like a board.

A vibration in the palm of her hand sends a tingle down her arm. She opens her hand, and the pretty red orb begins shining brighter than before. The orb begins to rise off her hand, leaving Emma breathless. The moment is magical, which makes her feel a little bit better about her bee situation.

She hears a howling wind come rushing from behind her, so fast she can barely make out the cloud of black smoke from the corner of her eyes. She panics, snatching the floating orb and begins crawling as fast as she can as the black smoke blows past her like a dust storm. All she can do is fall to the ground, close her eyes, and hope for the best.

All is calm. Emma can hear the dust settling through her pounding heart. She opens her eyes, and staring at her is the dullness of the red orb. Her forehead wrinkles, and her eyes widen to focus through the blur. She frees her eyes from the dirt, grabbing the orb before coming to her feet.

"Where am I?" Emma asks herself. Then, a tickle in her hands draws her eyes to them.

Pigmentation of a porcelain color fade her fingertips to a dull gray that spreads down her arm and scatters throughout her skin like an evacuation order.

"What?"

The color swiftly leaves her body and spreads expeditiously throughout the environment around her. She gasps, and her head lowers while her eyes examine the awkward environment surrounding her.

"What's going on?"

Everything looks similar to before, but colorless and dead. The ground and walls resemble dark gray flesh with bones showing through the rubber-like texture, which rises and low- ers like its breathing. She feels like she is in the middle of her worst nightmare.

Gripping its mangy claws around a piece of rock that protrudes out from the wall above her is a crow, who mocks Emma's cries with a series of caws.

She stops in her tracks when a vibration rattles her shoe-laces and runs up to her head, tickling her nose. A whirling like several drones whooshes all around her all at once.

She's frozen there in terror, scared to look, when out of the corner of her eye, she catches something that isn't a drone at all. Its yellow-and-black rings wrap around its oval-shaped body with eyes as large as chicken eggs. It's a massive bee whose body is the size of a professional football. Its stinger is quite terrifying and is the size is of a large screwdriver and is strong enough to penetrate through concrete. Three of them hover out in front of her ready to pounce on her at any second.

She gazes at the orb's bright glow as its magic is the only thing that can protect her right now. She uses its brightness as a flashlight. She thinks hard, trying to remember the magic word Mr. Lee said to make fire come out of his hand.

"Incendia." Her hand reaches out, aiming right at them. Still, nothing is happening. "What am I doing wrong?"

Several more of those nectar suckers swarm like enemy aircraft ready to dive in and take out whatever they can.

"Boy, do you guys look mad? I'm so sorry guys for invad-ing your home, I was leaving. I know I may look like a pretty orange flower but I promise you I'm not."

Pleading with them didn't seem to work. Their one track mind became more aggressive with every dreading second.

"Good bees. Nice bees."

She gives up on begging and decides to make a run for it. She gives it her all, trying to outrun those jumbo-stinging monsters, sliding over loose rocks as she drifts around the cor-ner. The first bee rushes in so fast it splats against the wall at the curve of the tunnel.

"Help, I don't want to die down here. Please."

Emma punches the wall, like that was going to do anything. She spins around to a buzzing sound. There are four of those bees staring at her taunting her as if they were enjoying it. As one of them flies in close to her face, she can feel the wind off its wings. Her hands reach to her sides for something to grab, and she feels the smooth texture of what feels like a root stuck inside the flesh-like wall. She reaches in to grab it, but misses.

"Come on." Her nose scrapes the edge of the bee's stinger. She weeps, unable to control her tears as her fingers crawl across the rock wall.

The bee rears back with its mighty stinger pointing it right at her eye, while the other three bees linger like they're waiting in line for their turn. One lunge forward after another, she dodges the stingers vicious attack as it drives into the rock wall behind her.

Upon the rock wall clings the spirit of tree roots and ivy vines that veer off like creases in a hand. Hanging ivy tickles her ear giving Emma a jolt that takes her breath away. She flips around holding her breath and lashing out in a blood-curdling scream but the dangling vines that sway gently brings her to ease with a long exhale.

"Yeah, this ought to work."

Her hand reaches through the vines as they tap against her. She jerks at the annoying sound of buzzing from behind her. Submerged into the darkness, her hand bumps into something kind of hard but it wasn't the wall. With one tug, then another, from the wall. She waves the root around to hopefully scare them off.

"Get out of here, you stupid bees."

Swing after swing, she keeps missing them. She never played softball before. She wishes she would have now. She keeps swinging the root, looking back, ready for the right time to run again.

The bees buzz into the tunnel's shadows. She can hear them whispering to each other, planning their next move when the buzzing culminates to pure silence. A mind full of wonder at what seems to be an endless delay when out of nowhere comes a whooshing sound, followed by a thud, leaving her more nervous than she already is.

A tip-toe backwards into a dark that's darker than the blackness behind the eyelids and with eyes aiming in every direction, she's cautious with every step she takes. Smack, crack, bam, pow, boom. What is making those sounds? She's light on her feet, about to make a run for it when footsteps leave her breathless. It must be him. That evil fire monster. Before she can attempt an escape, a figure in a brown cloak holding a golden stick reveals himself from out of the shadows.

"Let's go. We don't have much time."

By the sound of his voice, Emma can tell it is a man, but his identity is hidden in the darkness of his hood.

"You're one of them. You're a Reaper."

"Child, there's no time for guessing games. Unless you wanna deal with them, I suggest you come with me."

She's terrified, but Emma trusts him. Behind her are more of those super bees zooming in toward her. She has no choice but to trust him.

"All right, smarty. How we getting out of here?"

He's confident and patient, but his lack of words leaves her unconfident and unsafe. She drops to her knees. Her shaky hands cover her eyes with closed fists. She would scream if she had the breath for it.

The buzzing is like nails on a chalk board with enough decibels to shred her eardrums. Before she can cover her ears her jittery hands become still as the buzzing of the blood-thirsty nectar suckers fades away in the darkness.

"Child, open your eyes. He's here."

It's quiet. She holds her breath as a rush of calm cradles her. Those innocent eyes peel open. She looks around for any sight of danger. A smile grows on her face when she realizes everything's back to normal. She exhales when a footstep and clinging chains dangle behind her.

"There you are, Chrissie," says a sinister voice.

Before Emma can get a look, she becomes weightless. Watching her feet leave the ground, she searches for a reason why. How?

Her neck contorts from out of her control. With every aching muscle, she forces her neck downward and with a gasp she realizes she's off the ground, floating there with no explanation.

She shivers; her eyes flutter around to find the grim voice. Her breathing is labored and her palms are slick with sweat. Her pounding heart can burst at any moment. Out of her peripherals she spots another one of those Reaper monsters. Unlike Tate and Ira, this one is dressed in black and seems full of evil.

"Where are they?" the scary creature tilts his head to the side, impatiently awaiting her answer. "Now," the creature flicks his finger.

Her head slams back. Black particles spin above her like a swarm of flies spiraling around ready to swarm onto a tiny crumb of scrap food.

Through her weeping tears, she fights to force the words out, but her quivering lips won't. She can't gather enough oxygen to release a single word.

"Fine, I'll find out for myself."

"No." Emma sobs.

The dust spinning over her head begins to make their spiraling descent into her eyes. Her chestnut-brown irises alter to black as the particles pass into them. It is all like a dream. She can no longer see the swirling black particles, or the shadows that blanket the rocky ceiling.

Immediately the scary creature enters her mind. The trip came in a flash with a glare like arms that reach out to grab her as she zips back through the tunnel and back into the basement where Robert and Jessica were pleading for Emma's release.

Before she can whiff the smell of moist, wet earth she's back at the basement with Mr. Lee, Mrs. Hill, and those scary Reapers.

The one in black is there, lurking around and watching the conversation, but no one can see him but Emma, who remains furtive but alert.

"Please, leave us alone. We want to leave. We have the wordless book you want. I'll give it to you in exchange for Emma." Robert reaches for his bookbag and is immediately halted by Tate.

"There it is," growls the black-cloaked monster as the specter prowls toward Robert.

"The wordless book, huh? It's far from being wordless. It's no good to me anymore. I got what I wanted from it. What I do want is the broken end of my fire orb. I see you know how to use it. The girl for my orb. Do we have a deal?"

The monster in the black cloak sticks his intangible head into Robert's bookbag. Peeping inside, he gawks at the wordless book with a sigh of relief.

"Ahhh, there you are, my love."

Emma stands there like a puppet without strings, stiff as a board. All she can do is watch as his penetrating words whisper to her.

"Thanks to your memory, I now know where my book is. Don't worry; I can't take it yet. Not while I'm in your brain. I'm quite found of memories, you know. Unlike people, memories don't lie."

The evil one slinks around them, mumbling words of requite for Tate's disloyalty. A hint of skepticism boils to vengeance at the thought of his right-hand man betraying him and his rules.

"Why do you lie? Your loyalty has been voluminous."

"Are you backsliding, Tate? The things I've done for you. You're digging yourself a hole you can't crawl out of. You broke the rules and you know what that gets ya."

The book begins to rattle in Robert's bookbag, and a voice rises from out the book. "Robert, don't you give him that orb," says the voice from the book.

"You got this, Tatety boy. I'm gonna rest here for a moment. These nails look like shit. Since hot stuff and I are an item, he gives me immunity to annoying people like yourself. Make it quick, pookie. Momma needs a makeover."

Sparks fly as Tate presses his blades together. "Come on. Let's go."

"Giving advice, huh, old man? Well, you'll pay for that. Looks like you're off the hook for now, Tatety boy. We'll have our talk soon enough. Meanwhile, I have to pay someone a visit first."

Before Ira can crack her frost-bitten fingers, a sudden pulling sensation gives Emma a feeling of motion sickness as she whips into an abstract glare of colors of another memory. She can hear her own voice through the crackling flames. As the smoke clears, she can see herself through the blazing tunnel.

"MR. LEE! MS. HILL! Please don't be dead." Cough, cough, cough. "Please don't be dead."

Emma can't see them through the blazing ruble. Her knees buckle. Cough, cough. "I'm so dizzy." Her eyes widen in the smoky haze. She can somewhat make out a shiny red thing through the debris. She leans in reaching under the broken drywall with all her might as she searches for it.

"Ah, got ya." The tip of her middle finger scoots the orb toward her hand.

An abrupt stop of Emma's memory reminds her of where she is. The taste of smoke in her dry mouth gives her the desperate need to wetten her gums to rid the cotton-taste in her mouth. Every inhale burns her nostrils more then than the one before.

A swift gust of wind swirls through her hair as her head snaps back and her eyes widen. Emma lashes out in a blood-curdling scream, while the black grim particles escape the irises of her eye's. The latch around Deaths summoning hand, slithering into his glowing black orb.

A series of flickering flashes bounce off her reddened cheeks. One second, their tinted an orange hue from the flames in the blazing basement, and secondly, they glow a yellow hue from the tunnel's yellow light bulb that hangs above her head.

His sick twisted game of memory magic or telepathy is over with. Her exhausted body goes limp, and gravity hits her like a ton of bricks as she thuds along the rock ground and she is out like a light.

The sinister and vile voice of Death echoes into Emma's reviving mind. "You can hand it over now. Come on; I know you have it," says the black-cloaked monster.

Her eyes peel open to a blur of earthly browns and shadows that all seem to blend together. She holds her aching head as she stumbles to her feet. Unfurling her finger's, the broken red orb glares into her eyes. She gasps, all safe and secure, tucked in the palm of her hand. She has a slight smirk that grows upon her lips with a bit of relief, now aware of the orb is still in her possession.

"No, you can't have it." Emma draws the orb in tight into her chest to hide it from the one in black.

"Don't worry, Chrissie, I'm not going to take it from you. I wouldn't harm a hair on your little head. But they might."

"What, who?"

From out of the ground rise the skulls of two Death Deader's. Disgusting worms crawl out of their nose hole and eye sockets.

"Shhhh. This is the good part." The hideous black-cloaked monster places his boney finger against his lips like this is fun for him.

He claps his hands excited for what's to come. Clumps of dirt spill away from them as they rise to their feet. Black smoke and leftover dirt crumble out their mouths as they rear back with a vicious growl.

What are those things? You-you you're a-a monster. What made you this way?"

Both skeletal creatures walk next to the evil monster, waiting for his command. She wants to run, but she knows she has no chance. She bites her thumb nail to the quick, nibbling off what little remains, and with a swish and a gargle she ptooey's the remnants toward the Deaders.

"These bone heads here work for me. What I say, they do. Capisce? What they are is pretty obvious. Now, what were they? That's the question you should be asking. So, before I take your puny soul and take back what is mine, let me tell you a story. It'll be your last."

She peeps at her clinching fist, easing it open to gander at the dull red orb with great vigilance. Its dullness leaves her hopeless and sick to her stomach. She gulps, waiting to hear what she's sure is a stupid story, sneaking the red orb around her back and into her bookbag. Shoot, the more he talks, the longer she's still alive "Whatever," Emma leans against the rock wall with a sigh and a slight roll of the eye.

"I'm listening."

SIXTEEN
COAL MINE MASSACRE

t was August 7, 1995, and I was, well, human like you. After I escaped that dreadful place I was once from, I became a coal miner. All of it was an act. A means to survive while I enlisted a team of loyal cohorts to work for me. I had to plan and wait. Wait till I was strong enough to claim this world as my own. I wasn't a miner for long, though. I was a mere peon, slinging shovels and pickaxes. Real honest hard work."

30 YEARS AGO

"Hey, new guy, get over here and take over. I'm getting too old for this crap. I need a break." The rookie was standing at a doorway when he walked over to help out an elderly man by the name of Bill, a seasoned gentleman who hadn't touched his salt-and-pepper beard in years. His face was covered in wrinkles, his hands likewise, but also sandpaper rough. He had a welcoming smile and a humbled soul, though most knew him as a teller of stories.

Several men scattered throughout the tunnel have hammered away at the coal covered walls, while others shoveled their loose fragments into separate carts. The rookie began to hammer away at the wall, becoming more and more violent with each and every swing.

"Don't get yourself worked up, now, New guy. You got to conserve your energy, or you'll tire yourself out. We still have seven hours to go."

The new guy was quiet; he swung away at the wall and gathered the attention of the other coal miners nearby. Anger filled his face as he swung the pickaxe repeatedly until he cracked the pickaxe head where it wrapped around the handle.

A high, keening whistle pealed out in the air around them. It was lunch time, and while holding a ham sandwich close to his mouth, the new guy debated on whether or not to take a bite before tossing it on the ground. He never liked pickles much. He took a drink of water, and a rat ran over to a ketchup covered pickle lying next to his sandwich in the dirt.

Out of anger, he tossed a piece of coal at the rat, missing it before its clever paws could snatch it. While gazing at his ant-covered pickled sandwich, Bill limped around the corner, holding his thermos of hot coffee.

"Rookie, why don't you come and eat with us?" Bill read his face loud and clear. His eyebrows were slanted under his wrinkled forehead. His mouth clamped shut hiding his teeth as they ground together. "Sorry, I'll be on my way."

A glow in his coverall chest pocket took his attention. He pulls out a beautiful multicolored orb he acquired not long ago. It was Teal, Red, White, and Purple. Part of it was black but it broke off a few days ago.

While embracing the enchanting orb amidst a daydream of clamor, the loud and unsettling demonic sounds from within the multicolored orb brought a malicious grin to his face.

The daydream was quickly drawn to a halt by the sounds of nearby footsteps. He secretively tucked his precious orb back into his coverall chest pocket.

"Sam, my office. Now! Bring your pickaxe."

Sam followed his boss to his office, leaving his lunch behind, and only taking his pickaxe.

"Have a seat."

The metal chair groaned under his weight, squeaking like a frightened mouse. He left his pickaxe leaning along the right side of the seat.

"Have I done something wrong, Mr. Shanti?"

"Well, for starters, are you having problems at home? How's your wife?"

It's as quiet as the grave. There's only the hum of Mr. Shanti's worn-down refrigerator and the awful creaking of his chair as he rocked in it. Sam tapped his hand against his trembling leg. Emotion built up in his face, staring a hole through the wall as he could hear the screams of his wife.

"Sam, put it down. What the hell are you doing? Stop it you fucking psycho! Put the damn knife down! No, stop it! Ahh!"

The sounds of her pleading for her life were authentic, as if time took him back to that terrible night. The world seemed to spin around him until he was taken out of his daze by the snap of Mr. Shanti's fingers.

"We've been arguing lately, but that's it."

"Okay, then why are you so angry? Bill told me about your little fit you had earlier."

He grabbed the handle of the pickaxe, grinding his hand around the handle and tapping his foot on the floor. While he was debating what to say, Mr. Shanti pulled off his glasses.

"Listen, son, I'm sorry about whatever it is you're going through, but this is a workplace. There's no room for violence and those kinds of behaviors here. Well, I'm gonna have to suspend you."

He shook his head in disbelief, pretending for a moment he was innocent. But in a way, he really was. He couldn't tell his boss the orb made him do it. It made him kill his wife. How crazy did that sound? Who would believe that?

"It's for three days. Use this time to fix your marriage, get your head straight, and I'll see you Monday. You're a hard worker, Sam. We can't afford to lose you."

"Is that it? Am I free to leave?"

"Yeah, leave your pickaxe where it is. I can see it's cracked, anyway. I'll give you a new one when you get back. You can see yourself out."

The bottom drawer squeaked and clanged as it fully opened. Mr. Shanti pulled out a black folder and dropped it on his desk. His hand rested along his forehead to block the desk lamps bright lights from his eyes. Mr. Shanti was so busy, he forgot Sam was even there. He was too distracted with job hazard assessments and the stress of his actions.

Without warning, one end of the pickaxe drove through the skull of Mr. Shanti. With a pull and a few tugs, the broken end of the pickaxe broke off into Mr. Shanti's head, sending his head smacking into the desk, submerged in a pool of his blood.

He gawked at his broken pickaxe. His lips curled into a smile, loving how it taken the newly formed shape of a scythe. Black smoke rose off his flesh. His eyes were consumed by a sinister slime like oil. The same ooey gooey texture rested on the edge of his nostril and slurped back into his nose. His voice deepened with a sinister laugh. "Yes."

The end-of-lunch whistle blew. The long tunnel, which was empty is now manned with full-bellied men off their lunch break and hard at work. He walked with prominence down the tunnel with a stern stride.

Bill, the kind old man and Sam's pickaxe wielding partner, approached him, concerned. "Are you all right? Where the hell's that smoke off your skin coming from? You look a mess."

Sam ignored Bill, walking past as if he didn't exist until another co-worker found blood dripping off the broken end of his pickaxe.

"What the hell did you do?" Clearly frightened, he scurried away, bumping into Bill.

Bill remained surprised and speechless. "Look, I'm sorry, Sam, but I had no choice. You've been acting weird lately. What did Shanti say to you?"

He held there, taking it all in, visualizing the chaos with a malicious grin.

"Man, you're freaking me out right now."

He was quite irritated at Bill's concerns. Its rather annoying really. Sam felt more powerful with every angry thought crossing his grim mind. Steadily, his neck contorts into Bill's direction. He appeared emotionless, soulless, and full of hate as he advanced toward Bill. Grabbing his throat, he pressed his fingers into Bill's throat gradually lifting him off the ground.

"As you already witnessed, I don't like rats."

Black smoke reached out from his eyes like stringy cheese pervading off of him, grouping together into a ball. His mouth cracked in black sludge as he smiled at Bill's misery.

Gasping for air, Bill grabbed his hand in hopes of loosening his grip. With a deep inhale, Sam was able to consume his soul. He enjoyed watching Bill's soul leave his body. First, his eyelids slammed shut, and the lack of blood flow to his face caused his skin to sink. His entire body went limp. The last of his pure soul fled his pale white lips in a spiral downward into the black ball of smoke before his pale, lifeless body dropped to the ground.

Demonic whispers of an unknown dialect spoke out. Few words were comprehensible while most weren't. "Leader. He mustn't be harmed," hissed the slithering voice. The black ball of smoke swooped down to Sam's feet and spiraled upward around him.

Smoke swirled around the wooden pickaxe handle peeling off splinters like paint to unveil its new form: a black handle, stretching out longer into a fierce and masterful kusarigama. The blade became wider and much sharper than the pickax. Bill's lifeless body shimmered off its glazed surface. The length of the black handle is about the length of a baseball bat with a chain and spiked ball that shakes the earth as it clashes onto her covered surface.

"I'm the guardian of the Death orb," growled the menacing voice. Continuing around his legs, the sinister smoke shrouded him with a black cloak. His face was concealed in the hood of the most unfathomable darkness. The smoke dissipated, revealing a fully cloaked figure. The ball of oozing smoke converged to form the Death orb. Gradually, the Death orb floats into his chest.

"It's Sam." A coworker's voice shivered in unmeasurable fear.

He jerked his head at the pleasing sound of vulnerable fear from an innocent soul.

"I'm no longer Sam. I'm the Death Reaper."

The chaos of terrified coworkers was pure ecstasy for him. Their outcries animated his sadistic soul and his hateful black heart.

He geo leaped to the second victim, cutting him clean in half with the blade of his kusarigama, taking his soul before he landed.

The third victim thought he was getting away, but Death threw the spiked ball of his chained kusarigama into his back, and its sharp spikes like dragon's teeth dug into his flesh and spine. On impact, he jerked the chain, pulling the victim off his feet while ripping out the spiked ball simultaneously.

He caught the chain, whipping the spiked ball around over his head, throwing it at his next victim. The chain wrapped around the coal miner's legs, and with a single yank, the victim slammed to the ground. Death geo leaped to his begging victim and, without remorse, slit his throat. Blood oozed out of the coal miner's neck, staining his teeth and cheek red as it spread across his flesh.

His soul, a mixture of smoke and particles twirled skyward as if the wisps were countless screaming souls being whisked away into the raging black hole of his Death orb. The particles filled the Death orb like salt in a saltshaker. The orb's glow brightened amidst the echoes of his sinister laugh.

NOW

Emma's exhausted but is still able to balance herself against the tunnel wall. She rocks there, fighting to stay awake in fear of what may happen to her if she fell asleep.

She's barely able to make eye contact with him after that terrible story she just heard. Slightly able to make eye contact with anything for that matter.

Each approaching step Death makes toward her elevates her breathing. She rubs her fluttering eyes as if she is trying to keep them from leaping out of her sockets.

Her entire world is closing in around her completely snatching away her peripherals. It is her and a mere speck on the adjacent wall. The darkness takes her completely when her body loses function and she slumps over. Death stoops to her level gawking at her limp unconscious body.

"Good night, Chrissie. See you soon." Death overshadows Emma's unconscious body with an ominous laugh. From out of the reflection of the Death orb, Emma's unconscious body lies on the floor in a completely different coal mining room. Death towers at her feet, dropping her pink bookbag next to her still body.

Death scuffs his feet along the dirt while advancing to the dead-end wall, where, dangling above the dirt, are black Brahma boots with loose strings skimming along the ground as his feet sway gently.

Flashes of red calmly pulsate in his dead-end fingertips. Creeping up the wall are black cargo pants and a half-tucked white T-shirt. Dry crusty blood covers his neck and stains his chest with a thick coating that has already coagulated. The smell is so thick of heavy copper, Death can taste it on his tongue.

His head is drooping over, and dirty black tangled hair hangs off his head. His hands are restrained by chains clinging into each other above his head. Death's nose snuffs over the man's blood-covered shirt.

The man's jaw moves. He winces, still tasting the gritty dirt coating his mouth. He licks his gums to wet them, edging his head up exposing his battered face caked in dirt, dry blood, and sweat. Death gloats over Robert's misery, holding the wordless book in one hand and the fire orb in the other.

"I love the smell of blood and fear. Now, with my book in my possession, the cause can finally begin.

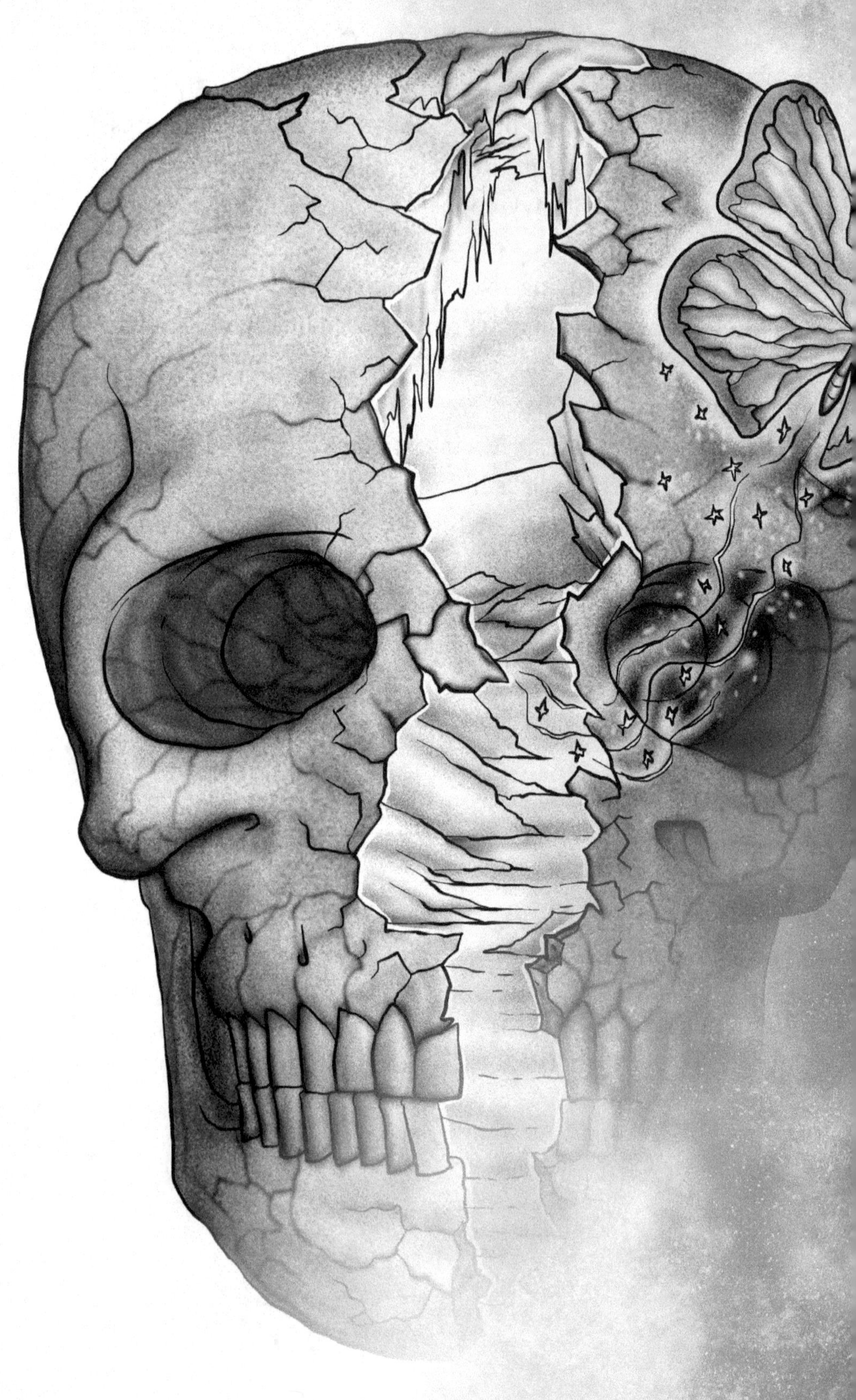

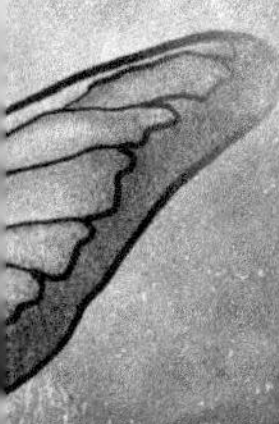

SEVENTEEN
CRACK IN THE WALL

Edges of broken gray glass invite the eyes to see the settling dust reflecting off an old rusty pipe. Each water droplet lands in a small puddle, running down a sloping concrete floor and into a drain.

Blind wind cares not if the edges of the glass are sharp or dull, or the width is too narrow or broad. The tempest carries the aroma of death and random debris, both gliding and crashing down over the graveyard of the Impossible.

Distant screaming whooshes past the broken window like an oncoming missile. *Smack! Thud, Thud, Thud!* Groans of pain mixed with mumbling are not at all lackluster for the unlucky soul. *Squish Squash, Squish, Squash* through the muddy terrain. The door creaks open when his muddy bare feet enter the castle.

"Ah, no, no, no, no. I can't believe it. How did she do it?"

He scurries over to a filthy drain. It takes a moment for those shaky knees to reach the cold stone floor. Luckily, the drain is big enough for his frail hand to fit through.

"There you are."

A pucker of his lips and a squint of his eyes trigger him, making him aware of how unsure he is of what he has between his fingers. Its sticky skin lathers along his fingertips. Several soft and squishy bumps remind him of dipping his hand in a full bag of marshmallows.

"Ribbit."

In the cup of his hand is a frog. But this is no ordinary frog. Its eyes are uglier than slime-dipped marble. Its flesh is as dark-purple as grapes.

His nerves are a bit shaky as he lowers the frog down to the slippery wet drain. Its tongue flicks out and snaps back. Sticking to its gooey, dripping-wet tongue is a moldy Polaroid picture. Voltage courses through its sticky body as it sits there, waiting for the man to free it from its burden.

"Ah, don't you dare shock me, you little varmint."

He peels off the photo from the frog's rough syrupy tongue before it hops down the drainage pipe, emitting a bluish-purple flash of electricity. The man shakes off the wet picture, flinging water droplets like a sputtering faucet, drying it off against the wool fibers of his sleeve.

"Woooo, it's okay." He breaths a sigh of relief, fighting back the tears.

Weak in the knees, he slides down the nearby wall, using it for support. A gander at the moldy over-exposed photo of a little girl riding her bike brings his head to a tilt. He slides the back of his hood off his head, revealing an elderly man with wrinkles in his eyes, a low ponytail, and a full gritty gray beard. The old man gently brushes his finger over the picture.

"I miss you and your mother so much. You look just like her."

The printed picture makes him feel like he's with her again. He can see it all as he remembers the day when the picture was taken.

THIRTY ONE YEARS AGO

The town is an ordinary cobblestone city upon the pink-russet sunrise gifting the town's residents with peace and love. Shopping centers display cases lined in fall decorations and delicious treats. Store owners flip their Closed signs to Open, ready to start their day.

Past the town and into an unearthly rainbow color burning woods are trees of different color flames with an ambience speaking of visual poetry.

Glissading burning leaves twist and twirl gracefully like geishas transitioning into baby phoenixes before grazing their talons along the ground. Delicately, they swoop back into the air, taking flight above the trees, giving sight to a marvelous bird's-eye view over the burning woods.

All the burning trees are harmless as light with an opening they can walk in. Covered in flame and sparkles of the same color, several albino deer drop off children into the woods and disappear inside the sparkling hole from within the tree's trunk.

"Whoa. Here's fine. Good boy. Hold there, Chris, and I'll help you off."

"Wow, Papa, that was so fun. When will we do it again?" Chris pets the albino deer, giving it the sweetest hug ever. "You're in school now; were gonna do this a lot. Exciting, isn't it?"

"Super cool. Can I do the thing, Papa? Please."

Her squinting eyes and widened smile were too cute to say no to. Marley stood still, his hand covering his mouth pretending to be thinking about it but was only delaying his answer to tease her.

"You remember how to do it?"

"Come on, let's go." She beats her Papa inside the tree's trunk, bouncing up and down with excitement.

The trunk is full of a pretty purple light with a sprinkle of purple sparkles, like looking at the many stars through a telescope. The tree's entranceway closes with them inside like elevator doors. Sparkles follow her finger as she draws the outline of a butterfly.

"Look, that's so cool Papa?"

"Ah, look, you did it."

The brilliant sparkly butterfly transforms into a key that glides down into the keyhole, unlocking the trunk's doorway, giving way to a heavenly light.

Marley can still hear her heavenly voice calling out to him through the glistening purple light. It was blissful, every cell in his body generated a peace that flowed through him like rippling waters when a single tear drips onto the polaroid picture.

A luxurious Angel Oak treehouse rests on the side of a mountain community with many cliffs, each holding their own treehouse. Leaves are like angelic butterflies changing colors as they flap their heavenly wings. The trunk rests in a dreamy lake reflecting the many colorful leaves off its pastel purple surface with waves that roll a rhythmic pulse to the sound of dreamy music.

He's making memories in the backyard with his precious daughter, watching her outrun the butterflies on her bike. Between the cosmos flowers and sweet smell of honey crisp apples, every breath is as lovely as the next.

"Marley, look. I'm riding with no hands."

"Who's Marley? Who am I?" Marley walks over and tickles Chris, who laughs uncontrollably.

"Hey, Papa, that tickles."

"That sounds better. Look what I fixed."

"Teddy! You fixed him. Ah, Marley."

"Marley? I guess you don't want your teddy bear, then."

"I'm joking with you, Papa. Mom called you Marley. I thought it would be funny if I called you Marley, too. Let me have it." Chris laughs, admiring her teddy bear.

"How did you fix him?"

"I sewed it up. Do you see the stitching?" Chris folds down the ear of her teddy and spots the string sticking out of its head slightly.

"There's more."

"What do you mean, 'there's more?'"

"Press its belly."

"Hi, sweet pea." Chris begins to tear up. "Mommy loves you." The gentle sound of her mother brings joy to her heart. Chris runs to give her dad a hug. "Thanks so much. You're the best dad in the world."

NOW

The joyous sound of his daughter fades away as he stares at the only photo he has of her. A single tear trickles down his face. "Somehow, someway, we're going to see each other again, my precious daughter."

A gentle breeze blows past, fluttering the polaroid and bringing the sound of a gentle whisper. "Marley."

"What? Hello? Who said that? I must be going crazy."

"Marley."

There it is again. He comes to his feet, putting the picture in the inner pocket of his cloak. The voice leads him to a long dark corridor with torches scattered throughout. A steady crackle and popping takes over the corridor's void as Marley pulls a torch off the adjacent wall.

"Hello. Who's there?"

The basement door creeps open with a lingering creak. He draws the lower half of Magmus's golden staff from the inside pocket of his cloak, ready to attack whatever's on the other side. The staff rattles against the door as he uses it to ease the door open. So far, so good. Marley can't stop shaking, taking a gamble with a gradual first stride to the first step past the door. His shadow towers over him like a blood thirsty vampire as he tiptoes down the spiral stairway.

"Hello…anyone there?" His feet scuff along the concrete with each step all the way to the bottom.

"Hello? Show yourself. I must be losing my mind."

Reaching the bottom, he waves the torch around, trying to catch a glimpse of who or what was calling his name. The echo of his own voice floods his mind with thoughts of confusion and disbelief. Maybe his cluttered mind of mystery and doubt is brought on by the stress of the Impossible, or maybe it is his old age getting to him.

A chuckle occupies his lips at the amusement of his wandering imagination. "Hum, I must be losing my daburn mind." With a soft sigh and eyelids that slip closed, he turns away toward the stairs when a flickering from the wall lights scintillate randomly.

"What, who's there? Those darn lights haven't worked in years."

The walls lighting fixtures shatter along the ground like empty bullet shell casings in a deadly war. The concrete under his feet splits, a crack that zigzags like a fleeing mouse from cat. Continuing halfway up the wall the crack comes to an immediate halt.

A loose piece of concrete dangles there in the split-open wall. All is still but the twitching of his hands and the chattering of his teeth. He gulps, swallowing as little hope as he can. The dangling piece of rock breaks loose tumbling down the wall and across the concrete floor.

Something odd, something curious, something mysterious draws him to the crack in the wall. He inches his way forward, tilting his head, trying to unravel what is happening. The crack is lined in tree bark. His fingers skim along its ridged edges.

"Could it be?"

Unlike the dull and pale colors bestowing this place, there is a rich and vibrant white and sky-blue butterfly emitting snow from behind its fluttering wings while passing through the crack in the wall. Before the joyous laughter comes, its anticipation flips his expression. Dry, labial hills erode into wet-licking lips of imminent joy.

Evil and a fool for thinking you'll get away with this. I'll do whatever I have to do to save anyone I can from you."

"Why do you care so much for others? They certainly don't care for you."

"There's a lot of good people. None of them deserve to die."

"Die. The people I kill don't fully die. I make them my servants. You've seen them. What do you think of my Deader's?"

"I think you're sick."

"Tell you what: I'll let you choose what one you want to be."

"Go to hell."

"Fire Deader it is. I'll make it happen nice and slow. Don't move; this may burn a little."

Robert can see the fear on his own face in the glassy reflection of Death's orb. A flash of transparent red pulsates through its entirety.

"I love it when you fear me. It fuels me." Death snarls, his footsteps echoing sharply off the prison chamber's wet walls.

Death approaches Robert, holding the wordless book against the side of his swaying shroud. Ink dust trickles from the book's pages, killing unwelcome strands of green that colonize through the crevices of the concrete floor.

Burning embers of ash rise out of the dark one's decayed and rotted flesh, prowling in cadence over Robert's forearm.

He winces, and his knees buckle forward but the tension of both ankle and wrist restraints prevent him from smacking his knees against the ground. His jaws clamp down, scratching his lower gums and staining his teeth in blood. Individual hot ash presses into his flesh, forming burns all up his arms and through his white T-shirt.

Death laughs in his twisted amusement. Both eyes squint, his fists ball up, and each chain jangles as his restrained hands tremble.

Yelps merge into wailing while his flesh begins to blister. Through the unbearable pain, all Robert can think of is Emma when Death catches his exhausted eyes glancing at her with great empathy.

"Don't worry, Robby boy. She'll be next. I'm thinking of a Snow Deader. Those are fun to watch."

"Let her go! Don't you touch her."

Emma calmly becomes aware of herself. She senses a slight pulse beating in her neck. Her eyelids open the tiniest amount, revealing the dark blob of Death through her foggy vision. Her arms stretching tightly at her side. The faint sounds of screaming and laughing are nauseating. She uncurls her fingers, pressing her hand against the dirt to help lift her head off the ground. Her foggy vision clears. All the pieces are back in place like a puzzle.

"Ah, my head. Mr. Lee, you're alive?"

"Shut her up. Her voice annoys me."

Two Death Deader's drag Emma into the rooms corner, re-griping, and fighting to keep control of her thrusting feet. She's stuck there, sobbing and frozen in fear.

"Watch her. Sneaky little shit. The last time I took my eyes off Chrissie, she stole my precious orb. Your death will be enviable, you little brat."

"Enough! Make it stop. Please! We've never done anything to you."

"What are you talking about? She's the reason why I was trapped at the Impossible in the first place. Not to say I didn't like the place. I did create it, and my beautiful book, which I've been separated from for far too long. All I wanted was to-" Death growls, clinching his fist in frustration. "But she had to get in my way. Well, not this time. Ha ha ha."

"I don't see what's so funny? Your precious little book is missing some pages."

"What?" The Death Reaper scrambles through the book, making the pages blur.

Coming across the missing pages, the Death Reaper geo leaps in close to Robert's face with a loud enough roar to crack and crumble the concrete wall behind him. "Where are the missing pages?"

"Stop torturing me."

"Be careful how you speak to me. The next time I feel disrespected, I will cut out your tongue with the blade of my kusarigama."

With a wave of Death's hand, the burning embers drop to the ground. Their burning edges sizzle to a cool temperature.

"Speak. The merger may not happen now without them."

Sweat overflows Robert's pores, running over his many burns and blisters. He gasps, trying to ignore the pain and regain his composure.

"I said speak. I won't ask again."

"I don't know. I don't know."

"Sadly, I believe you."

Before the next few words slip out of his mouth, he peeps his head around Death. His eyebrows rise, wrinkling his forehead. His mouth hangs open loosely at the sight of Emma under the Deader's control and terrified for her life.

"What, you think she's getting away? You can't save her."

With the broken fire orb in Death's loose grasp, Robert is sure there is enough slack in the restraints to reach out and grab it.

Death guffaws at Emma's expense, leaving him distracted from Robert's desire for the fire orb. Robert is reticent in reaching for the fire orb in Death's fingertips. The dark one's hand sways, giving Robert a much more difficult time fulfilling his motive. He calmly waits for the right moment. Butterflies flutter in his stomach as Death's rotten fingers rest back at the Reaper's side.

"I can feel your bones quiver. It makes me happy to see you so frightened Robby boy. I'm gonna miss torturing you," the dark one says.

Before the evil one can twist his neck in Robert's direction, a moment, an opening for a way out twinkles in the broken fire orb like it is giving him a wink. Robert makes his move and snatches the fire orb from Death's grasp.

"Abeamus," Robert mutters with a smirk.

A cluster of black-and-red particles and smoke swirls into the wordless book before the book can smack along the dirt floor.

Landing hard in the Impossible graveyard, Death slams into the ground first with a clump of his cloak in the clinch of Robert's grasp. They tussle amongst the dead's grave, rolling along the ground and bumping into standing caskets.

The rolling comes to a halt when Death gets the upper hand, ripping the fire orb out from his grip and tossing him through an open casket. Broken pine wood surrounds Robert as he lays there in its splintery mess. Pine splinters and dead grass adheres to the back of his white T-shirt as he struggles to his feet.

"Nice try, but it looks like your little plan didn't work. You messed up. Chris now belongs to me. As far as I'm concerned, until I find my missing pages, you can stay here and rot." The Death Reaper's jaw bones creak as he smirks a sadistic smile that is mostly hidden under the shadows of his hood.

Black smoke climbs up the cloak of the sneaky evil snake. Robert sways with little strength to hold his balance. With one last ditch effort to gain control of the Fire Orb, he bursts forward with his hand extended outward. His hand traverses through the dry hazy gloom with bowels that deliver a sharp sting like a serpent's bite.

He jerks his hand back which sizzles like butter in a frying pan. His melted flesh runs downward, as if made of slime, dripping onto the dead grass. A sharp acidic smell permeates off his flesh wound, strong enough that no amount of scrubbing could ever take the stench away.

The black smoke ascends the somber skies toward the ominous skull cloud, leaving Robert's heart submerged in a sea of hopelessness.

"NO! What have I done?"

A trail of black smoke, compacted tight as a cluster a fleeing Crows, twirls skyward with wisps like wild beasts, guarding their king amongst a vigorous war. The enemy launches toward the weary grey, the portals mouth opens wide with a devilish chuckle, ready to receive its welcoming master.

Disheartened by his grave mistake, Robert stumbles beaten, burnt, and bruised toward the castle.

"Emma's in danger, and I'm not there to protect her. I might as well have sent her to her Death. Hello? Hey, come out and talk to me, please! I don't even know your name. Man in the cloak. I need your help."

He shoves open the double entrance doors to the castle, leaving an echo down the dark corridor with cries stinging even deeper.

"Come on, man, she's going to die if you don't help me!"

Continuing down the corridor, shoving doors open on

both sides only to find out they are empty. A surge of hope gusts through his veins like a crashing tidal wave as he observes a different door that is slightly open. The door stands there like an invitation to a new adventure, creaking like a beating drum. He remains vigilant as he descends the spiral steps.

"Hello? I need your help."

An echoing thump of each descending step mixes with a continual cling and clang, fusing with some moderate grumbling, keeping him on high alert. The grumbling becomes louder and easier to interpret as he approaches the bottom of the steps.

"Come on, it's right there. I want to go back home."

It's the cloaked man. Robert verifies that he can barely see him through the yellow and orange hues of his torch nestling securely in a wall mount. He is thrusting a golden rod into a cracked wall, splintering tree bark with each chop.

"Hello."

"Ah, it's you again. Unless you want to help me, I advise you to go back to where you came."

"Now, how do I do that?"

"The same way you got in here. The orb."

"That's the thing—the Death Reaper has it."

"What? You idiot! Why did you let him have it?" The cloaked man is clearly frustrated tossing his golden staff across the room.

"I didn't give it to him. He took it from me. So, I'm stuck here till you tell me another way."

"Looks like you're stuck, then, because there is no other way out. If there was, I would have been gone a long time ago. I can't leave with this stinking bound curse anyway. Where's your friend?"

"Jessica? She didn't make it. She bled to death from Ira's boomerang."

"I'm sorry to hear that."

"Listen, this place this disgusting evil place was once beautiful. It was where I was from. This crack here, it's got to be home. It has to."

"It's a crack."

"Look at this butterfly. They don't live here. They're called 'snow meadows.' See the snow trail they leave behind?"

"Wow, super cool."

"This snow meadow is from the Possible. My home. See the tree bark here. It's like it's making its way back. Like it's bleeding through. But how?"

"Look, there's not much time. Emma's in trouble."

"Who's Emma?"

"She's a student at Happy Oaks Middle School. She was on a weekend retreat to Camp Wolf Creek."

"Wait, wait, is that place still open? Have you seen her? My daughter, Christen Honeycutt?"

"Wait a sec—you're Marty?"

"Marley actually. Please tell me you've seen my daughter?"

"I've heard your story. You've been here this whole time?"

"Yes, yes. Now, have you seen my daughter?"

"Sorry, I've never met her."

"Damn it. I never should have left the Possible. What was I thinking? We could have stopped him before he left, and none of this would have happened."

"What's the Possible?" Robert asks hesitantly, knowing the old man probably won't hear him anyway due to the man's spastic actions.

"Yesterday, my life was normal, now this. Could things get any stranger than now?"

"Actually, yes, they can. Follow me."

Marley lifts the torch from its wall mount. The flame sizzles like bacon with orange and yellow stripes swaying like a sleeping ghost. The grays of the man's smoky beard shimmer off its glow.

Ascending the drafty concrete steps the flame gives light to spider webs and mildew thick as paint. The torch in Marley's grasp gives the man a yellowish aura that surrounds him like a light bulb.

"That little girl you mentioned. Emma, was it?"

"Yeah. That's her."

"Was she 'bout thirteen, brown-haired, and wearing an orange camp shirt?"

"How do you know Emma?"

Each click and clack up the spiral stairway gave an echoing beat in rhythmic quality and a counterpoint to the old man's gritty voice.

"The stranger part is, somehow, I was taken from here. Suddenly swept away. I landed in some sort of coal mine when I heard the voice of a little girl screaming. She was terrified. After I saved Emma, I was right back here. I've been here for over twenty-three years, and that's not happened to me. Not once."

"You're not the only one who has questions," Robert murmurs as they enter the chilly oppressive corridor, thudding the basement door shut behind them.

The walk down the corridor toward the main entrance is rather odd. The old man is quiet. The tension boils in the pit of his stomach, a tension so hot his stomach is about to spit and sputter acid up his intestines.

"You wanna defeat the Reapers and save this Emma? Well, you're outta luck. I've tried to save my daughter and failed. I couldn't beat them. Neither can you."

Marley slams the large double doors shut, leaving Robert outside, helpless and alone. His heart skips a beat at the sound of two clicks. With clenching fists, he pounds on the doors.

"You mentioned your daughter. What's her name?"

The wind whooshes through dry dead grass and withering leaf litter, blending with the echoes of his pounding fists off the double archway doors.

"You can't just do nothing, man! Lives are at stake here!"

An aquatic voice carries on the gust of wind pushing against the grass, over a broken headstone, through the crack of a swaying casket door, and over his shoulder.

"Looks like I'm not the only one who acts my age."

Robert jerks his head around to observe Seth standing there like a samurai warrior amongst a battle. His teal cloak blows in the wind like a super villain's does before causing chaos. His trident pierces the cold hard ground. Teal vapors rise off his legs and feet like an oncoming fog that evaporates before reaching his waist.

"What do you want?"

Thunder rumbles in the muggy skies. Seth leans back, glancing at the somber clouds. Both aquatic eyes roll toward the rumbling thunder.

"It's about to rain. I can feel it."

"Why are you here, Seth?"

"Well, since you don't know where the missing pages are, you're pretty much useless—plus, you've seen us. We can't risk our motives to be tarnished by your kind."

"The Death Reaper said he would leave me here."

"He changed his mind. After what you did to Ira, he sent me here to kill you."

"Is she dead?"

"You're not going to be alive long enough to know."

Thunder shakes the dark and gloomy skies, drawing Robert's attention upward. A single raindrop falls from the dull grim abyss and splats on his forehead. He wipes the wetness off his brow with a slide of his hand.

"What's the matter? Are you scared of little a water? You should be. This ought to be terrifying."

A sudden rumble behind the tree line frightens the murder of crows, and they take flight. The Impossible tremors with a monstrous quake. In the midst of the horizon, dead elm trees scatter, making way for crashing tsunami waves. From out of the second wave, two massive aquatic hands the size of battle ships charge through the branches and trees like an explosion.

The Impossible tremors under the presence of the mighty sea beast, shaking the ground like waves churn in a storm. Many tentacles adorn its octopus face. Its head alone is taller than any mountain. Both aquatic arms are a ménage to a family of squirmy tentacles that trample the shoreline, leaving craters under their weight.

"Ah, fuuuuuck." Robert fights to keep his balance under the tremors it causes.

His belly grumbles as the beast stares into his shivering soul. The ginormous water beast rears back with a vicious roar, sending a spray of monstrous goo hammering into him.

"Robert, meet Mokud. Mokud, meet Robert." Seth's laugh

reverberates like a submarine's sonar system with enough power to rupture his lungs.

One aqua tentacle barrels into the castle tower like a cannon ball plows through a pirate's ship. Broken brick debris whizzes past him after a lucky tumble out of the line of fire.

The sea beast's many tentacles rise high above the bell tower, stretching out and curling into a ball, ready to crush Robert with enough weight to make him implode. Fear becomes a tangible, aqua living force creeping over him like some hungry beast, immobilizing him; his brain is holding him captive. He wants desperately to run for safety, but his feet will not allow him to.

Mokud's colossal tentacles come splashing down one after another with enough force to flip the earth. Robert can feel his flight response kick in, increasing his heart rate, flooding him with much-needed adrenaline. He somehow manifests the strength to get out of the way, and its devastating impact stifles a splash, throwing him forward like a rag doll with a spine-aching bounce and a slide across the graveyard, bumping into an open-doored casket lying on its side.

His blisters have busted, and are now irritated by the gritty layers of dirt covering them. He digs deep to ignore the pain, and he catches movement out of his peripherals. The moving brown blob brings him to a fright. He stiffens up covering his face with his hands, as the open casket rolls over on him.

It's pitch-black other than the small amount of light making its way in from under the casket. The smell of rotten burnt meat isn't his only concern. It is the amount of weight holding him down and who's lying on him that makes him cringe.

A tiny but noticeable thud smacks the ground next to Robert's waist. He wiggles his shoulders and arms to stretch his hand under the limp weight. He rummages his hand, curling his fingers like a creeping spider after its meal. His fingers strain, skimming across the cold smooth texture of something like metal.

"You're not playing hide and go seek with me, are you, Robert? This game is so fun."

Robert is literally in his own death-bed and may be there permanently if he doesn't figure a way out. He drags the piece of metal with his outstretching fingers. He wiggles his neck from under the dead body, straining for a peek. The moon's beam scarcely passes through, and the silver light shines onto what looks like a Zippo lighter.

"Is that oh, please, please, let it be."

The lid clicks open. He spins the coarse flint wheel with his thumb, producing sparks, bringing the wick to an orange flame.

"Yes." Robert bursts with laughter.

He brings the flame close to his face, and the torches scorching mouth swallows the shadows revealing the burnt fleshy face of Blake, who's as charred as coal.

"Arghhhhh, Shit!"

A rush of adrenaline boils in his veins. He shoves a crispy Blake and the casket off of him, and Seth halts the colossal aquatic tentacles with the command of his closing fist, sending Mokud back into the lake with a simple wave of his hand.

"Look what you did. Looks like Natsu really did a number on him. Ha, looks like a hotdog. After I kill you, the old man has a mess to clean up."

Here come the rain drops all at once, falling from a sky of dingy gray like a pack of hungry wolves ready to devour their prey. His lungs work to bring in much-needed oxygen. Immediately, he regrets breathing so heavily, as the cold and bitter taste of polluted rainwater splashes off his tongue.

"Why don't you stop this?"

"I'm sorry, Mr. Lee, but a little rain can't hurt you. Or maybe it will."

Each strand of gray grass dances like cobras charming each rain drop. Robert numbers their splashes against the toe cap of his work boot, and each water droplet comes to a screeching halt like an intense traffic jam. He reaches his hand in to touch the levitating raindrops, and their rubber-like texture bounces off his hand like a rack of pool balls breaking up by the cue.

Each water droplet abruptly transfigures into glass, one of them lacerating his finger. He places the cut between his lips. The taste of his own blood brings him to his own mortality. He goes weak in the knees, hitting the ground like a bomb, then army crawls between headstones and caskets, looking for a safe place to take cover.

"Oh, now a game of tag. Looks like I'm it."

Seth sends hundreds of perfectly still bladed rain droplets from high above; they come barreling toward Robert like whiffle balls.

"Oh, shit."

He crawls past a gravestone, taking cover behind the security of its concrete wall. Ting, ting, clank. All the aqua blades slam into the headstone. Glancing around for his next move the only standing casket seems like the best option he has.

Peeping his trembling head over the headstone, his unnerved eyes spot Seth gloating at his expense.

"You can't hide from me."

Robert's hand slushes into the mud as he picks himself off the ground and, in full sprint, runs for his life into the last standing casket with an etching that reads Charlie Baskins on the casket's outer door. Another round of aqua blades whirl from behind him and into the closing casket door, missing him by inches. His eyes slam shut, and his arm shields his face, hoping one is not stuck in him.

A brief silence gives Robert a moment. Catching his breath is difficult since space is limited. He has a sudden sense of claustrophobia. He can smell the putrid acrid odor of Charlie's burnt rotten flesh as his dead body presses against his.

His heart feels like a wild animal trying to escape its cage. He wants to surrender, stand there, and let Seth kill him so his torment will all be over with.

An artillery of cold water droplets pelts the casket and ground from angry clouds, unleashing their mighty fury of many aqua blades from the command of Seth's trident. Aqua blade after blade pierces into Charlie's chest, shaking him like an electric shock.

Robert knows he can't stay in there forever. With a shove of the door, the remaining screw falls out the hinge, dropping the door to the ground and sending Robert and Charlie's body tumbling into the mud. He tastes the mush of mud and the crunch of grass between his lips.

"Looks like you got a little mud on ya, Mr. Lee."

A tentacle wriggles out from Seth's cloak creeping its way over to Robert before he can stand on his feet. It slinks around his ankle and with a hard yank Robert crashes to his face and cracks his nose in the slippery wet mush. Blood, mud, and worm guts smears up his cheek as his exhausted muscles pushes himself off the slimy mud.

Seth's tentacle begins to retract back under his cloak, dragging Robert away from Charlie's dead corpse and closer to Seth's wrath. Robert becomes weightless; the tentacle constricting around his legs lifts him off the ground. The overwhelming pooling of blood drains to his brain, slowing his heart rate down considerably as he is dangling over Seth by both legs. Gravity sends his organs over his lungs, making it difficult for him to breathe.

"Are you ready to die now?"

"You're gonna let the Death Reaper boss you around huh? What, you can't make your own decisions?"

"Any last words, loser? I'm getting very impatient. I am a child, you know," Seth says as many aqua tentacles emerge from out of the back of his cloak.

"What the hell is that?"

Tentacles slither over to Robert, wrapping around all his limbs. He can feel their grip tightening around him. Each tentacle's tension stiffens, threatening to pop his joints out of their sockets.

"Okay, okay." Robert quivers, stuttering.

"I'm done playing with you, mister," Seth says as the tentacles' grip loosens dropping Robert like a bad habit.

"Damn, you didn't have to drop me."

His body aches with a ruthless groan, cracking his neck as he sits up. A faint scream fights through the raging winds and piercing rain so dense he'd be better off wearing a blindfold.

Lightning illuminates a brilliant pathway, lifting his eyes toward a teal blur.

"Robert! Robert! Get Over Here! Now!"

He recognizes the voice and moves closer. His eyes follow the wave of voltage coursing through Seth's body, moving them down to a puddle he's standing in. Robert tries to locate the source of electricity. Bubbles emerge from the puddle as he leans in to take a closer look. Pop after pop, the bubbles flow into ripples, fading away, exposing Seth's hand convulsing in the puddle's reflection.

From out of the puddle, a dark purple frog jumps out, spooking the bejesus out of him. Volts flow through its slimy body before it hops away.

"What the hell?"

He gazes around, unable to scc much past the vapors. Seth's quivering comes to a halt, and he drops to his knees. Smoke rolls off his cloak like steamy rice, and through its denseness, a figure emerges from a cloudy wall.

I s that you, Marley?" Robert yells through the unrelenting wind.

"We don't have much time. Listen to me! This is your way outta here! You must take his orb and transport your-self out of here before Seth can wake up."

"Why don't you come with me?"

"I can't! Because of the bound curse, the orb won't work for me. I have to stay here. Take the orb!"

"Wait, how do you kill them?"

Robert reaches for the water orb, digging and thrusting his hand into the surface of Seth's chest which is like sticking your hand into a mud puddle. His slimy fingers anchors se-curely around it. Seth's eyes spring open before Marley can answer. His eyes illuminate through his hood with the richest teal color. The wind ruffles past his hood, unveiling his cheek through the darkness of his hood.

"Get off my orb."

"Robert, you must collect all the orbs and…"

"Surprise. Abeamus!" Seth commands.

Both Seth and Robert teleport into the skull cloud of the Impossible like a rocket. The rush of fierce air slams into Robert's flesh like a vicious hurricane, making it difficult to open his eyes. Seth's cloak flutters and his soppy skin ripples against the howling air as they tussle amongst the squall. Robert tugs and yanks at the water orb, fighting to free it from Seth's chest.

The exquisite teal smoke trail is ethereal between the vapors, resembling a waterspout which is quite a picturesque sight. Condensation builds up, spraying cool mist into Robert's face as they flip and turn.

The earthly smell of dirt is all but pleasant as it whirls around Robert like a tornado skimming over his burns with its grittiness.

One second, Robert is weightless amongst the air, and the next comes a splash. He is soaking wet. His body is heavy, like anchors are pulling him down into the abyss.

The water is freezing cold, like a thousand sharp icicles thrusting into his body, colder than the Antarctic ice on the coldest day of winter. The shooting pain feels like countless piranhas ripping off his flesh. On top of that, he can't swim. The thought of drowning tears into his subconscious like a butcher's blade.

Seth is holding him under water, deep beneath the cenote. Robert grabs at Seth's wrist, pushing and pulling to free himself from Seth's grasp. He claws and scratches but it does no good. His chest weighs heavy, like a submarine is lying on it. Bubbles float out his mouth as the oxygen leaves his body giving it no choice but to sink into the bottomless abyss.

"It's okay to die, Robert. I'll visit your dead corpse from time to time," Seth says with a mighty voice with sound waves vigorous enough to traverse through the dense waters.

His bookbag floats there above the surface. Into the rippling water, the refraction of light passes through. A blurry figure of the Death Reaper stands there stalking him, gripping the wordless book tightly against his side. His harrowing sadistic smirk leaches into the depths of his very soul.

Before Robert can focus his blinking eyes, the Death Reaper is gone. He continues his descent with his T-shirt in the clinches of Seth's fists.

Every second, he is less aware of his surroundings and even himself. Everything is closing in. Holding his breath is involuntary. Tunnel vision creeps in as his grip surrenders from Seth's cloak. The fight leaves his hands as they sink to his side.

With Robert's limp dead body in his clutches, Seth swiftly bursts upward, leaving behind a mixture of accomplishment, ripples, and Robert's body.

The darkness washes over Robert. At once, the coal mine or, in fact the world is non-existent. Piece by piece, the loneliness consumes his dead body.

Above the surface, the sound of a continuous drip of water from the stalactites splats onto his bookbag. The darkness is thick as a moonless night.

Robert's lifeless body rises out of the water, floating motionless on his stomach. Steadily, the current drifts his body across the caves spring, smacking along a rock wall.

The last fragment of brain activity reminisces about the beautiful day that once was: The tedious bus ride full of happy children, his head rested on the warm embrace of Jessica's shoulder. All the activities, even the canoe ride, which was not all that bad. Travis, Dale, Katelyn, Zoey, Caleb, and Emma. Poor Emma. Last time he saw her, she was in this coal mine guarded by those Deader's. Hopefully, she was able to find a way out, if she's even alive.

Lastly, his precious Jessica. The sun's rays radiated off her sunrise golden hair. She had a glow, an aurora around her that made his heart dance. He misses her deeply. Her beautiful face. They had an endless love, an unstoppable force that could move mountains.

Robert treasures all those moments. Every waking minute, every second, every breath, every heartbeat, elates his soul, moving him through the deadliest storms. Everything he learned from her. Everything she learned from him. Piece by piece, every moment fits together perfectly. They are one complete puzzle, one life, one spirit formed together by love and now destroyed by death.

His camp, passed down to him from his mother and father, has suffered, practically destroyed thanks to those monsters. Fire-trucks park along the camp's pathways. Their twirling lights paint the camp red. Stressing firefighters hold the line, manning hoses spraying over a burning cabin eight, while another team battles the raging woods, its length stretching across the camp. Treehouse after treehouse crumbles to the ground, kicking up dust and embers, drizzling down through the thicket of black smoke rushing toward the heavens like an exploding volcano.

Brakes hiss as the tires of the Happy Oaks Middle School bus come to a screeching halt. Linda leads the line of terrified young teens escorted by a firefighter who is ensuring their safety onto the bus.

"220 to command, that's the last of the adults and children. They're en route to the planned gathering point for meeting back up with their parents."

"That's a copy, 220."

Tap, tap, smacks the firefighter's hand against the bus's fender. "Thanks, Debra for your help. That's all of them but the two missing adults and the missing girl. Go home and get some sleep."

"I'm gonna try. I sure hope they find Emma."

"Rumor is, the FBI's getting involved. If anyone can find her, it'll be them. You take care now."

The bus door slides closed, and the engine growls as the Happy Oaks Middle School bus takes off toward the camp's exit. Walking off donning his helmet, the firefighter ventures off toward the blusterous burning woods.

Black branches writhe like the tendrils of a horrifying unseen beast, snapping like twigs by the uproar of an impeding gale and crashing to the ground by an unforgiving force of gravity.

Leaves kick up from the impact, uncovering a frightened squirrel firmly secured in a pile of dry leaves. It hops away in a panic, scrambling up an oak tree, its claws digging into its bark's dry outer tissue, making sure to grab an acorn along its journey, scurrying to the tippy top overlooking the destruction of camp Wolf Creek.

Patches of fire scattered through the camp's entirety resemble lit lanterns in the deepest abyss of an ominous cave. The black smoke kisses the gloomy skies, painted in a black that is the darkest dark can be. Its edges glow a purple hue, the color of a raisin, a majesty amidst the thunderous rumble bringing forth the first tear from the angry void.

From within the heaven's tear lies the reflection of the camp's destruction, barreling into an opening of a mountain at Hollow's Peak like an atomic bomb, splashing into the cave's spring and next to Robert's floating body.

Beneath him, tiny air bubbles emerge from the water, popping around his submerged head. His still hands sway gently in the water. His fingers curl, tightening his fist in a shake of rage. Both eyes fling open. Happy to be alive, his lips roll upward into a smile.

Robert's alive.

ACKNOWLEDGMENTS

First off, I'd like to start by saying that this story has been a long time coming. Sixteen years led by the wild animal of trial and error. It started back in 2008 as a video game idea; my journey was long, dark, and cold. From writing a script, to paying for character, and environmental art. At one time, I even bought a cheap program to do it myself but it didn't work out too well. So, I went on the search for someone to make it for me when I found an outsourcing company to make it but it was very costly. So, I ran a Kickstarter campaign to raise money for it. The campaign ended with only fifty-eight dollars raised. I took a break for a while but I didn't give up. Scrapping my script I went on to write a novel instead. I knew I could do it. So in January of 2020, I began writing The Wordless Book. Just four years and learning from many YouTube videos, this story has finally reached the surface and I couldn't have done it without all of the people involved.

I'd like to thank my most precious wife and two daughters for being patient and believing in me. Without you're love, I would have given up years ago. You guys worked so hard on helping me promote this story through filming promotional pieces and trailers and I know deep down you didn't want to, but it goes to show how special you guys are. Through the many sleepless nights with a notepad and pen in my hand, you and I have found myself in my little world pondering on the next paragraph. I couldn't ask for a better family than the one I have. I'm very lucky and I count my blessings. Just know for now the story is written so now I can finally rest my mind. For now.

Next on the list is Mata Tridatu, also known as B.A.W, who designed ninety-five percent of the amazing interior art for this novel. We found each other through a post I've written on social media requesting an artist for my story. Lo and behold, an angel walked in and since January 2nd, 2021, we began working together. One of the things that makes this story so special is the brilliant artistry bringing this story to life. I never had not one issue with him. It's almost like he could see in my mind. His art always turned out perfectly the first time. I am lucky to be working with him on this project and I look forward to what we can do in the future.

Connie is another important piece to this puzzle. She has an incredible eye for detail and her artistic detail really made this novel shine. She is responsible for allot of the chapter art that decorates the pages of The Wordless Book. She is really kind and understanding, delivering her finished work expeditiously.

Renee Springer is an extraordinary person and beta reader who has taken her time fleshing out most of my proofreading errors. She took the time to answer my questions and even checked in on me from time to time. She's also an avid reviewer and arc reader.

Sian Jones is another beta reader I am lucky to have worked on The Wordless Book. She has been very helpful, pointing out some of the flaws from all sides of the editing process. Sian also edited my synopsis as well which I'll always be grateful for.

My line editor Kristen Corrects was a pleasure to work with. She's been so kind and understanding. My writing journey began with her four years ago and I think she will be very happy with the result.

Well over fourteen thousand editing mistakes later Kristen was the start of my learning career. She was so patient and only an email away to help out any way she could. Thanks, Kristen, for all you do.

I would like to thank Tim Marquitz, who has been my Copy and Developmental editor. He also has been kind and very patient. Before him, this story was full of tension and POV errors. He's opened my eyes greatly to keeping track of each word I write. Whether it's presence or past tense, I owe him my gratitude for his knowledge. Thanks, Tim.

Oren Eades proofread my novel with near perfection. His close attention to detail and intense knowledge really gave my manuscript what it needed to become its strongest self. My concerns for the finished quality were laid to rest after reviewing all his edits. He was very kind and left me some really positive feedback that put my mind at ease and made me excited for readers to read this novel.

Yosbe Design. Need I say more? She is an amazing book cover designer. I'm lucky and delighted she was interested in teaming up with me to create something amazing. We worked so well together and on top of that, she was professional and prompt with her work. I look forward to working with her in the future.

The professionalism from Enchanted Ink publishing is beyond exceptional. The level of formatting is stunning and visually appealing that really makes this novel stand out as one of a kind. His overall quality is a work of art indeed and it shows with every flip of the page.

I would like to thank my followers on social media. You guys stuck with me when things were quiet, and it seemed like I gave up, you continued to follow me, and I will always appreciate it.

Last but not least, I would like to thank my readers for purchasing this book. I gave it my all to give you a story I hope you'll love. You keep me motivated day in and out. It is my dream to make people smile and enjoy themselves in the most entertaining way I can.

Thank you all.

LEARN MORE ABOUT THE AUTHOR

WWW.THEWORDLESSBOOK.COM

Instagram:@thewordless_book

Twitter:@thewordlessbook

YouTube:@thewordlessbook

Facebook:@thewordlessbook

www.linkedin.com/in/thewordlessbook

SHAWN SPENCER

I currently live in the buckeye state with my wife Amanda, two amazing children, two dogs, one rabbit, and one cat. Years ago I spent the majority of my childhood in baseball and martial arts. After I graduated I joined the military where I was involved in the Iraqi freedom war. After four years and an honorable discharge I ventured to Texas where I went to school for auto body and painting. Through my classmates I was informed of a karate dojo that was close by. Wanting to stay in shape I began training at the Rising Sun Karate dojo under the amazing Kyoshi Frank. After Texas and an auto body certificate I came back to the buckeye state and got married to my most precious wife Amanda where I now work as a Elementary School Custodian.

www.ingramcontent.com/pod-product-compliance
Lightning Source LLC
Chambersburg PA
CBHW071227300726

48975CB00002B/319